FLIGHT PATHS OF THE EMPEROR

FLIGHT PATHS OF THE EMPEROR

STEVEN HEIGHTON

Granta Books
London

Granta Publications Ltd, 2/3 Hanover Yard, London N1 8BE

First published in Canada by The Porcupine's Quill, Inc., 1992
First published in Great Britain by Granta Books 1997

A CIP catalogue record for this book is available from the British Library.

1 3 5 7 9 10 8 6 4 2

Typeset in Bembo by M Rules
Printed and bound in Great Britain by
Mackays of Chatham plc, Kent

CONTENTS

To the memory of Eleanor Mary James
(1896–1990)

and for Nori, Sam, Hiro, Masaki, Miki-san and Mr Ishii

★

For their advice, encouragement and support I'm indebted and grateful to Mary Huggard and her family, my own family, and the editors of the magazines and anthologies that published the stories – especially John Silkin, Giles Gordon and David Hughes. I'm also very grateful to Anne McDermid, and to Frances Coady and the team at Granta Books – Becky Hardie, Isobel Rorison and Claire Paterson.

I especially want to thank John Metcalf for his invaluable advice, criticism and support.

The traveller who enters suddenly into a period of social change – especially change from a feudal past to a democratic present – is likely to regret the decay of things beautiful and the ugliness of things new. What of both I may yet discover in Japan I know not; but today, in these exotic streets, the old and the new mingle so well that one seems to set off the other ...

Lafcadio Hearn, Glimpses of Unfamiliar Japan, 1894

... but your dead forget you as soon as they pass the portals of the tomb. They wander alone among the stars and never return ... To us the ashes of our ancestors are sacred and their resting place is hallowed ground. You wander far from the graves of your ancestors and seemingly without regret ...

from a speech made by Seattle,
chief of the Duwamish, upon ceding the lands
of his tribe to the American government in 1854

The old Buddha has passed away, the new is yet unborn. As for me, I am born in a dream, what shall I see as real?

from the Noh drama

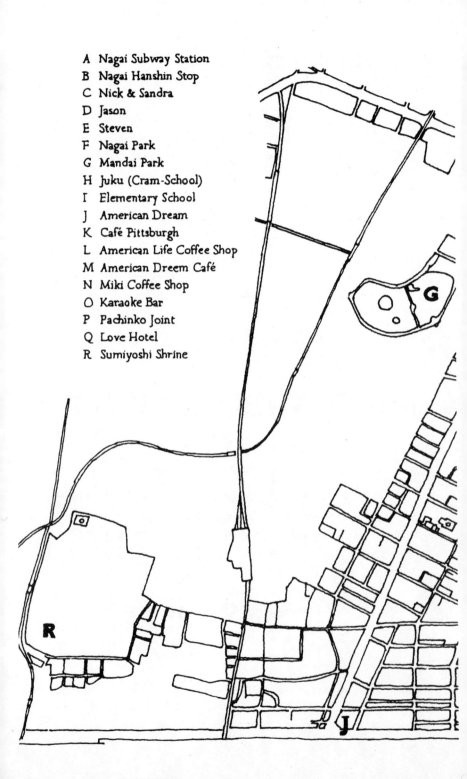

A Nagai Subway Station
B Nagai Hanshin Stop
C Nick & Sandra
D Jason
E Steven
F Nagai Park
G Mandai Park
H Juku (Cram-School)
I Elementary School
J American Dream
K Café Pittsburgh
L American Life Coffee Shop
M American Dreem Café
N Miki Coffee Shop
O Karaoke Bar
P Pachinko Joint
Q Love Hotel
R Sumiyoshi Shrine

大阪市住吉区街区図

In the Sumiyoshi ward in Ōsaka, Japan, the area near Nagai Park and around the Nagai train and subway stops is a place of cheap accomodation where a good number of foreigners live — though often without ever meeting. Most of them teach English to Japanese students in the burgeoning schools of downtown Ōsaka.

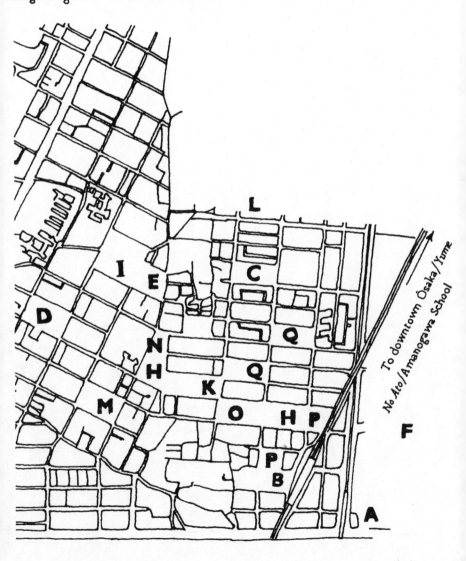

1

FIVE PAINTINGS OF THE NEW JAPAN
A NATIONAL GALLERY

I   SUNFLOWERS

I was the first foreigner to wait tables in the Yume No Ato. Summer enrolment was down at the English school where I taught so I needed to earn extra money, and since I'd been eating at the restaurant on and off for months it was the first place I thought of applying. It was a small establishment built just after the war in a bombed-out section of the city, but when I saw it the area was studded with bank towers, slick boutiques, coffee shops and flourishing bars and the Yume No Ato was one of the oldest and most venerable places around. I was there most of the summer and I wish I could go back. I heard the other day from Nori, the dishwasher, who works part-time now in a camera store, that our ex-boss Mr Onishi has just fought and lost a battle with cancer.

'We have problems here every summer,' Mr Onishi sighed during my interview, 'with a foreign tourist people.' He peered up at me from behind his desk, two shadowy half-moons drooping under his eyes. 'Especially the Americans. If I hire you, you can deal to them.'

'With them,' I said automatically.

'You have experienced waitering?'

'A little,' I lied.

'You understand Japanese?'

'I took a course.'

'Say something to me in Japanese.'

I froze for a moment, then was ambushed by a phrase from my primer.

'*Niwa ni wa furu-ike ga arimasu.*'

'In the garden,' translated Mr Onishi, 'there is an old pond.'

I stared abjectly at his bald patch.

'You cannot say a sentence more difficult than that?'

I told Mr Onishi it was a beginners' course. He glanced up at me and ran his fingers through a greying Vandyke beard.

'How well do you know the Japanese cuisine?'

'Not so well,' I answered in a light bantering tone that I hoped would disarm him, 'but I know what I like.'

He frowned and checked his watch, then darted a glance at the bank calendar on the wall.

'Morinaga speaks a little English,' he said. 'He will be your trainer. Tomorrow at 1600 hours you start.'

'You won't be sorry, sir,' I told him.

'I shall exploit you,' he said, 'until someone more qualitied applies.'

★

Nori Morinaga leaned against the steam table and picked his nose with the languid, luxurious gestures of an epicure enjoying an after-dinner cigar. He was the biggest Japanese I'd ever seen and the coke-bottle glasses perched above his huge nose seemed comically small.

'Ah, *gaijin-san!*' he exclaimed as he saw me, collecting himself and inflating to his full height. 'Welcome in! Hail fellow well-hung!'

I wondered if I'd heard him correctly.

'It gives me great pressure!'

I had. I had.

Nori Morinaga offered me his hand at the same moment

2

I tried to bow. Nervously we grinned at each other, then began to laugh. He was a full head taller than I was, burly as a linebacker but prematurely hunched as if stooping in doorways and under low ceilings had already affected his spine. He couldn't have been over twenty-five. His hair was brush-cut like a Marine's and when he spoke English his voice and manner seemed earnest and irreverent at the same time.

'Onishi-san tells me I will help *throw you the ropes,*' he chuckled. 'Ah, I like that expression. Do you know it? I study English at the University but the *gaijin-sensei* always says Japanese students must be more idiomatic so I picked up this book' – his giant hand brandished a thick paperback – 'and I study it *like a rat out of hell.*'

He grinned enigmatically, then giggled. I couldn't tell if he was serious or making fun of me.

Nori pronounced his idiomatic gleanings with savage enthusiasm, his magnified eyes widening and big shoulders bunching for emphasis as if to ensure his scholarship did not pass unseen. I took the book and examined it: a dog-eared, discount edition of UP-TO-DATE ENGLISH PHRASES FOR JAPANESE STUDENTS – in the 1955 edition.

'We open in an hour,' he said. 'We are *oppressed for time.* Come on, *I'm going to show you what's what.*'

Situated in a basement, under a popular *karaoke* bar, the Yume No Ato's two small rooms were dimly lit and the atmosphere under the low ceiling was damp and cool, as in an air-raid shelter or submarine. I wondered if this cramped, covert aura hadn't disturbed some of the earliest patrons, whose memories of the air raids would still have been fresh – but I didn't ask Nori about that. The place had always been popular, he said, especially in summer, when it was one of the coolest spots in Ōsaka.

A stairway descended from street level directly into the dining room so on summer days, after the heat and bright sunshine of the city, guests would sink into a cool aquatic atmosphere of dim light and swaying shadows. The stairway was flanked on one side by a small bar and on the other by the sushi counter where I'd eaten before. An adjoining room contained a larger, more formal dining space which gave onto the kitchen through a swinging door at the back. Despite the rather Western-style seating arrangements (tables and chairs instead of the traditional *zabuton* and *tatami*) the dining area was decorated in authentic Japanese fashion with hanging lanterns, calligraphic scrolls, a *tokonoma* containing an empty *maki-e* vase, *bonsai* and *noren* and several framed, original *sumi-e*. The only unindigenous ornament was a large reproduction of Van Gogh's *Sunflowers* hung conspicuously on the wall behind the sushi bar.

'Onishi-san says it's for the behoof of the American tourists,' Nori explained, 'but I'd *bet my bottom* he put it there for the bankers who come *in the wee-wee hours*. It's the bankers who are really interested in that stuff.' He sniffed and gestured contemptuously toward *Sunflowers* and toward the *sumi-e* prints as well, as if wanting me to see he considered all art frivolous and dispensable, no matter where it came from.

I didn't realize until much later the gesture meant something else.

Nori showed me around the kitchen and introduced me to the cooks, who were just arriving. Kenji Komatsu was head chef. Before returning to Japan and starting a family he'd worked for a few years in Vancouver and Montréal and his memories of that time were good, so he was delighted to hear I was Canadian. He insisted I call him Mat. 'And don't listen to anything this big whale tells you,' he warned me affably, poking Nori in the stomach. 'So much sugar and McDonald's the young ones are eating these days ... This one should be in the *sumō* ring, not my kitchen.'

'*Sumō* is for old folk,' Nori said, tightening his gut and

ironically saluting a small, aproned man who had just emerged from the walk-in fridge.

'*Time is on the march,*' Nori intoned. '*Nothing can stop it now!*'

Second chef Yukio Miyoshi glared at Nori then at me with frank disgust and muttered to himself in Japanese. He marched toward the back of the kitchen and began gutting a large fish. 'Doesn't like the foreigners,' Nori grinned indifferently. 'So it is. You can't pleasure everybody.'

The swinging door burst open and a small dark form hurtled into the kitchen and disappeared behind the steam table. Nori grabbed me by the arm.

'It's Oh-san, the sushi chef – come, we must hurry.'

Mr Oh was a jittery middle-aged man who scurried through the restaurant, both hands frantically embracing a mug of fresh coffee. Like all the elder folks, Nori explained, Mr Oh worked too hard ...

We finally cornered him by the walk-in fridge and Nori introduced us. Clearly he had not heard of Mr Onishi's latest hiring decision – he flung down his mug and gawked as if I were a health inspector who'd just told him twenty of last night's customers were in the hospital with food poisoning.

The *yukata* which Mr Oh insisted I try on looked all right, and in the change room I finally gave in and let him Brylcreem and comb back my curly hair into the slick, shining facsimile of a typical Japanese cut. As he worked with the comb, his face close to mine, I could see the tic in his left eye and smell his breath, pungent with coffee.

'You look *marvellous,*' Nori laughed on my return, 'and you know who you are!' He winked and blew me a kiss.

Mr Onishi entered and snapped some brusque truculent command. When the others had fled to their stations he addressed me in English.

'I hope you are ready for your first shift. We will have

many guests tonight. Come – you will have to serve the aliens.'

From the corner of my eye I could see Nori clowning behind the grille, two chopsticks pressed to his forehead like antennae.

As I trailed Mr Onishi into the dining room, two men and a woman, all young, tall, clad smartly in *yukata*, issued from behind the bar and lined up for inspection. One of the men wore a pearl earring and his hair was unusually long for a Japanese, while the woman had rich brown, luminous skin and plump attractive features. Mr Onishi introduced the other man as Akiburo. He was a college student and looked the part with his regulation haircut and sly, wisecracking expression.

With patent distaste Mr Onishi billed the long-haired man as 'your bartender, who likes to be known as Johnnie Walker'. The man fingered his earring and smiled out of the side of his mouth. 'And this is Suzuki Michiko, a waitress.' She bowed awkwardly and studied her plump brown hands, the pale skin on the underside of her wrists.

My comrades, as Mr Onishi called them, had been expecting me, and now they would show me to my sector of the restaurant – three small tables in the corner of the second room. In this occidental ghetto, it seemed, Mr Onishi thought I would do the least possible damage to the restaurant's ambience and reputation. Michiko explained in simple Japanese that since my tables were right by the kitchen door I could ask Nori for help as soon as I got in trouble.

The *tokonoma*, I now saw, had been decorated with a spray of poppies.

'We open shortly,' Mr Onishi declared, striding toward us. His manner was vigorous and forceful but his eyes seemed tired, their light extinguished. 'We probably will have some American guests tonight. Your job will be to service them.'

6

'I'll do my best, sir.'

'And coffee – you will now take over from Michiko and bring Mr Oh his coffee. He will want a fresh supply every half-hour. Do not forget!'

For the first hour the second room remained empty, as did the tables of the front room, but the sushi bar was overrun within minutes by an army of ravenous, demanding guests. 'Coffee,' cried Mr Oh, and I brought him cup after cup while the customers gaped at me and hurled at Mr Oh questions I could not understand. The coffee yellowed his tongue and reddened his eyes, which took on a weird, narcotic glaze, while steam mixed with sweat and stood out in bold clear beads on his cheeks and upper lip. Orders were called out as more guests arrived. Mr Oh's small red hands scuttled like sand crabs over the counter, making predatory forays into the display case to seize hapless chunks of smelt or salmon or eel and then wielding above them a fish-silver knife, replacing the knife deftly, swooping down on speckled quail eggs and snapping shells between thumb and forefinger and squeezing the yolk onto bricks of rice the other hand had just formed. Then with fingers dangling the hands would hover above an almost completed dish, and they would waver slightly like squid or octopuses in currents over the ocean floor, then pounce, abrupt and accurate, on an errant grain of rice or any garnish or strip of ginger imperfectly arranged, and an instant later the finished work, irreproachable and beyond time like a still life or a great sculpture, would appear on the glass above the display case from which it was snatched within seconds by the grateful customers or attentive staff.

The process was dizzying. I was keenly aware of my ignorance and when I was not airlifting coffee to the sushi bar I was busy in my own sector studying the menu and straightening tables.

Around eight o'clock Mr Onishi entered the second

room, carrying menus, followed by a man and woman who were both heavyset, tall and fair-haired. The man wore a tailored navy suit and carried a briefcase. The woman's hair was piled high in a steep bun that resembled the nose-cone of a rocket, and her lipstick, like her dress, was a pushy, persistent shade of red.

'Take good care with Mr and Mrs Cruikshank,' Onishi-san murmured as he passed me and showed them to their seats. 'Mr Cruikshank is a very important man – a diplomat, from America. Bring two dry martinis to begin.'

Mr Cruikshank's voice was genteel and collected, his manner smooth as good brandy. 'How long have you been working in this place?' he inquired.

'Two hours,' I told him, serving the martinis.

'Surprised they'd have an American working here.' With one hand he yanked a small plastic sabre from his olive, then pinched the olive and held it aloft like a tiny globe.

'I'm not American,' I said.

There was a pause while Mr and Mrs Cruikshank processed this unlooked-for information.

'Well surely you're not Japanese?' Mrs Cruikshank asked, slurring her words a little. 'Maybe half?'

Mr Cruikshank swallowed his olive then impaled his wife's with the plastic sword. He turned back to me, inadvertently aiming the harmless tip at my throat.

'*Nihongo wakaru?*' he asked in plain, masculine speech. *You understand Japanese?* I recognized his accent as outstanding.

'Only a little,' I said.

'I'll bet he's Dutch,' Mrs Cruikshank wagered. 'The Dutch speak such beautiful English – hardly any accent at all.'

'You'll find it hard here without any Japanese,' Mr Cruikshank advised me, ignoring his wife, drawing the sword from his teeth so the gleaming olive stayed clenched between them.

'*Coffee,*' Mr Oh called from the sushi bar.

'I'll only be serving the foreign customers, sir.'

Mr Cruikshank bit into his olive. 'Some of the foreign customers,' he said, 'prefer being served in Japanese.'

'Or maybe German,' said Mrs Cruikshank.

'I can speak some German,' I said. 'Would you like it if –'

'*Coffee,*' cried Mr Oh from the sushi bar.

Mrs Cruikshank was beaming. 'I was right,' she said, lifting her martini glass in a kind of toast. '*Wie geht's?*'

'We'd like some sushi,' Mr Cruikshank interrupted his wife, who was now grimacing at her drink as if trying to recall another German phrase.

I fumbled with my pad.

'An order each of *maguro, saba, hamachi*, and – why not? – some sea urchin. Hear it's full of mercury these days, but hell, we've got to eat something.'

'Yes, sir.'

'And two more martinis.' He pointed at his glass with the plastic sword.

'Got it.'

'*Danke schön,*' roared Mrs Cruikshank as I hurried from the room.

While waiting for Johnnie Walker to finish the martinis I noticed an older guest rise from the sushi bar and stumble toward the washrooms. As he saw me, his red eyes widened and he lost his footing and crashed into the bar, slamming a frail elbow against the cash register. He righted himself with quick slapstick dignity and stood blushing. When I moved to help him he waved me off.

Johnnie Walker smirked and muttered as he shook the martinis and for a moment the words and the rattling ice took on a primitive, mocking rhythm, like a chant. The older man began to swear at him and reached out as if to grab his earring, his long hair. *Shin jin rui*, the old man muttered – *Strange inscrutable creature!* I'd heard it was a new phrase coined by the old to describe the young.

'Wake up old man,' Johnnie snapped in plain Japanese as he poured the martinis. 'Watch out where you're going.'

The man lurched off.

'Always drunk, or fast asleep in their chairs.'

'*Coffee*,' cried Mr Oh from the sushi bar.

II   THE DREAM

'Tell me something about the restaurant,' I said to Nori, sweeping my hand in a half circle and nodding at the closed bar. 'How old is the place?'

Nori finished his Budweiser and balanced the empty tin on a growing tower of empties. 'It was built after the war ends,' he belched – and I couldn't help noticing how casually he used the word *war*. His expression was unchanged, his voice was still firm, his eyes had not recoiled as if shamed by some unspeakable profanity. That was how my older students reacted when The War came up in a lesson. No doubt Mr Onishi would react the same way. But not Nori. For him the war was history, fiction – as unreal and insubstantial as a dimly remembered dream, a dream of jungles, the faded memory of a picture in a storybook. He wasn't much younger than me.

'What about the name,' I said, 'Yume No Ato? I mean, I can figure out the individual words, but I can't make sense of the whole thing.' *Yume*, I knew, meant 'dream', *no* signified possession, like an apostrophe and an 's', and *ato*, I thought, meant 'after'.

Nori lit a cigarette and trained a mischievous gaze on my hairline. His capacity for drink was larger than average for a Japanese but now after four tins of beer he was flushed, theatrical and giddy. He wrinkled his broad nose, as if at a whiff of something rotten, and spat out, 'It's a line from a poem we had to study in the high school. Ah, Steve-san, university is so much better, we have fun in the sun, we make whoopee, we live for the present tense and forget all our yesterdays and tomorrows ... I hated high school, so much work. We had to study this famous poem.'

He stood and recited the lines with mock gravity:

> 'Natsu kusa ya!'
>   Tsuamono domo ga
>   Yume no ato.'

'It's a *haiku*,' I said.

'Aye, aye, captain.' He slumped down and the tower of beer cans wobbled. 'Do you watch *Star Trek*?'

'I'm not sure,' I said, 'that I understand it.'

'Oh, well, it's just a TV show – about the future and the stars.'

'I mean the poem, Nori, the *haiku*.'

'Ah, the poem – naturally you don't understand. It's old Japanese – old Japanese language, old Japanese mind – not so easy for us to understand either. It's Matsuo Bashō, dead like Shakespeare over three hundred years. Tomorrow and tomorrow and tomorrow. We had to study them both in school. Full fathom five and all that.'

'But about that last line ...'

'*Yume no ato?*'

I nodded.

'That's the name of the restaurant. You see, when Mr Onishi's uncle built the place after the war he gave it that name. It's a very strange name for a restaurant! Mr Onishi was just a boy then.'

'What does it mean?'

'I don't think Mr Onishi would have called it that, but

11

when his uncle went over the bucket he didn't want to change the name. Out of respect.'

I finished my own beer and contributed to the tower of cans. The other staff had gone upstairs to the *karaoke* place but they'd drunk a lot of Bud and Kirin beforehand and the tower was growing high.

'I wonder,' I said, 'if the words mean "when the dream is over?" '

Nori took a long drag on his cigarette. 'I don't think they do,' he finally said. 'And besides, the dream had only just begun. The uncle was smart and he built Yume No Ato to attract foreigners as well as Japanese and it's done really well, as you can see.' His eyes brightened. *'We're going great guns.'*

Mr Onishi's telephone began to ring from the back of the restaurant, where he was still working. We heard him answer.

'The first line,' I said, 'is "Ah! Summer grasses", right?'

Nori seemed to be weighing this, then blurted out, *'Yume no ato* means ... it means what's left over after a dream.'

Mr Onishi's voice could be heard faintly. I surveyed the shaky tower, the ashtrays, the skeletons of fish beached on the sides of our empty plates.

'Leftovers,' I said, ironically.

'There's another word.'

'What about vestige? No? Remnant?'

Nori stubbed out his cigarette like a game-show panelist pressing a buzzer. *'Remnant!'* he cried, *'your choice is absolutely correct, for five thousand dollars and a dream home!'* Suddenly he grew calm, thoughtful. 'So many foreign words sound alike,' he mused. 'There's a famous Dutch painter with that name.'

'You mean Rembrandt?'

'That's him. A bank here in Umeda just bought a Remnant for nine hundred million yen.'

'Yume no ato,' I said, 'must mean "the remnant of dreams".'

Nori furrowed his brow, then nodded.

'Funny name for a restaurant,' I said. 'You like game shows?'

As if in a fresh wind the paper *noren* in the doorway behind the sushi bar blew open and a haggard phantom came in. Mr Onishi. He seemed to look right through us. Nori suggested we clean up and leave. We began to pile the chopsticks and empty plates onto a tray. I glanced up and saw Mr Onishi beckoning Nori.

'Please go examine the guest toilet,' Nori told me.

The washroom was immaculate – I'd cleaned it myself two hours before – but I spent a few minutes checking it again so that Nori and Mr Onishi would know I was thorough. For the second time that night I was intrigued by a notice in the stall, pencilled on the back of an old menu and taped to the door –

TO ALL FOREIGNERS:
OUR TUBES ARE IN ILL REPAIR, PLEASE
DO NOT THROW YOUR PEEPERS
IN THE TOILET.

When I came out of the washroom Mr Onishi was gone. 'The boss looks awful,' I whispered to Nori, my smile forced. 'When he was on the phone before – maybe a guest was calling to complain about the new waiter, eh?'

'Possibly,' Nori said, 'but more likely it was a banker.'

'What, at this time of night?'

Nori shrugged. 'The elder folks, I told you, they're working late. And early, too – there was a banker here first thing this morning to talk at Mr Onishi.'

'Bankers,' I scoffed, shaking my head. 'Not trouble, I hope ...'

Nori laughed abruptly. Arm tensed karate-style he approached the tower of cans.

III   THE KERMESS

KAMPAI!

A month has gone past and the whole staff, *gaijin-san* included, are relaxing after a manic Saturday night in the Yume No Ato. August in Ōsaka: with other waiters and students and salarymen we sit in a beer garden under the full moon above twenty-two storeys of department store merchandise, imported clothing and cologne and books and records, Japanese-made electronics, wedding supplies, Persian carpets and French cigarettes and aquariums full of swordfish and coral and casino-pink sand from the Arabian Sea, appliances and appliqué, blue-china chopstick-holders computers patio-furniture coffee-shops chefs and friendly clerks and full-colour reproductions of well-known Western portraits, etchings, sketches, sculptures, landscapes that Japanese banks are buying like real estate and bringing back to Ōsaka, anything, anything at all, SPEND AND IT SHALL BE GIVEN, endless armies of customers and ah, summer tourists billowing like grain through the grounds of Ōsaka's most famous department store. SURELY, quoth the televangelist from the multitudinous screens, SURELY THE PEOPLE IS GRASS.

(For a moment the tables shudder as a tremor ripples through toxic earth under the Bargain Basement, and passes.)

KAMPAI! Western rock and roll music blasts from hidden speakers. In a few minutes the *O-bon* fireworks are due to start and we've got the best seats in the house. The plastic table sags and may soon buckle as another round of draft materializes and is swiftly distributed. A toast to this, a toast to that, *kampai*, KAMPAI, every time we lift our steins to take a drink, someone is proposing another toast: in a rare gesture Komatsu toasts the wait-staff (Akiburo and Johnnie and Michiko and me) because (this in English) we were really on the balls tonight and made no errors at all. *Kampai!* Akiburo toasts Komatsu and Mr Oh and second chef Miyoshi in return, presumably for turning

14

out so much food on such a busy night and making it all look easy. *Kampai!* Mr Oh raises his glass of ice-coffee in thanks while second chef Miyoshi, drunk and expansive, in a rare good mood, toasts Nori for not smacking his head in the store-room when he went back for extra soy sauce, KAMPAI, (this translated by the delighted Nori, who immediately hefts his stein and decrees a toast to Michiko, the waitress, simply because he's mad about her and isn't it lucky she doesn't speak English?).

The blushing Michiko lifts her heavy stein with soft plump hands and meekly suggests, in Japanese, that it might be possible, perhaps, to maybe if it isn't too much trouble drink a toast to our skilful bartender, Johnnie Walker, without whom we would hardly have survived the night, it seems to me, after all, or maybe we might have? *Kampai! Kampai!* The flesh of Johnnie's ear lobe reddens around his pearl stud. He smirks and belts back another slug of whisky.

'To Onishi-san,' he says in English. 'To Yume No Ato.' And he quickly adds some other remark in harsh, staccato Japanese.

'KAMPAI!' I holler, hoisting my stein triumphantly so that beer froths up and sloshes over the lip of the glass. But no one has followed suit. They are all gazing without expression at the table or into their drinks. Johnnie Walker's head hangs lowest, his features hidden.

Komatsu glances at his watch and predicts that the fireworks will start in thirty seconds.

I turn to Nori. 'Did I do something wrong?'

Miyoshi and Mr Oh both snap something at him. I can't make out a word.

'Well, not at all,' says Nori, softly, 'I guess people just don't feel like talking about work after a busy night.'

I purse my lips. 'I have the feeling you're not being completely honest with me.'

'Of course I'm not!' Nori protests – and I wonder if we've understood each other.

At that moment the fireworks start. Everyone at our table looks up, relieved. '*O-bon*,' Nori says to me, relaxed again. 'Tonight the ancestors return.' Flippantly he rolls his eyes, or only seems to – I can't be sure because his coke-bottle lenses reflect the moonlight and the fiery red glare of the first rockets. One after another they arc up out of the dark expanse of Nagai Park, miles to the north, then slow down and pause at their zenith and explode in corollas of violet, emerald, coral, cream, apricot and indigo. *Hanabi*, they call them in Japanese: fire-flowers. The steins are raised again, glasses rammed together, toasts made and spirits drawn skyward by the aerial barrage.

My flat is somewhere down there on the far side of Nagai Park and now I picture a defective missile veering off course and buzzing my neighbourhood, terrifying the old folks, plunging with a shriek like an air-raid siren through the ceiling of my flat ...

Nori grabs my arm with steely fingers. 'Steve-san, listen – do you hear what I hear?' I'm still concentrating on the look and sound of the exploding flowers, but suddenly I pick it out: the bouncy unmistakable opening bars of 'Like a Virgin'.

'It's the Madonna!'

'I hear it, Nori.'

He lumbers to his feet. 'You want to dance? Hey, get up! Come off it!'

Michiko and Johnnie Walker are already up beside the table, strobelit by the fireworks, shaking themselves to the beat, Michiko with a timid, tentative look and Johnnie with self-conscious abandon. The older staff sit motionless and watch the exploding rockets. Nori glances at them, at Michiko, at me, and I can tell he doesn't want to lose her. As she dances her small hands seem to catch and juggle the light.

'Life is so curt,' he pleads. 'You only lived once!' He gives

16

me a half-smile, a sly wink, and I'm no longer sure he doesn't know exactly what he's saying.

KAMPAI! Nori hauls me to my feet and heaves me from the table in a blind teetering polka, out towards Johnnie and Michiko, his big boorish feet beating a mad tattoo on my toes. Komatsu and Mr Oh, the elders in the crowd, link arms and start keening some old Japanese song. Steins raised they sway together to a stately rhythm much slower than Madonna's, their voices rolling mournfully over the antique minors and archaic words. The rockets keep exploding. Their sound takes on a rhythm which seems to fall between the beats of the opposing songs – then as I watch, one of the rockets fails to burst. Like a falling star it streaks earthward in silence and disappears over the city.

IV   GUERNICA

I woke early the next morning with a headache and a burning stomach. I'd been dreaming. I dreamed Michiko had come home with me to my flat and we stood together hand in hand on the threshold, staring in at a gutted interior. The guilty rocket, however, had not actually exploded – it was resting in perfect condition, very comfortably, on an unburnt, freshly-made futon in the centre of the room.

Michiko took me by the hand and led me into the ruin. When the smoke began to drown me she covered my mouth with her own. Her breath was clean and renewing as wind off an early-morning sea and when she pulled away the smell of burning was gone. She removed her flowered kimono and stood naked before me. The nipples of her firm small breasts were now the accusing eyes of a seduced and betrayed woman – then I was naked too, and utterly absolved, and we were lying side by side amid the acrid wreckage by the futon. She climbed

17

atop me and took me inside her, slowly, making small articulate sighs and rolling her head back and forth so her dark bangs rippled like a midnight waterfall across my nipples, and the blue-black hair was curved as space-time and full of sparks like the Milky Way, which in the Japanese tongue is called *ama no gawa*, the river of heaven.

I wanted to come, to fill the gathering space inside her, and I wanted to run my tongue down the soft pale line of hair from her breasts to her belly and on up the wooded mound of Venus and lick the nectar from her tender orchid, as the Japanese poets say, but then it came to me that Nori had meant to tell me something important – about Michiko? About a poem? Or was there something I'd asked him that he hadn't answered?

Summer grasses ... Something left over after dreams ...

What a stupid time to be thinking about poetry.

I woke embarrassed but with a feeling of desperate tenderness for Michiko, to whom I'd hardly ever spoken and who had inspired, I thought, no more than a generic interest on my part. It was like missing a lover who'd slept beside me all night and had just left and gone home before I woke ...

Well, I reflected, a dream like that was better than the waitering nightmares I'd had all the time till recently, and still woke from now and then. Usually I'd enter the restaurant and be told I was two hours late and none of the other wait-staff had shown up and the restaurant was full and we were booked solid till midnight. Other times I would realize I'd forgotten a couple or threesome who'd been seated two hours ago in the back corner of the second room and would they believe now it was just an honest mistake and I'd really been busy and meaning to get to them all along? Sometimes they were the Cruikshanks, and sometimes Mr Sato, who (Nori had told me) had been a professor at the university in Kyōto but was demoted and now taught primary kids in Nagai, and that was why he drank so much and was so cold and pedantic when he spoke to you. In fact the unrequited dream-diners could be just about anyone, because the summer had been busy and now I was serving both foreigners and Japanese alike.

It had been the busiest summer in years, Komatsu said, and we were attracting more tourists than ever before – so why the visible anxiety whenever talk after hours came round to the restaurant? Mr Onishi did not look like a man with a flourishing business. Perhaps he was ill and everyone was worried? I'd been reading articles lately about the soaring incidence of cancer in Japan, the spread of big business and factories into the countryside, toxins in the soil, polluted water, poisonous seafood ...

'I think you'd better level with me,' I told Nori the night of my dream.

Miyoshi was standing by the walk-in fridge, reading the *Sangyo Keizai*, and Komatsu was behind the steam table chopping onion. But I had the feeling they were listening to us, and so did Nori.

'*Not here*,' he whispered.

'Ah, such good news,' growled Miyoshi, lowering his paper with an unpleasant smile. Since he hardly ever spoke English I knew the remark was aimed at me. 'Such good news about the yen!'

Nori shook his head. 'For some the war has never ended.'

'*Nihon ichiban!*' Miyoshi cried. 'Japan is number one!'

'And he wasn't even born till after,' Nori grumbled. 'I don't understand.'

'Maybe we should talk somewhere else,' I said.

Nori nodded but Komatsu set down his knife and said quickly, 'No. It's all right. Steve-san is part of the restaurant now – we should tell him the truth.' Eyes pink and glistening, he walked out from behind the steam table and pulled the newspaper from Miyoshi's hands.

Miyoshi scowled, did an about-face and marched into the fridge.

'Look at this,' Komatsu sniffled, handing me the paper.

'You know I can't read Japanese.'

'Of course. Don't read, just look – the pictures.'

In the lower right-hand corner of the front page several well-known pieces of European art were reproduced in hazy black and white. One was a Rousseau, the second a Gauguin, the third a Brueghel. I couldn't read the caption beneath but I could make out the name of a prominent Ōsaka bank, written in *romaji*.

'And Van Gogh,' Komatsu said, frowning. 'I hear they have just bought another costly painting by Van Gogh – so many paintings they are buying and bringing to Japan.'

We could hear Miyoshi in the fridge, muttering to himself, furiously shifting things around.

'They're buying everything in their sights,' Nori said, his usual gusto tangibly absent.

I told them I knew a bit about these purchases, but didn't see what they had to do with us.

'Well,' Komatsu started, 'they need some place to put these paintings ...' His voice tapered off on the last words. I sensed I was being counted on, in customary Japanese fashion, to finish the sentence mentally so that everyone would be spared embarrassment.

'Chagall, too,' Komatsu resumed, 'and Rembrandt and Picasso.' *Bigasshole*, it sounded like, but I knew who he meant. 'Costly things ... they need to find a place to put them all ...'

'Like an art gallery,' I said.

Komatsu rubbed his eyes with a corner of his apron. 'I'm afraid so.'

It had been just like *Dallas*, Nori groaned, describing how the bank had first made polite offers to the dozen businesses operating in the block where they meant to build, and most

20

were politely accepted. But several proprietors (including Mr Onishi and the owner of the Idaho Caffeine Palace, a large coffee shop dating from the late forties) had refused to consider them. Secretly the bank made more attractive offers, then a final offer which the firm's representative begged Mr Onishi to accept, because if a negotiated settlement proved necessary then payment would revert to the level of the initial sum – or, conceivably, somewhat less.

Mr Onishi had ignored the bank's covert threats and a negotiated settlement proved necessary. Unfortunately it did not involve negotiation. The bank produced lawyers who showed that actual title to the land had belonged to the bank till the end of the war and they argued that the transfer of deeds had been improperly handled by the over-worked civil authorities of the time.

The young lawyers (I could just hear them) moved further that since the art gallery would be a public facility of great benefit to all citizens of the prefecture and would attract hundreds of thousands of foreigners to Ōsaka, it was in effect a civic institution, albeit privately owned, and the city should urge Mr Onishi to come to terms.

'The court is asking Mr Onishi to accept,' Nori said, 'but he just says no.'

Nihon ichiban, we heard faintly from the fridge.

Komatsu took the newspaper from me and walked back around the steam table. He began to giggle, like a bad comedian setting up a punchline. 'They're going to tear us down,' he said, laughing openly. 'Soon!'

Nori was chuckling, too, as the Japanese often will when speaking of their own misfortunes. Komatsu was laughing harder than I'd ever seen him, so I knew he really must be upset.

I paused respectfully. 'Listen, I'm really sorry to hear this.'

Komatsu roared with laughter. Nori continued to cackle.

I asked them if they knew when these things were going to happen.

'There's no time like presently,' Nori said, slapping me on the shoulder a bit harder than he needed to. 'Come on, it's a busy night tonight, we'd better get happening.'

'Please take coffee now to Mr Oh-san,' Komatsu giggled.

Miyoshi was still marching around in the fridge.

V   THE STARRY NIGHT

September in Ōsaka is just as hot as July or August, and this year it was worse. Though many of the tourists were gone, the Yume No Ato was busier than ever: Mr Onishi's struggle with the bank was now common knowledge, so old customers came often to show their support and the sushi bar was crowded with curious locals. Meanwhile enrolment was picking up at the school and I had to cut back on my hours as a waiter.

Mr Onishi was upset when I told him, but since I knew now of the epic struggle he was waging each day in the courts (Nori got the details from Komatsu and passed them on to me) I found it hard to feel angry in return. The boss, after all, was showing tremendous pluck. Sure, he was of another generation, a hardy breed of industrious survivors, and as a child he would have absorbed with his mother's milk the bracing formula of *bushidō*, but this was valour way beyond the call of duty. He was giving Japan's second biggest bank the fight of its life. Already the original date for demolition was three weeks in arrears ...

I heard that after receiving the court's final decision, Mr Onishi sighed and said, '*Yappari, nah*. It is as I expected. They will build a museum and a new country and fill both with foreign things.'

The demolition was set for the end of September and the Yume No Ato was to close a week before.

On the last night, a Saturday, the dining room was booked solid from five till closing with regular customers, both Japanese and foreign. We assembled by the bar a few minutes before five to wait for Mr Onishi, and at five sharp he emerged from his office. He marched up to us, a menu tucked under one arm like a swagger stick, then briefed us in a formal and highly nuanced Japanese that I could not follow, though the general tenor of his speech was easy enough to guess. Or was it? Sometimes I wondered if I'd ever done more than misimagine what these people felt and believed.

A current of laughter rippled through the staff and Nori nudged me appreciatively, forgetting for a moment that I did not understand.

Mr Onishi dismissed us and we hurried off to complete our preparations as he climbed the stairs and opened the door. A long shaft of dirty sunlight pierced the cool gloom, and a few seconds later our guests began to descend, bringing with them the hot muggy air of the street.

'Meet me in the back,' I told Nori.

We stood in the kitchen on either side of the open rice machine, slowly filling it with the contents of two clay cooking pots. Thick billows of steam rose between us and Nori's face was intermittently clouded, his eyes nacreous, indistinct, like a man under a foot of water.

'So what did Onishi-san just say,' I asked, scooping the soft, sweet-smelling grains into the machine.

'He was apologizing.'

'Apologizing,' I said.

'Sure. He was apologizing for letting the bank close the Yume No Ato. He says it's all on his shoulders. He feels responsible for the jobs we will lose. He says he is sorry because he has felled us.'

The steam was thinning and I could see Nori clearly. His big face was pink and sweating.

23

'He says his uncle was a soldier in the old navy and after the war he built this restaurant with his own two hands. So he says that by losing the restaurant he has felled his uncle, too.'

'But isn't his uncle dead?'

Nori put down his pot and gave me a faintly disappointed look. 'For many years. But so the old people believe – they can fell the dead as well as the breathing. Like being caught *between the devil and the deep blue sea, neh?*'

I nodded and stared into the rice cooker, its churning steam spectral and hypnotic.

'I feel sorry for him,' I said.

'So it is, all the while. The big fish eat the little.'

There was a harsh grating sound as he scraped rice from the bottom of his pot.

It was the busiest night of the summer but the customers were gentle and undemanding and the atmosphere, as at a funeral reception, was chastened and sadly festive and thick with solidarity. The foreigners left huge tips and Mr Oh grunted graciously whenever I freshened his coffee. It fell to Michiko to serve the disagreeable Mr Sato for the last time and though he usually deplored the grammar and fashions of her generation, tonight he was tolerant and even remarked at one point on her resemblance to his own daughter. The Cruikshanks were among the last to arrive. When they left, just before closing, Mrs Cruikshank said she trusted I wouldn't have to go home to Germany just yet and surely with my good English I could land another job ...

The last guests, our oldest customers, intoxicated and teary-eyed, staggered up the stairs around midnight and we dragged together a few tables and sank down for a last meal. Mat and Nori and second chef Miyoshi filed from the kitchen bearing platters of steaming rice and salmon teriyaki; at Mr Onishi's behest Johnnie Walker opened the bar to all staff. And now, though I'd felt more and more a part of things over the last

24

few months, I sensed my saddened colleagues closing ranks, retreating into dialect, resorting to nuance, idiom and silence, a semaphore of glances and tics and nods. Nori loomed on the far side of the table with Michiko beside him. They were talking quietly. In the shadows by their chair-legs I could see two hands linked, like sinuous sea-creatures, twined and mating in the deep.

Johnnie had finished the last of the Johnnie Walker Red and was now working on a bottle of Old Granddad. Mr Oh was not drinking. He sat mutely, his agile hands wrapped around one beer tin after another, crushing them and laying them to rest among the plates and ashtrays. Komatsu and second chef Miyoshi were smoking side by side, eyes half-closed, meditating on the fumes that rose and spread outward over their heads.

Mr Onishi, I suppose, was in his office. At one-thirty he came out and told everyone it was time to leave. There were some last half-hearted toasts and deep bowing and then we all stumbled upstairs and outside. The night air was cool and fresh. We looked, I thought, like a beaten rabble. As if wounded, Nori tottered over and proffered a scrap of paper the size of a cheque or a phone bill. 'Here,' he said, his speech slurred, 'I almost forgot. That poem they called the restaurant for ... Remember?'

He and Michiko swayed before me, their features painted a smooth flawless amber by the gentle light of the doorway. Behind them the brooding profiles of bank and office towers and beyond those in long swirling ranks the constellations of early autumn.

I took the slip of paper and held it to the light:

Ah! summer grass / this group of warriors' / remnant of dream
(this poem by Matsuo Bashō, lived same time as Shakespeare)

So long and take care of yourself. Nori.

He shrugged when I thanked him. 'We had to study it back then. A real pin in the ass.'

'Drop by the school sometime,' I said. 'Please, both of you ...'

I knew they wouldn't come.

Gradually the rest straggled off alone or in pairs and I headed for the station. Waves of heat rising out of sewers and off smokestacks and the vacant pavement set the stars quivering, like the scales of small fish in dark water. In the late-summer heat of 1945, after the surrender, Japanese armies had trudged back through the remains of Ōsaka and there was little where these buildings now stood but rubble, refuse, dust and blowing ash. A stubble of fireweed and wildflowers bloomed on the ruins, rippled in the hot wind. There was nothing for the children to eat. I heard these things from a neighbour, a toothless old man who had been a soldier at that time, and I heard other things as well: how faceless Japan had been, how for a while it had been a different place – beaten, levelled and overrun, unable to rise – waiting for the first touch of a foreign hand. For a sea change, into something rich, and strange.

On the train to Nagai I had a half-hour to experiment with the words on Nori's farewell card. By the time I got home I had the translation done, though the line 'Yume no ato' was still troublesome and I found it hard to focus on the page.

> Ah, summer grass!
> All that survives
> Of the warrior's dream ...

I keep thinking I should send a copy to Nori.

2

THE BATTLE OF MIDWAY

TŌKYŌ – John Cruikshank, the controversial American attaché, has refused to retract allegations that school textbooks published recently in Japan whitewash the nation's role as an 'aggressor' in World War II. He also refused to comment when asked whether American textbooks deliberately ignore the 'racial implications' of the U.S. bombing of Hiroshima and Nagasaki. Mr Cruikshank, who is fluent in Japanese, returns to America tomorrow. [From THE JAPAN TIMES, October 16, 1988]

It was our first visit to the house of Mr Fujita Masatomi. It began with a formidably ample meal during which we scandalized our hosts by enjoying raw tuna, then clam, then squid, then (Mrs Fujita having to make a special trip to the kitchen, driven by a sense of baffled desperation and patriotic duty) – several quivering gobbets of raw sea-urchin.

Sensing our hosts' bewilderment and anxiety I diplomatically confessed that while I could stomach the sea-urchin it was not exactly to my taste. I coughed faintly and covered my mouth, as if politely concealing a grimace of disgust.

The day was saved. National pride was salvaged and restored. My wife deftly consolidated this little victory by preferring coffee when offered either that or Japanese tea.

The time had come, our host solemnly decreed, for interesting conversation. I fell back on a trusty gambit. I told him, in Japanese, that I found his house very comfortable and his *tokonoma* particularly impressive. Mr Fujita turned to his brother and wife and the rest of his large family and told them, in Japanese, that I found the house very comfortable and the *tokonoma* particularly impressive. In clear English his daughter told us I was being unnecessarily polite: it was an old house and nothing to get excited about. Mr Fujita and his family, who did not understand English, grinned and nodded as if to corroborate this remark, which I therefore took as a standard expression of modesty. No, I insisted in formal Japanese, you are quite wrong, your house is actually very nice.

My words seemed to come as a bit of a surprise to Mr Fujita but he turned and repeated them to his family as before. His daughter maintained that the house was unremarkable, was in fact rather ugly, and noted there were problems with the plumbing. In Japanese I told her the plumbing had seemed fine on my last visit to the washroom, which, in conventional Japanese manner, I compared favourably with our own humble facilities.

Mr Fujita shot a quick glance at his daughter. She said in English that she hated living at home and would certainly leave if she were a few years older. In Japanese I told Mr Fujita he had a charming girl. *Not at all*, he said, resorting to the traditional phrase, *not at all* ...

It had been a heavy lunch. We were all getting tired. My wife's face had that ominously inflated look that shows she's smothering a yawn; Mr Fujita's brother leaned back from the low table, stretched himself full-length on the tatami floor, and did not stir for the rest of the afternoon.

'The old folks are always sleeping,' Mr Fujita's daughter complained. 'Sometimes it's impossible to wake them up.'

Mr Fujita barked a command in brusque Japanese. His children wheeled a television set and a VCR into the room while he selected a tape and loaded the machine. Everyone (except Mr Fujita's snoring brother) moved briskly to their new stations.

Cups and scraps of food were efficiently evacuated. I had the feeling that if the premises were searched, a detailed schedule of the afternoon's proceedings would sooner or later appear.

'*Karaoke*', Mr Fujita announced, beaming in anticipation. He drew a large microphone from a drawer under the VCR and plugged it into the speaker of the TV set. For some time I had been expecting this to happen.

Mr Fujita performed scales to warm up.

'*Karaoke* means "empty orchestra",' Mr Fujita's daughter explained. I told her in Japanese that I knew it. 'Empty,' she went on in English, 'because there is only music and no voice.' She swept her hand in a full circle to take in all present, then pointed at the microphone.

'We make the words ourselves,' she said.

'You mean we read them,' I corrected her, nodding toward the television where a glowing white pellet, like a grain of cooked rice, romped from character to character as a lyric crossed the screen ...

A Western model rode a black stallion along the edge of the Inland Sea as Mr Fujita crooned a traditional lament in his excellent baritone. Mr Fujita's daughter sang 'My Way' – a Western song that almost every Japanese knows. My wife and I were urged to sing a duet. A quick survey of programmes showed that only one other English song, 'Yesterday', was available to us, and finally Mr Fujita found it on an old disused cassette. He hoped the quality was still reasonable.

It was. The video featured a Brylcreemed teenager brooding among cherry trees over a walletful of tiny photographs. The woman in the photographs was visibly blond.

We bungled the song badly before returning the microphone.

Suddenly the footage accompanying the lyrics switched from garish colour to the shuddering, scratchy black-and-white of vintage newsreels. Small airplanes swooped in formation towards a burning aircraft carrier, big guns fired from the armoured decks of battleships. Two Zero fighters could be seen crashing into the sea. Mr Fujita's cozy den was filled with the sounds of battle.

I nudged my wife. '*Pearl Harbour*?' she whispered, her lips contorted like a ventriloquist's. I told her it looked like Midway. I wondered if our hosts were hinting that it was time to leave.

Mr Fujita's face was now the blanched tint of the raw cuttle-fish we had eaten an hour before. His kneeling body was perfectly rigid yet seemed somehow to be inching towards the television set, like a machine on hidden ball bearings. Music had started up, the voiceless score of an old Beatles tune, and Japanese lyrics crossed the screen in silver spurts like the glimmering tracks of tracer bullets.

'I think it's "All You Need Is Love",' my wife whispered, beginning to giggle. I pinched her foot. 'Don't you dare,' I hissed.

Some of the children watched the screen while others played around Mr Fujita's peaceful brother, who lay like a casualty on the deck of a destroyer. His daughter watched the battle with rapt attention, as if she had never seen anything like it before.

Mr Fujita had now manoeuvred his mysterious body to within striking distance of the vcr. He grinned immensely as his hand shot out at the on-off switch beside the screen. He missed. The volume rose to a deafening pitch and the den thundered with explosions and the sound of tubas and trombones straining towards a crescendo. The fallen brother twitched in his sleep, as if having a bad dream. Mr Fujita's fingers found the on-off switch and the television went dark, just as a Zero fighter on a *kamikaze* mission whizzed into the deck of an aircraft carrier.

'*Mā, jūbun desu,*' Mr Fujita said. 'That's enough television for now. The children tend to watch too much, you know. The daughter especially.'

The daughter frowned. 'He's full of it,' she said in English.

Mrs Fujita burst from the kitchen with a fresh pot of coffee. The daughter began to whisper in my wife's ear; my wife struggled to contain a smile. Kneeling by the blank television Mr Fujita glanced up, his wide eyes darting like searchlights as the children flew around him with their arms stretched out, swooping and banking and making engine sounds. The brother trembled again in his sleep.

3

SOUNDS OF THE WATER

The old pond, ah!
A frog jumps in –
The water's sound.

–Bashō

Jason holds the shower nozzle above his head and feels icy water course through his hair and over his face. His eyes are tightly closed. In his nostrils and around his lips the white water sprays and surges, like a stream cascading over gaps and fissures in a tropical cliff. Jason breathes steadily, enjoying the illusion that he can survive in two elements.

He is a frog, or some scaly exotic amphibian – a member of a scarce and endangered species. A cliff-toad peering from a ledge through the veil of a waterfall, vigilant for predators. An injured bullfrog, tired and hungry, bathing its wounds in the dim pool of a Kyōto garden. The old pond, ah!

Jason's mother has begun to call him. He can barely hear her through the locked door and over the sounds of the water. Her voice reaches him in baritone spasms – much like the voice of his father, or like ripples of thunder during the monsoon. A light quick tinkling is the ping of raindrops on stepping stones outside a Chinese teahouse (or the emergency key twisting in the bathroom lock).

As the door bursts open he leans back into the tub and submerges. His wide-open frog's eyes stare up through the water at a dim unfocused form which raises wobbling arms to its head and emits a muffled scream.

★

It is Christmas and I am a child of ten. My sister and I sit by the drooping tree among empty boxes and tangled scraps of tinsel and dappled paper. In the curls above my sister's ear I have set, like some rare Pacific flower, a magenta bow. As the lights on the tree flicker the bow glitters in her hair and her calm face is suffused with a marvellous light. I reach out to her with another bow. In my lap is the marble-green globe I have just pulled from a cardboard box.

Father was a full-time world traveller of part-time renown, a renegade, a rogue male, a foreign correspondent who did not correspond, an absence and a distance, a jumbo-jet gypsy with a rakish leer and leather briefcase full of farewell cards and polyester flowers. Our house was too small for him. Likewise our town and our family. He was a lady-killer – no mean suburban beau but a gallant cavalier whose ambitions were truly global. In winter he wore a great fur coat and clapped his hands and breathed long streams of mist into the freezing air as he talked of Mongolia. He used words my sister and I could not understand and did not notice or did not care that their meaning was lost on us. He was alien and exotic. When we met him at the airport his arms were always bursting with strange gifts and he carried in his clothes and on his breath faint odours that were new to us. He was the Craw, the great furry ursine beast that pursued us through the dark basement and up half-lit flights of stairs and even into our dreams as we squealed in an ecstasy of fear. He was venerable and distant, a compelling will roaming the house between assignments, a brooding absence when he was away.

Beside him mother was staid and pious, gentle, competent and methodical, perpetually consoling. All the photographs we have of her are slightly blurred. Someone seems to have tampered with my memories of her, for her face always has a soft focus, as if in deference to an actress prematurely aged. We can

33

see now that her compliance and reserve dissembled a mounting despair, and we can feel, as of course we could not feel then, admiration for her stamina. My father knew what he was doing when he married her. Perhaps he was as surprised as we were the one time she fell from character (the actress, prematurely aged) and became a foreigner to us, as he had always been.

David, I heard my mother begin, *please, we have to talk. It's all right, Jason and Dora are upstairs.*

In those days I was always in retreat, always searching for undiscovered corners. In anonymous nooks and clefts and attics, pantries, cupboards and crawl-spaces, in steamer trunks or hidden in the laundry hamper under father's well-travelled clothing, I would stow away for hours.

I was never hungry; I did not get bored. A menagerie of illusions sustained me and like an emperor's magician I could assume the outward form of any creature in the Animal Kingdom. That morning, like a cub or a tree frog, I had wedged myself under our Christmas tree and was gazing up into the living room through a dense blind of twigs and needles. Bulbs winked a few inches from my eyes, ornaments dangled. No one knew I was there. Through all the foliage, flickering lights and clustered ornaments, I could not see the expressions on my parents' faces, though of course I could make out their words and the tones that gave them meaning.

My mother, with great caution: 'David, you know it wasn't what he wanted.'

'Sometimes it's best to get things you think you don't want.'

'David. David, look, you know why you gave him the book. We both know why. Because it's what you would have wanted at his age. What you'd still want.' Surprisingly firm. Gathering momentum and with it confidence. Becoming strident.

'Well? How else can I decide what to give him?'

'You don't know who he is. You don't care. You think he's just a shadow – your shadow. You want him to be your shadow. You want him to grow up to be like you, to think like you ...' With a kind of disbelief, as if airing the words has crystallized a terrifying, latent recognition.

'And you don't.'

'Why should I? You think I want to be abused by my own son?'

'Who's abused? I bought him a nice book. He loves it.'

'It's you who loves the book, David. You don't know the first thing about how he feels. You don't know how any of us feel you're so wrapped up in yourself. You never listen when the children tell you things or ask you questions and you never listen to me.'

'You never speak.'

'I make a point of speaking to you whenever you drop in. But nothing gets through to you, does it? When you're happy the whole world should sing with you and if it won't you blame us all for upsetting the harmony. When you're mad because an assignment's not going well or you're blocked then everyone else had better sympathize or else they're cruel and insensitive and –'

'Marilyn, for God's sake, it's *Christmas*.'

'You make me feel as if it's my fault.'

'Are you so sure it's all mine?'

'You expect me to take the blame for everything. Fifteen years. You act as if *she's* my fault too. I'm letting myself go, I don't watch what I eat, I'm always asleep by the time you get to bed – and then you hint how much better things would have been for you if you hadn't married me –'

'This isn't like you, Marilyn.'

'You don't know what I'm like. You don't *care*. Why don't you just – just go live with her in Halifax if that's what you –'

'*Marilyn*, for Christ's *sake!*'

35

I coughed then – as an animal caught out of its element might struggle for breath. I coughed again, louder. I knew my father would do angry things soon after he used those words. *For Christ's sake.* I knew the pale, featureless orbs turning sharply in my direction were the faces of my parents. Their sudden silence was more terrifying than their voices had been.

'Jason,' my mother's voice said, 'Jason, we didn't know you –'

'What do you mean by hiding under there while we're talking, Jason? Come out from under there. Now.'

'Jason, darling, Daddy and I –'

'Out of there. Come on.'

'– didn't know that –'

'NOW.'

I saw my father's body squatting and waddling toward the tree. His movements were awkward. He did not belong down here. His face was still obscured by the cool-smelling boughs – an aroma of resin like the scent around ponds in Kyōto. I clutched the globe and the book he had given me, *A Journey through Asia*, and stole back towards the farthest edge of the tree. An enormous hand reached under the rustling boughs and groped directly towards me. Shaken ornaments swayed and rattled. One fell and shattered on the floor. *Leave him alone,* my mother cried, *leave the boy alone.*

'The Craw,' my father called. 'The Craw wants his Christmas dinner!'

'No,' I yelled feebly. 'Go away.'

I felt the hand on my wrist. I willed it away. I saw my father's vast red face follow his arm into the open under the boughs, like a moon setting in a jungle clearing. 'THE CRAW WANTS HIS TURKEY!' the face cried. 'But I'm a frog!' I screamed. And shut my eyes so I would not have to see.

★

36

It was no ordinary globe my father bequeathed me. Though I lost it years ago I can recall clearly how it looked, how it felt in my hands. Where the land met the cobalt sea it was green as our neighbours' lawns and if you moved your finger along the coast-lines you felt the shore rising out of the water. The land continued to rise – you could feel it with your finger – and turned sallow then sunburnt brown then chilly white for the snow-covered peaks. The poles were a frosty, monotonous silver. When I slid my fingers over Antarctica I could trace the rise and fall of massifs under the ice-sheet and imagined I felt the biting cold of the glaciers. The deserts were a dusty yellow, the coast of Siberia a barren grey, and the scattered volcanic islands of Japan reared suddenly from the sea's trenches. And most of all I remember the high plateau of Tibet, its egg-shaped swelling crowned with a craggy shell of silver; how I loved to travel my fingers along its roughness and, as if it contained a code, a passage in Braille, I derived images of the day I would stand there, hours above the rest of the world, over the steaming succulent jungles of Thailand and the vast grainfields of China (my fingertips, journeying), over the war-torn countries where my father often went, over Burma, over Nepal, the boreal forests of Siberia, the Indonesian archipelagos, the seething metropolises of India and the outskirts of Brampton, Ontario.

In the days between Christmas and New Year's, the globe and the book *A Journey through Asia* were always in my hands. In favour of these gifts all stuffed animals, save two, were ousted from my bed. Only Agnew the patched tattered lamb and Bashō, the stuffed frog my father had just brought back from Japan, escaped closet exile.

When he came home my father brought gifts for my mother, too, but for some reason they always made her cry.

On New Year's Eve, Pandora and I were playing the globe-game in her room. One of us had to wear a blindfold while the other held out the globe; the blindfolded player would reach out and feel the proffered surface and on that flimsy basis name the part touched.

My sister was deplorably bad at this game. I was always giving her clues. 'Dad went there last Easter,' I'd say. *But Jason, he's always going places.* 'Last Tuesday,' I'd venture, 'do you remember what Mom made for dinner last Tuesday?' *Nope.* 'Lamb curry! She made curry!' *I hate lamb curry.* 'A kind of ink,' I'd hiss, 'beginning with "I". Elephants. Sitars. Silk.' *I give up.* 'So do I,' I'd groan, giving the globe a slight turn.

'Now,' I said to her, 'try again.'

'Ummm ...'

'Come on, it's easy.'

'Maybe with a little hint ...'

'Pearl Harbour,' I whispered tentatively. 'Chopsticks.'

'It feels like a little mouseturd under my finger.'

'You idiot. Do you know what the samurai would do to you for saying that?'

'I give up. Let's play another game.'

'Ah so! Honourable sister-san not want to continue!'

'Germany! It's Germany! Miss Schmidt always says "Ah so" in gym class.'

'You're hopeless,' I groaned, braining her with the cardboard globe to make her stop laughing. But she would not stop. And I wanted to hit her again. The more ridiculous her mistakes were, the more she giggled. It frustrated me that my triumphs failed to chasten her or make her more serious – it wasn't at all like winning a game against boys. But at least she was impressed by my talents. I knew the globe so well that I could guess the correct place almost every try. I bragged that I could even tell the icy chill of the North Atlantic from the Indian Ocean's placid warmth – and though I used coastlines to help me discriminate, I almost believed my boast was true.

Finally she stumped me on Southern Ontario. 'Brampton!' she cheered. 'It's our own place! Don't you know?'

I didn't. But this little lapse didn't affect her admiration for me; she insisted we show Mom and Dad what I could do. 'Dad can write an article about you for the travel magazines,' she crowed. 'Now he won't have to go away to find his stories.'

We walked together up the dim hall to my parents' room. I cradled the globe under my arm like a helmet. Their door was closed, they would be readying themselves for the neighbours' New Year's Eve party.

I heard voices from beyond the door but they were not my parents'. I could not make out the words. I heard a sharp sound. I tried to say something to my sister but in her excitement she had already turned the knob, pushed open the door. 'Daddy! Mommy! See what Jason can do!'

At odd times ever since, I have seen them again as they were, momentarily frozen as in a Christmas tableau. I have a good memory. The scene does not change. Framed within the doorway they are two exotic natives surprised in the front room of their hut by an intrepid photographer. Familiar features of the room and of their persons have taken on a primitive, and alien aspect, an air of inscrutable treachery: Father standing in profile, his back to the mirror, facing my mother who is facing us. Her eyes meeting ours but not acknowledging this accident. Their bodies tensed, faces still. Suddenly a small dark bead like a jewel forming at the corner of my mother's mouth and trickling down her chin.

My father's eyes turn toward us slowly, inexorably as in a dream, his thin lips snarling *The doorbell, can't either of you hear the doorbell? Go and let the babysitter in.*

At breakfast the next morning his parents are hung over and in no mood for his games.

'Take off the blindfold, Jason,' his father growls.

'Do what your father tells you,' says his mother.

Pandora giggles hysterically for a moment then begins to cry.

Jason explains that the blindfold is part of the globe-game, which he offers to demonstrate after breakfast, but father says he has to call the travel agent after breakfast and mother says she doesn't feel well and will lie down. Jason has never heard his mother say anything like this before. He is having breakfast with two strangers who may or may not turn out to be friendly.

Pandora asks their mother if it's her mouth that's bothering her because she has a cut there doesn't she and Jason is glad he is wearing the blindfold so he does not have to see the cut or watch his mother's face as the question hits home.

'Your blindfold, Jason,' his father rumbles. 'Take it off.'

'That's not in the rules,' Jason says with pressed dignity, stumbling from the table and feeling his way toward the stairs.

The blindfold curtails Jason's studies but he has read enough of *A Journey through Asia* that he can imagine and extrapolate and surmise. He turns the globe slowly in his hands and hears through the wall of the study his father's voice arranging and reserving flights for an excursion to Tibet. Usually he hears little through the wall but in the short time since he began wearing the blindfold his hearing has become preternaturally acute, like the faculties of some nocturnal creature.

First his father is talking softly, there is a sense of urgency in his voice, urgency and explanation. Now another call, a different tone. Clearer. There will be fighting in Tibet very soon, he hears, and if you get me in now before they close the borders I'll be there when it happens. Yes. Yes. I may have to stay awhile. A photographer too. Fine. One of the new hotels. Lhasa via Hong Kong and Chengdu? Yes. Fine. Jason moves his fingers over the Himalayan plateau and its oval shape feels to him like a swelling tumour or permanent scar. Fighting there. But who? In *A Journey through Asia* Tibet was a peaceful kingdom (his father's voice stops and a door slams as he lumbers out of his study) – a peaceful kingdom high up above the rest of the world: the ravenous tiger-eyed jungles of Burma, the bloody banks of the river Jordan, barren tundra along the frozen seas, the starving cities of Bangladesh and the outskirts of Brampton, Ontario. In Tibet all the people had serene meditative expressions because the air was too thin for fighting. If you tried to argue you would hyperventilate and if you actually swung your fist at someone you would have a heart attack and die. Jason had not read these exact things but his inferences were solidly founded. In Tibet the thin air made people giddy and they laughed at everything you said. There were no comedians in Tibet because the idea of needing to make people smile was alien to the Tibetans. The Tibetans never dreamed. There was no need to escape through dreaming, or by any other means, like some amphibian forced to change elements to survive. In Tibet everyone inhabited the same element: in the crisp vivid air of the high plain, things appeared as they really were and the light was too brilliant and clear for lying. Lamas walked through the temples, gentle furry mammals in orange robes, the sacred cows of Tibet ...

Jason's father is in the study again speaking rapidly and quietly on the phone. Even with his superior hearing Jason can catch only a few words. *No ... overseas soon ... any more ... court? Marilyn* (his mother's name) *... Marilyn.* And the word *childsupport.* He has never heard this word before. It makes him think immediately of his mother. *Marilyn,* he hears again. *Yes ... Yes ... Goodbye.* His father's door slams. He hears him calling his mother to come upstairs. Putting the globe down, Jason slips quietly through his door and into the bathroom. He locks the door and climbs into the tub. For the first time in several days he removes his blindfold – and has to close his eyes at once because of the unaccustomed light. As his parents begin to argue somewhere in the distance he holds the shower nozzle like a phone receiver above his head and feels icy water course through his hair and over his face. His eyes are tightly closed.

At dinner Jason is scolded – no doubt for locking the bathroom door and terrifying his mother. This is his deduction, based on the infrequent words that penetrate his silent world. He has stuffed both ears with wads of cotton. He has refused to remove his blindfold and will say nothing but the word 'No.'

To hell with it, he makes out distinctly. *Let the kid do ... he wants. Your ... son.*

But at bedtime first his father then his mother come into his room. Though their voices are filtered out by the cotton plugs, he understands them, as a cat or a dog might, by their changing tone and the odd recognizable word. He hears his father: *Jason ... Doctor?* He shakes his head to signal no. The word itself now seems an extravagant concession.

Eyes ... hurting?

Go away, he commands him in his mind, reckoning slyly that his father's obedience is sooner or later assured. In fact he gathers his father is leaving in a few days. And now some kind of promise is being made – probably of gifts from Tibet.

Suddenly Jason speaks. Will his father see the Dalai Lama?

No ... exile ... India. Look, take that ... stuff ... of ears.

'Exile!' Jason cries. 'How could they ever send him out of his own country? Why would they want to do it?'

Politics, he hears faintly, *politics*, as if the word is being shouted over a vast distance.

Why ... blindfold?

'But he's just an animal,' Jason pleads, 'he's innocent!'

His father says something he doesn't catch, but in the dull distant rumble of the voice, like a whirlpool nearing on a wide river, he feels an undertow of sadness so unlike his father he wants to tear off his blindfold and see who is there. But he is afraid. He senses the huge, whiskery head brooding above his own and wonders if the doubt and indecision he feels are his own or his father's. The two faces hover in the darkness together, like a planet and a moon. Jason pictures a pool in a lush jungle brimming with moonlight, in the breathless moment before the predator springs, and senses there is still something he might say. But he does not know what it is.

Jason will not remove his blindfold. After a gentle, clumsy kiss his father's face breaks away from him and backs into the darkness.

When his mother comes in she says nothing – or perhaps she is only whispering. He senses her beside him, inhabiting the silences, warming and disarming them. When she kisses him goodnight he feels the moisture on her cheeks and around her lips.

Jason plays the globe-game with Pandora or sits alone in his room. For her he will take out his cotton plugs. She is sad because she never sees Mommy and Daddy. They are always in their room talking or going out somewhere in the car again and again. They go out suddenly and though they are never long they leave no babysitter and Dora is afraid. Mommy isn't being Mommy any more. There's never any dinner. And Jason – aren't you getting hungry? How long is it since you've ate?

She wonders if they'll both go away to China this time. He tells her no.

One day in his father's study he removes his blindfold and finds a pair of genuine earplugs. The picture on the tiny packet shows a passenger in an airplane sleeping peacefully while two strangers rant and gesticulate beside him. With some difficulty Jason extracts two sticky wads of cotton from his ears and inserts the traveller's earplugs. Only the loudest of sounds, the packet guarantees, can violate them.

Probably it is only a day or two but it seems that many

months go by while Jason hibernates in his soundless world. His mind roams without agenda over an uneven past and through the Asia of his Christmas reading – and finds Asia by far the more hospitable locale. As he stumbles by accident onto the scene where his father refuses absolutely to have animals in the house, No, not even the Shepherd puppy that has trailed Dora home from the park, he struggles to escape and finds himself in the bow of a golden schooner in some Asian sea. But in Asia there are disturbing visions, too. More vividly than many things he has actually witnessed he sees the photograph in his book showing a statue of the fasting Buddha. Sharp, appalling bones protrude through the figure's skin like the ribs of the crucified Christ his mother retrieves from the basement each Christmas. The statue sits by a pond in a Kyōto garden. Behind it, silhouetted against the water, is the bough of a plum tree heavy with fruit. What is it that makes the stone figure so reluctant to eat? Why are the sunken eyes closed so resolutely on that tranquil scene? A caption reminds readers that at last the Buddha renounced his austerity and chose the path of moderation, but clearly there had been a time when he was unable to accept and assimilate anything his surroundings held. Jason thinks of Lamas sauntering up the halls of their hermitage towards the refectory, their blunt velvety snouts sniffing air perfumed with the scents of tea and *tsampa* ... But some of them were in exile now. They would be isolated and hungry.

His belly growls and like a lion-tamer he quells it with a brisk slap. He has eaten nothing. This has not been like a real Christmas at all, except for the book and the globe and the games he and Dora played and the Christmas tree with its coloured lights which seemed as magical as ever. Last Christmas was not real either, or the one before that, but mother was more in control then and the troubles were quieter, present but contained, like something packed deftly in a delicate box. He remembers unwrapping *A Journey through Asia* on Christmas

Eve and thinks of those Asian kings in the passage his mother always asks Father to read them then: *now when Jesus was born in Bethlehem of Judaea in the days of Herod the king, behold, wise men from the East came unto Jerusalem ...*

Where had the wise men come from? And how? His father couldn't tell him. One was from Japan, he thinks to himself, and wore armour studded with jewels and brought with him a jade statue of the enlightened Buddha. Another from India rode a tattooed elephant and carried silks and nutmeg, twigs of cinnamon, mangoes and diamonds the size of pelicans' eggs. The third was the Dalai Lama himself, ambling on his gentle hoofs, bearing on his saffron-robed spine exotic testaments and maps and scriptures. And they were wise. That was a rare thing. Something that would dwell, furtive and endangered, in the very heart of Asia. Perhaps his father was looking for it on his travels. Someday Jason must go.

On the last day of the Christmas holidays he and his mother and sister accompany Father to the airport. Like a seeing-eye dog, his sister leads him through the terminal's automatic doors. Even through earplugs Jason can hear the crowds and he is dazzled by electric lights when he finally takes off his blindfold because his mother has knelt beside him and removed one plug and begged him please to be sensible, Father is leaving for a long time, won't he be a good boy and say goodbye?

At the time he attaches no significance to his father's visit to the counter of a domestic airline before checking in for his international flight, but he knew even then with the deaf-and-dumb intuition of a child that his father would not be coming back, ever. His mother is crying discreetly and his sister giggling the way she still does now when she's nervous or afraid of betraying some delicate emotion.

His father will not face any of them directly. His face like an ancient statue's, perfected in its stolid grief, as if resolved not to crack into pitiful decay despite its antiquity. He sees it that way now. He recalls nothing of his actual feelings as he and Dora struggle to lift an unprecedented second suitcase onto the scale and his father disappears into customs after rushed kisses and a vague guarantee of gifts on his return.

Years after making his own journey to Asia, these scenes he thought he'd escaped return to him. He is in his apartment, alone, watching a *National Geographic* special on the Bering Strait. From Alaska the camera pans over a dark expanse of water hemmed in by fog, while an authoritative voice explains that in clear weather one can see hills on the coast of Asia. Abrupt cut to a view of the same water under sunny skies and there they are, as promised, pale hills rising over the Siberian coast, hills the voice describes as the remnants of the Great Bering Land Bridge. '*By which men once crossed from Asia to North America,*' the voice goes on, becoming animated as it explains that since the bridge vanished the only animal able to cross the strait is the polar bear. '*What amazes the crews of isolated Bering Sea oil rigs are the bears that will sometimes appear in the surrounding water, as much as sixty miles from Siberia, the nearest land, and a hundred miles from the Alaskan coast where the bears must have originated ...*'

As the scene cuts to the deck of an oil rig, Jason sees big men in parkas lining the rails and cheering at a small unfocused spot of white bobbing in the rough grey seas. The camera zooms unsteadily and a white bear is seen to turn its head for a moment as if to acknowledge the crew's attention, then continue aloofly on its way.

Wandering back through the enormous airport, struggling with holiday crowds, we pass curved counters spoked with long queues and giftshops full of paperbacks, postcards on rotating stands. Our mother is perfectly composed. She is herself again, patient and predictable, vulnerable, necessary. Smiling her kind conspiratorial smile she reaches down and pulls the remaining plug from my ear. Dora has stopped giggling and is pointing with wonder at a huge globe revolving above a ticket counter. Our mother nods and smiles. As we pass a restaurant she suggests we get a meal.

4

Magi

It wasn't like the falling star that crosses the night in a split-second, catching your eye as it vanishes. The light was brighter than any meteor, brighter than the other stars, and like a signal flare it fell slowly, pulsing, from a point high above the skyline.

We watched for a while in silence before Richard, the oldest of us, decided it was an airplane. And that it was going to crash.

There's nothing else it could be, he told us.

And after he'd said it we began to notice the faint glimmering tail following the light as it descended. Accelerating, little by little.

None of us spoke. The others may have been listening, like me, for the cinematic sounds we'd come to expect: a long subsiding wail, a baritone roar as the falling craft met earth in a bubbling orange fireball.

But there were no explosions, no fearful screams. Around us the fields hummed with a dull, hypnotic rhythm, cicadas chanted in foliage by the path. A drone of cars on the highway a mile off through the wood, and our anxious, unsteady breathing.

Maybe he can still pull out of it.

Murmurs of agreement. *He's still not dropping too fast.*

He is – can't you see he's speeding up?
Come on. Pull out of it.
He's really going to crash.
We've got to do something – come on.
But Richard told us it was too far.
Even if we run?
Too far. A hundred miles, maybe. A thousand.
A cluster of fireflies rose from the field beside us and
drifted across the path. The falling speck was glowing brighter
as it neared the skyline.
I wonder if the pilot's afraid.
Of course he's afraid. Wouldn't you be afraid?
And someone added, *He's all alone.*
Which was a strange thing for any of us to say, because the
light could have been a thousand things for all we could tell, a
jetliner from Asia with hundreds aboard, a returning satellite or
approaching warhead. But no one objected. The light was soli-
tary and small and we knew whoever it carried must be alone.
And now the ghostly tail trailing the light began to
change, to fan out and pulsate with a prismatic glow. Soon the
light would touch the skyline.
He'll never pull out now.
Maybe he can jump – maybe he's got a parachute.
We'd never see it from here.
And in the watchful silence that followed, like the vapour
trail behind the falling light, there was agreement. We knew the
pilot would not get out. Something told us. Perhaps the brittle,
expectant stillness of the fall air – or did we sense something in
the light's resemblance to a star, its timeless arc across the night-
sky compressed to a few seconds?
But we were only children.
For a moment more we froze in that constellation, David
behind me, Richard to my right; the others had slipped away.
The light reached the dense blackness of earth and we waited

for the explosion. Some day we would trace our scattered, soli-
tary orbits to this place.

Richard raised his hand for silence; we waited intently.
But the light was too far off and crashed behind the skyline or
into deep forest, or was swallowed by a lake, for it vanished suddenly and left the sky infinitely darker. The air had turned
cool. From far off the almost-human shriek of some bird.

The stars themselves were clearer now that the sharper
light was gone; the Milky Way pulsed and blazed and to the east
Mars glistened like the eye of a reptile. The Magi might have
seen the heavens with the same transfigured wonder when the
star of Bethlehem finally fell, and the rough desert track they
were following home to their kingdoms vanished into the dark
...

I craned my head back to see Orion and count the
Pleiades, but before I was done I lost my balance and stumbled.

5

AN APPARITION PLAY

I

Sharon's face was as Japanese as her mother's had been and held no shadow of her father's features. The old innkeeper spoke to her first. There was a small place up the way, she said, that served local food and was popular with tourists, but as it was off-season they should have no trouble finding seats. Surely, though, they were not about to rush off so soon? They had only just arrived and the weather was unseasonably cold – so much snow this early in December!

Helpless, Sharon shrugged and smiled at the woman, then turned on her father with a fierce look:

'What did she say?'

Adam Fuller ignored his daughter. He was rummaging for a deft response to the old woman's Japanese. *Forgive us*, he finally brought out, *but my daughter is hungry and I'm ready for a drink. I think we'll go straight to the restaurant.*

Ah, the innkeeper sucked in her breath, *a daughter!* She performed two rapid, shallow bows, the sleeves of her winter kimono fanning the still air. *Forgive me, I did not realize ...*

Fuller shrugged off her mistake as if it meant nothing. Yet she had taken his daughter for a wife, or a lover, and no doubt thought he was younger than his thick frame and ashen hair would suggest. And now she exclaimed at his 'excellent Japanese'; the grim nostalgia that had struck him with the wind as they got off the train from Kyōto seemed to fade.

Sharon frowned up at him. She seemed to know she was being discussed. She smiled at the woman, her eyes hopeful, keen, and said softly, 'My mother came from here.'

The woman shrugged politely and looked to Fuller.

My wife was raised in the town, he explained, and the rest tumbled out like a flustered confession: *We met in Ōsaka years ago when she was a student and I was here in Japan as* – he paused and frowned – *as a missionary.*

The woman's faint eyebrows arched slightly but she made no remark. Fuller blushed and smiled at this fresh sign of her suspicion. The days *were* drawing nigh, he thought – a phrase from scripture returning to mind – when he would take no pleasure from life. It was good to be thought still vital, young.

Vanity, his father would have rumbled. *Vanity.*

'Father, can we go now? Please, I'd like to eat.'

But Fuller was not done. Nostalgia for his youth, for Aiko as she was then, for his last visit to the town twenty-three years before – all surged up from his chest in a heated flood. Had the innkeeper really not heard of the marriage? It didn't happen every day that a local girl married a foreigner! And surely she had known the Ogawas?

The woman said she had run a *minshuku* in Matsue till just last year and knew only that the Ogawas had passed away some time before.

Almost ten years now, Fuller said. *Aiko came back for the funeral.*

Ah. The woman looked down and smiled sadly. There was a pause, then she sighed, *Yes, come to think of it I do seem to recall something about the Ogawa girl marrying a foreigner.*

'Father ...'

And next winter on the ship home to Canada – he went on as if drunk – *this daughter* – he set his hands on her slim shoulders – *this lovely daughter was born.*

As he spoke, the woman nodded and gave little sighs of encouragement, her small shrewd eyes darting back to the girl's face again and again as if finding it impossible to believe that she too was a foreigner, like him. Perhaps the woman still thought he was some rich old tourist with a young girl from the city? The part about his being a missionary, he thought, did not sound convincing.

He pulled at his black silk tie, as if loosening a clerical collar. *I left the church years ago,* he said.

The innkeeper sighed encouragement but Fuller's urge to explain things was fading. He blushed, thinking of what he had already said. Far too much, he thought.

'Father?' Sharon squirmed free of Fuller's other hand and turned to face him. In these surroundings she looked more than ever like Aiko. 'Please, I want to go now. I'm hungry. I can't understand any of this.' Her eyes gleamed with frustration.

She would like to lie down, perhaps? the innkeeper suggested.

Fuller shot the woman a look. *She's hungry,* he told her. *I'm afraid we'll have to go.*

The innkeeper pursed her lips slightly as if priming another question, but she did not speak. Fuller could feel her curiosity – and now, rising to meet it, his own nostalgia and need to confess. He swallowed and gave Sharon a quick glance and muttered, *My wife passed away two years ago. Tomorrow we're going to visit the family tomb, and. Well.*

Fuller and the innkeeper smiled nervously, Japanese-style, as if at some private joke. *I'm so sorry,* the woman mumbled, bowing, stepping back into the hall so that her face fell into shadow, the eyes deeply caved.

When Fuller and Sharon came out into the cold night air she turned to him and said, 'You were talking about me and then at the end about mother, weren't you?'

Fuller gave a guilty nod; she groaned and clenched her fists. 'I don't like you talking about me when I can't understand, it's not fair. What did you say about my mother?'

Snow was falling into the street and thickening on the slate roofs of the wooden buildings.

'I did mention that she passed away.'

Sharon thrust her small pale hands into the pockets of her college jacket. Fuller thought again of the polite euphemism he had used for death: *nakunaru*, which means literally 'to disappear'.

'I can't believe you told her so much. You never used to talk to people that way. Are you going to tell her everything else, too?'

'Please, Sharon, not now.'

'You never talked to *me* that openly.'

'I said not now.'

'Why not now?'

'We've been through these things.'

She groaned. 'We never have. You always tell me no, not now, not now, we've been through these things, but we haven't been through them yet and if you have your way we never will. Father, I need to *talk*. I told you I was seeing someone when I was at school and he said I needed to talk to you.'

Fuller gripped her arm as a hunched old woman shuffled past them, seeming to stare; it was hard for him to tell. 'What do you mean you were seeing someone? You told me you broke up with your boyfriend.'

'*Someone*, Father, not a boyfriend. I was *seeing* someone.'

'Here,' Fuller squinted, 'this must be the place.'

'I mean a therapist, a shrink.'

'Keep your voice down,' he snapped, 'I know exactly what you mean.' He released her and roughly pointed up at a line of characters above an ornately carved door. Through a frosted window the inside of a restaurant could be made out, dimly.

'This is it,' he murmured. 'I can read the characters.'

'Father – did you hear what I just told you?'

'Of course I did.' He shook his head and looked up into the swirling air. 'Sharon, for crying out loud, why didn't you say something about this before? Your grandfather would roll over in his grave if he knew you were talking to a doctor about your problems. Why didn't you talk to me?'

Snow was melting on Sharon's upturned nose and forehead, her serious face was lighted by the window and it was the face of his wife, or nearly the same, twenty-three years ago in these streets.

You should know, the face seemed to insist, *you should know why I had to do it*, and he was stunned by the English words that stabbed out in her flat, ordinary accent – a familiar voice bursting from behind some exotic mask:

'What you did to her. Sometimes I can hardly stand to look at you.'

She smudged the back of her hand across her eyes to clear off the melted snow.

Fuller had his father's sulphurous temper, but had taught himself to control it. After a moment he said, in a measured tone, 'I think you must need something to eat.' He took her arm and climbed the steps to the door and led her through: the place was empty but for three burly young men cross-legged round a low table by the grill, leaning together over steaming cups of saké. Their faces were flushed and their red eyes, dazed and darting, soon came to rest with something like relief on Fuller and the tightly held girl.

II

Next morning when he woke, nauseous and exhausted, Fuller sat stiffly and rapped on the sliding paper door dividing the room. He waited a few moments then pulled it open, slowly. Sharon was already dressed in jeans and black sweater and stood between her *futon* and the window gazing out at a grey sky full of snow, the whitened eaves of a neighbouring house. It was cold and when he coughed to get her attention his breath, a dense silver cloud, burst away and diffused in the room's still air.

He had always liked to rise before anyone else. 'You're up early,' he told her.

'I suppose.' Her words fogged the window, haloed her head. 'I got up two hours ago and went out walking. It's so beautiful here. I climbed the hill behind the town – from the top you can see these beautiful mountains.'

'Like the view from our house?' (He saw Vancouver spread out before them, the mountains looming up behind, ghostly with snow.)

'No,' she said, 'it's different here. Purer, somehow.'

'Purer?' He chuckled, but he thought he knew what she meant; he and Aiko had climbed the hill several times on their honeymoon. It was May and there were others on the path – a few tourists and locals out for the air and to view the last of the cherry blossoms. An elderly Belgian man with a flowing white beard had taken a picture of them arm in arm on the wall of a ruined castle, and for years Fuller had kept a framed copy on his desk. He had thanked the man, mumbling a few words of clumsy French. Later Aiko had kissed him and said, in Japanese, *You could be my guide anywhere, you speak so many languages.*

In those days she seemed to worship him.

'Father – can we get something to eat?'

'Give me a minute,' Fuller mumbled, coughing.

A bell tolled somewhere in the town and he glanced at his watch: late, eight-fifteen. He looked down at the pale fabric stretched tight over his gut and sat up straighter. The bell was familiar from his first visit – centuries old, it was sounded at the monastery each day for ritual reasons he had forgotten.

'The snow's really deep now in the streets,' Sharon went on, her face averted, breath swirling in dense fumes round her hair. 'On the way back I passed the restaurant we went to.' She turned to face him. 'Can we go again tonight?'

'I think I'd rather not, Sharon.'

'Why?'

With shaking hands Fuller straightened his quilt and smoothed back his hair. 'I thought we'd try somewhere else.'

'It seemed like a good place to me,' she said, turning back to the window. 'The food was good – wasn't it?'

Fuller slid the paper door half closed and stood up. Dressing behind it he glanced again at his belly. For years he had been a thin man, pinched and gristly as his father had been till the day of his death, but since meeting Vida he had steadily put on weight. Vida said this meant he was happy now – that a man put on weight when he was ready to settle down. All the years before, she explained without a hint of malice, he had been starving, denying himself.

Now he no longer looked much like his father. That was a relief. Yet the extra weight had aged him.

'Father – can't we go back?'

Fuller frowned at Sharon's silhouette on the paper door, a dim shadow in snow. He thought of the young men who had sat across from them in the restaurant, the three faces flushed and huddled close over steaming cups. They were speaking softly and quickly and he had to admit that even the words he could make out were hard to understand. It was all dialect – and though he would not have confessed it to the girl he knew his Japanese was greatly reduced. *The devil's tongue*, that was how the first missionaries had christened the language, and even now, overrun with English words, it was a challenge. Still, he could tell the young men were talking about him, the *gaijin*, and the pretty Japanese girl and how well she seemed to speak English. He hadn't enjoyed his dinner. The *nabeyaki* and mountain vegetables were well enough prepared, but he kept sensing that the men, like the innkeeper, regarded him as some rich old American tourist with a lovely Japanese girl – and soon his feelings of pride gave way to anxiety because they were drunk and without women and they would resent him.

As the young men got drunker their voices grew loud. Finally the dark, broad-shouldered one pointed and directed some harsh remark at Sharon, who smiled back, nodding as if she understood. They seemed to be inviting her – no, both of them – to their table. They were gawking with the flushed, volatile bar-room grins that can turn vicious in a second. So Fuller sensed. He was about to ask for the bill when the manager came out of the kitchen and muttered something to the men, pointing at his watch; they paid him and left quickly.

Fuller hoped they had been asked to leave.

'We'll try another place today,' he told her, pulling his belt tight.

'Father,' she said, 'those three guys ... Why did they upset you so much?'

'I told you what they were saying, Sharon.'

'But I thought you couldn't understand them.'

He slid the door open and glared at her back. 'They were speaking too softly. A lot of it was dialect.'

'But you couldn't tell me what that one guy said when he spoke right at us!'

'He was drunk. Probably his friends couldn't understand him either.'

She turned from the window. 'Father, you don't have to know *everything*, you know. You're not some kind of *god* or something.'

'Of course I'm not.' He tightened his belt another notch. 'Why would you say something like that?'

'Because the man I was seeing at school told me you felt

you had to know everything and always have an answer and be perfect and he said I should tell you you don't have to be.'

'Nobody's perfect, Sharon, I've always said that.' He stalled for a moment, took a deep breath, then went on: 'Sometimes, though, you make me feel as if I should have been.'

She muttered something he didn't hear. When her face froze over, he thought, it was Aiko's: a death-mask mutely accusing him, passing judgement. And seeing her now in a shared room against a backdrop of *tatami* and paper walls painted with ghostly Japanese scenes ... He had the chilling sense that he was confessing to a dead wife, demanding absolution, not explaining things to a daughter.

'Look, you can't tell me one minute I don't have to be perfect and the next I was a lousy husband and father. I did my best, all right? When are we going to stop looking back and get on with our lives? That's why we came here, isn't it? I thought if we could come here together with your mother's – with the ashes —'

The wave of anger building behind Sharon's eyes seemed to break. Her slight body sagged and slumped back against the window.

'Let's try to be nice to each other,' he said. 'All right? Just for now, while we're here, all right? For her sake.'

A moment later she nodded, shivering.

Behind her the window shook and the snow brushed and fluttered fine wings over the glass.

★

The Ogawa family tomb was on a hilltop by a monastery a few miles away and they agreed to walk there over the quiet Sunday streets. On their way they would pass Aiko's old house and visit the 17th-century farming village maintained on the edge of town for tourists; he and Aiko had gone there on their honeymoon and he wanted to see it again.

Before leaving home, Fuller had had some of his wife's ashes sealed in a small wooden urn. Now Sharon carried it, as she had insisted, in a hand-woven Japanese bag she had picked out in Kyōto as an early Christmas gift. She carried it with a chastened dignity he had never seen in her before; his throat tightened as her budding adulthood was borne in on him.

After coffee and toast in a small shop they walked on into the outskirts of town. The snow had stopped falling and under-foot it was already beginning to melt. It took Fuller some time – he would not stop and ask directions, as Sharon kept urging – but finally he found the old Ogawa home, a small bungalow squeezed between a souvenir shop and a café, both closed. At some time in the last ten years, apparently, the house had been made into an inn, but it too seemed to be closed for the season.

Sharon mounted the step and pressed her face to the wooden slats of the door, then shook her head slowly and stepped down. A few snowflakes blew from the eaves and set-tled in her hair.

'I wish we could see inside,' she said.

'So do I,' he told her. 'Very much. But it would be differ-ent now.'

He remembered the room at the back of the house where the Ogawas had put them up – their daughter and her out-landish new mate. The old couple had been polite to him, even warm in the end, but then they had other daughters, other sons, so Aiko's impending defection with a gangling mis-sionary must not have struck them as a fatal loss.

Sunlight had entered that tiny room soon after dawn each morning. Awake beside his sleeping bride he had watched it creep over the weave of the *tatami* and fold its light in waves over the rumpled quilt that covered their legs. One time when the light had reached and climbed her upturned breasts his lin-gering guilt and astonishment were overcome, he leaned over and whispered her name, cupping her head in one hand and with the other hand embracing her, lifting her mouth toward his as if to drink ...

He was thinking of Vida, of making love to Vida. He missed her and wanted to write or call but he knew she would be unhappy if he reached her from here. The three years it had taken him to leave Aiko had almost killed her, she said, and though she had encouraged him to 'make this pilgrimage,' he knew she would not want to hear from him now.

When they reached the farming village the woman in the ticket booth was asleep and Fuller had to rap on the glass to wake her. Over a hill behind the booth they could see a range of high straw roofs, rich amber, so steep they were clear of snow. The old farmhouses had been built for extended families and they were huge inside, as big as country churches, with smoke-blackened beams at the crest of ceilings forty feet above the dirt floors. Each had a firepit where coals smouldered unwatched under simmering cast-iron pots. The space, the stained beams in the vaulted ceiling, the bitter drafts and rising smoke – Fuller recalled, aloud, the Presbyterian chapel in the Okanagan where he had preached for three years after leaving Japan, when Sharon was a baby.

She wanted to know if he ever wished he'd stayed a priest.

'Minister,' he snapped, irked that she could make such a basic error and wondering if it was deliberate. Yet the question *had* seemed sincere, conciliating ... 'I'm sorry,' he finally said. 'The truth is, I really don't think about it too much now.'

'You never go to church anymore,' she accused him. 'It hurt mother, you know – how you stopped going.'

'I stopped going a long time ago, Sharon. I never tried to stop your mother.'

'She said it hurt her. She said ... You know she converted for you, then you left the church. Then you stopped going.'

He tried to focus on the little crucifix lying on the cowl of her sweater. She had no interest in religion – none that he could see – but since Aiko's death she had taken to wearing it.

'It wasn't my life, Sharon, it was my father's. I guess it took me a while to see that.'

'Mother said you lost your faith.'

'I lost my *father*,' he burst out, 'my *father*, Sharon – that's what I lost.'

Her eyes seemed to fill and she looked away. *A loss of faith.* At one time it had loomed as something catastrophic and spectacular, but it turned out to be a long slow seeping, a slow bleeding, like the loss of a language. *The devil's tongue.* A slow bleeding, and the blood had first been drawn, he thought, by his father's hands when he was a boy in the thirties in a ragged clapboard rectory in Orangeville. The bleeding went on for years but he was finally, irrevocably drained, and healed, by his father's death; for seventeen years since then he had worked for a Japanese-import firm in Vancouver, and now a belief in his father's God seemed to him as eccentric and impractical as a belief in ghosts. He had driven himself hard in the firm and risen steadily. He had made a name for himself – the only drawback being that with each promotion his Japanese had become less essential. At home he and Aiko had long since settled into English, and so with time a great deal was lost. Yet while the hard-won vocabulary and grammar continued to decay, other echoes from his past came back to haunt him with a growing patience: hymns, commandments, passages from scripture, forever returning in the voice of his father, booming down from the pulpit, looming over the congregation and establishing with each divine, fiery cadence a sense of untouchable shame: *Vanity of vanities. Where wast thou when I laid the foundations? Thou knowest not the ways of the spirit, nor how the bones do grow in the womb ...*

Once, after returning from Japan, tried by the confines of a small-town parish and possessed yet again by his father's temper, he had reached down from the head of the table and slapped Sharon for some childish slip he could no longer recall. And afterward as she shrieked in the kitchen, Aiko trying to calm her, he had shut himself in his study and glared at his gaunt face in the tiny mirror behind the door. His father's face had glared back at him. Even here, in the mountains of British Columbia three thousand miles from home, he could not escape. The old man was sick then, dying in the rectory in Orangeville, and Fuller swore to himself he would leave the church as soon as he passed away. And never strike his daughter, or wife, again.

On both counts he had kept his word.

Sharon was watching him from the corner of her eye. 'Did you ... Father, did you start to resent Mother because she was more and more religious and you'd lost your faith?'

'That doesn't sound like you talking,' he snapped. 'It sounds like your therapist.'

'I'm just trying to understand what happened!'

'What happened is we *changed*, Sharon. Can't you – look, please, can't you try to understand?'

'You said some of the people in that town were prejudiced against her. Maybe, I don't know, maybe you started to feel ashamed? In history we've been studying the Japanese internment and, well, I've been thinking ...' She trailed off and squatted numbly by the fire, shivering hands outstretched.

'She was so thin at the end.'

'Sharon, please.'

'Like a prisoner of war or something.'

'Look, that's enough. You know I was never ashamed of your mother.'

'Then why? *Why?*' She buried her face in her hands. Swearing under his breath, Fuller dug at the dirt floor with his toe, then filled in the hollow. He saw she was determined, whatever the cost, to have everything out.

'We were wrong about each other,' he said softly. 'Both of

us. We couldn't really communicate well at first – not with words – but it didn't seem to matter.' He paused. 'People seem different, somehow, in another language. I know this is hard for you to understand. By the time your mother was speaking English – well, she didn't seem to me like quite the same person. And I suppose I was changing too.'

'You lost your faith,' she accused him, glancing up. Her face, lit from below, looked hurt, yet stern and unforgiving, like his father's.

'I told you, Sharon, I told you. It was my father I lost.'

'He *hated* her,' Sharon cried. 'Mother told me your father hated her. That made you change to her.'

'Sharon, please! Your grandfather – he was with the army in Hong Kong, a chaplain. You know that. You know very well what happened there with the Japanese. He never got over it.'

'But then, Father – I don't understand – why would you go to Japan?' She seemed to watch him with a cruel shrewdness. 'Why would you marry my mother?'

Fuller took a step towards her and stopped himself. He stared into the fire, shaking. 'Please, Sharon, don't make me angry. Please. Your mother and I – we were just in love, like anyone else. You know that.'

'I'm supposed to know everything,' she burst out, 'but how can I? When did you ever talk to *me*? Only her – she was the only one who told me anything. When I had no friends because I didn't fit in, not with the white kids or the Chinese kids and – you were always, always *working*.' She stood and faced him, body half-turned. 'I never saw you, and now I'm supposed to know everything. The man I'm seeing, he says it's typical –'

'Of what? *What?*'

Her eyes widened in fear. He forced himself to look away, into the small flames. *Weeping,* the old words came back to him, *like a crackle of thorns under a pot.*

A long time seemed to pass before Sharon said, 'Father, I'm cold. Maybe we should just go on.'

'I don't want to hear any more about this man you're seeing.'

Fuller turned from the fire and stalked out.

★

It was windy and fresh snow was falling by the time they got out to the road. There was a growing roar, then two headlights hurtled out of the grey air and at the last moment seemed to veer towards them and sheer away. Fuller's good wool slacks and jacket were drenched with slush. A pale hand waved from the window of a fading car.

'Those guys from the restaurant,' Sharon laughed hoarsely, waving, though the car had disappeared.

'I saw.' Fuller put a hand to his chest. 'You still want to eat there?'

'Think they can see us anymore?' She went on waving. Fuller gripped her arm and yanked it down. She wrenched herself free and glared at him, breathing hard.

'Shit, what is the matter with you? What is it – what do you have against those guys? They didn't mean to get us wet, we're hardly wet at all, they just wanted to wave. Last night you were giving them the meanest looks and for no reason – no reason. I can't believe they didn't get mad at you.'

'You don't know what they were saying, Sharon.'

'And now the way you're looking at me. Again. It's like you've got something against Japanese!'

Fuller spun away and walked quickly. Ahead through the driven snow a hill loomed, its white slopes bristling with the black spires of pines; beyond would be the monastery and its parish of old tombs, and among them the Ogawa tomb. He and Aiko had gone there one evening with lotus flowers for her grandparents, killed during the war, and she was so young and had knelt so supply in her spring kimono he could not have believed she would join them this soon. *In August*, she had said, gazing up at him, *even now, with things changing, there will be crowds here with candles and lanterns for the Feast of the Returning Ghosts.*

He had said a short perfunctory prayer of his own as she knelt before the stone.

They reached the crest of the hill and a bell began tolling nearby. The sound grew louder as they filed, Fuller leading, head bowed, onto a sidetrack that cut from the road and climbed through the trees – but by the time they entered the monastery grounds it had ceased. The cold air seemed to shudder with echoes. The bell stood on a dais in a snow-filled courtyard walled in by long, low, decrepit buildings. Fresh footprints led from the monastery door to the dais and back again.

'It's this way,' Fuller whispered, as if speaking in an empty church.

Sharon unslung her handbag and carried it gingerly, face pale, eyes anxious, damp. He tried to take her free hand but she withheld it.

When they found the stone, snow-capped, its inscription barely legible, Sharon turned from him, dug the urn from her pack and set it down by a vase of flower-stalks budding with fine blooms of snow. Fuller felt his throat tighten. Quickly he told her to wait for him while he went to the monastery to find the groundskeeper; he was afraid he did not have the strength to pry back the stone himself and place the urn inside with the others. Possibly there would be papers to sign.

As he rushed off he heard her coughing and thought again of her words: *What you did to her. Sometimes I can hardly stand to look at you.*

He thought of three young men in a restaurant, waiting.

On their way back the snow stopped and a range of mountains appeared to the west, then a faint sun adrift between darkening clouds.

★

The innkeeper explained that during the season several Noh plays were performed each night, but in winter there was only one per week, on Sunday evenings; if they hurried they could still see it and have their dinner after that.

Fuller didn't want Sharon to know about the play. He wanted to eat early in case the young men were out again, drinking – but when she asked him what was being said he reluctantly explained, and then, trying to appease her because the day had been such a trial, invited her to choose what they would do.

Sharon, more composed after an hour's nap, neatly dressed and made-up, wanted to see the play, very much, and eat later in the restaurant.

Only a few others were in the theatre when they arrived. They were issued programmes in ramshackle English describing the play and the genre of Noh to which it belonged; Fuller squinted and held the programme at arm's length and gave Sharon details. *Tsunemasa* was an Apparition Play by the famous Noh playwright Seami. Apparition Plays were about ghosts and were usually in two acts, the first short and the second long. There were two main actors – the *shite*, or 'doer', and the *waki*, or support player – as well as a chorus to narrate or comment on the action. In this play a wandering priest named Gyoki tried to find and confront the ghost of Tsunemasa, but could only hear the ghost's voice and the music his spectral fingers still plucked from Green Hill, the lyre he had played on in life.

The house lights dimmed and Fuller whispered to Sharon, 'I'll translate for you.'

His guts were knotted. He was afraid she would sense in the interplay of priest and phantom vague insinuating parallels – the same sort that made him writhe with guilt and disbelief when during his affair he would sit in a theatre with Aiko and Sharon while a film neatly exposed each twist of his own infidelity. He folded and refolded the programme till it fit in his clenched hand.

The drums and flute had a hypnotic, ethereal tone, and the dialogue, when it began, was in a language he hardly knew. It was stylized, antique and labyrinthine; he could barely translate a word let alone explain the play's subtler developments. What was the priest saying to the ghost? Why did the ghost always shy away? He had no idea and did not even pretend to know when Sharon asked him for help. He saw her amazed eyes widen in the darkness, the whites set off clearly by her eyeshadow, and he knew it was because she had grown used to his having an answer for everything – or venturing a bold guess when he did not. But he had changed, since Vida. Loving her, he thought, was the first thing he had ever done for himself, and he had changed and freed himself from the past before it was too late.

He shrugged. 'Sorry. At one time I could have told you.'

'But this is *important*. I want to know what they're saying.'

For a moment he thought of improvising: telling her the priest was asking pardon for not being at the ghost's side when it passed away, pleading that the death was unexpected, the priest thought of the ghost constantly and would do anything to be forgiven. But probably, Fuller thought, none of that was true. He had presided over enough funerals to know that for every one who mourns inconsolably there are two or three whose sharpest grief is their failure to grieve as they feel they should.

'Why did Tsunemasa die?' Sharon asked him as the ghost danced slowly into the wings, leaving only the priest on stage, still chanting in his haunted baritone. 'Do you understand why he died?'

'I'm not sure,' Fuller coughed. 'Maybe killed in battle.'

She leaned over, very slowly, and poured poison into his ear: 'I've been talking to my doctor about sickness, too.'

'Doctor? What are you talking about – you're ill?'

'The man at school. My therapist.'

Fuller let out a long breath. 'I thought you meant you were ill.'

'My doctor says I'm harbouring a lot of anger about mother's sickness.'

'But Sharon' – he tried to take her hand – 'Sharon, darling, it just *happened*. I understand how you feel, but there's no use being angry.'

'Well you see, that's just it. I'm not sure it just happened and even David – that's his name – David admitted he's read some things about stress and how it can bring on disease and everything.'

A tourist couple in the front row glanced back at them. The priest had knelt and now spread out his robed arms as if blessing the tiny audience.

'*Sharon*,' he hissed – but she ignored him. Which made her insinuations still harder to bear. She continued to watch the play. He forced himself to focus on the sumptuous robes of the priest, now retreating toward the pine at the back of the stage, and recalled something Aiko had said just weeks before he met Vida. One morning as he dressed before the full-length mirror in his room she had slipped in, still in her old nightgown, and looking him up and down, scowling, asked how he could face himself in such finery. And then unforgettably *she* had quoted scripture at *him*: *I gathered me also silver and gold ... I gathered me riches ... and whatsoever my eyes desired I kept not from them.*

So he had known finally that they were strangers.

The deep sockets of the priest's mask were filling up with shadow. In a few minutes they would be able to leave.

'Sharon – look at me.'

She obeyed.

'The man is not a medical doctor – is he? Well? He sounds to me like a quack. Cancer happens to people who've never had a day of serious stress in their lives and it would have happened to your mother no matter what I did.' His voice was thick, his throat tight, as if squeezed by hidden fingers. 'Don't blame me for everything, Sharon. You can't blame me for everything.'

The voice of the priest died out and the curtain fell. The tourists in the front row began to clap.

When the house lights came on Sharon covered her face.

★

She said nothing as they hurried to the restaurant but he could feel her anger building and he sensed everything she had said so far was a mere prelude to what would come. His guts were clenched. He felt no hunger. He did not want to play out another scene in their bitter little drama and he regretted the whole trip intensely. At first he had planned on coming alone – to commune in privacy with Aiko's ghost, or with his memories of her, which amounted, he was afraid, to the same thing – and now he saw how much better that would have been. How much better to be haunted by the dead, who can only touch you, if at all, with transparent, weightless fingers, instead of the anger and accusations of the living! He shivered and thought of Catholic confession, how even as a youth preparing for a very different ministry he had told his stern, disapproving father how the rite must be a great comfort, to some.

The restaurant was empty. He sat facing Sharon, his back towards the door, and ordered beer, tea, and a pot of hot saké. Sharon's painted mouth frowned as he placed the order. His father had been a teetotaller, but Fuller, defiant and unhappy, had learned to drink in Japan. At first Aiko did not object, but in Canada as years passed and she clung more and more to the church her mute disapproval had grown.

He took a long draught of beer and glanced at the booth where the young men had been last night.

After a second beer and some saké he felt calmer.

'I *don't* blame you for everything,' Sharon started, looking down at her cup. 'I'm just trying to understand things. I have to understand.'

'I know that, Sharon, I know.' He wanted to stay calm. 'Look, I'm sorry things have been so hard on you – they've been hard on all of us.'

'Harder on some than on others.'

He saw she was helpless to stop herself. Briefly his exasperation dissolved and her lowered head was the head of a small child, his child, so innocent, helpless, bereft. Throat tightening he drained another cup of saké.

'We haven't talked much about school,' he burst out. 'I know that's been tough too – all your switching around. I guess sometimes it's hard to figure out what you want ... But you've settled now on history?'

'Actually I might drop some courses and make history a minor. There're classes now in Japanese and I want to take some. I *hate* not understanding things here. I want to come back here and live.'

He forced a laugh. 'After you graduate, though.'

'Or before. I think I feel more at home here ... This trip's decided me.'

'But Sharon' – he smiled and shook his head – 'Sharon, your home is where you were born. What do you know about Japan?'

'You told me I was born on a ship in the middle of the ocean! And I know a lot about Japanese things. David encouraged me to write this paper on the internment because in some ways –'

'Where you were raised, then. Don't kid yourself, you don't belong here. My house is your real home – our house.'

'*Our* house? You expect me to live with you now that Vida's there? I don't even want to come visit on weekends.'

He raised his hand, then raked it through his hair. 'She's been good to you, Sharon. She'll be your friend if you let her.'

'I don't want her as a friend! I don't want her in my house! You – the two of you —'

71

Fuller looked up; the manager watched them from the back of the room. Fuller signalled for more saké. There was a crash of footsteps and raucous laughter and the rasp of a door sliding free. An icy draft plunged down his spine, his body betraying him with a long shudder.

Sharon looked up and he knew by her expression – spitefully pleased – that it was the three young men from the night before. He turned and watched them strut clumsily through the room, tug off shoes and position themselves in their booth. They nodded to him, smiling, and he saw for a moment how she could mistake those looks for friendly greetings. He knew they were not. She thought she belonged here but she understood nothing and he had to protect her from what she did not know.

He wished he could make out more of the young men's words.

'Maybe I should tell you now,' she said firmly, 'I'm going to have my name changed – by law.'

'What are you talking about?'

'I want to drop the Sharon and go by my second name.'

'Aiko,' he murmured, shaking his head. 'But why? Why not just ask people to call you Aiko if you want to go by your second name? That's what I did when I joined the firm – just had them use my last name. Why go to all the –'

'I've been thinking about it for a while and David said it would be good for me.'

'But Sharon –'

'Now that I've been here I know it's the right thing to do.'

She turned away and peered at the floor, then across at the young men. He felt them watching her, and him. He shot them a vicious look and they seemed to recoil. The manager rushed out with saké for both tables and refilled Fuller's cup.

'Sharon,' he whispered, 'listen, please ...'

'*Kampai*,' one of the young men cut in, raising his own

cup. It was the dark, broad-shouldered one who had called them over the night before.

'*Kampai*,' he repeated, face ruddy.

Sharon raised her steaming cup.

'Stop it,' Fuller croaked at her, 'stop it!' And he turned on the young men and hissed *Dame yo!*, thumping his fist so the china saké-pot leapt from the table.

The young men gaped at each other and began whispering in an urgent tone. Fuller turned back to Sharon, shaking.

'You're grown up now so you can do what you like with your name and you can live in Japan if you want to but since we're talking about changes I might as well tell you what's changing in my life. I thought you might take it as good news, I thought we could talk while we were here and sort some things out and – put the past behind us –'

'*Behind* us? What are you talking about? You want me to forget my mother. You think we can just leave her ashes behind!'

'In perspective then. You can't blame me for everything that happened, Sharon. People change. I had to leave your mother, we were living in different worlds.' He gulped down another cup of saké. 'And she wasn't the saint you make her out to be. She wasn't even Japanese any more but now that she's gone you've – gone and made her into some kind of idol.'

'I have not!'

'She was getting harder and harder to live with.'

'She was getting older. Older than Vida.'

'Vida and I are getting married.'

Sharon's whole body sagged and she curtained her face with her hands. Helpless, he watched her shoulders quake.

'Sharon –'

'*Aiko*,' she cried, looking out at him with a changed face. 'Aiko, my name is *Aiko*.'

The young men glared. *Don't stare at us*, he stammered in Japanese – *this is my daughter*.

He clutched at her shoulder, her arm.

'Sharon, stop it!'

The broad-shouldered one stood and said something, then repeated the words, louder. *Don't hurt her,* he was saying, *leave the girl alone.*

'You – bastard,' she coughed out. 'You weren't even there when she was dying. Just me. You were off with Vida.'

Fuller felt he would gag on the guilt and anger, the alibis he had choked down. 'But the doctors – I was told it was all right, she'd be fine for months, it was all right.'

'On a fucking holiday. Father –'

'We were legally separated! For two years!'

The broad-shouldered one took two steps toward them, and stopped. *Leave the girl alone.*

'My mother was dying and you were off – fucking another woman!'

Had he not been so drunk he would have caught her full in the face with his open hand and knocked her down. As it was he only grazed her mouth and the tip of her nose but it was enough, it was more than enough, the blow seemed to ring out like a shot and a line of blood took form above her lip. She was so stunned she did not even cry out but stared at him with dead eyes. He turned away. The broad-shouldered one was racing back from the kitchen with the manager behind.

I am afraid we cannot serve you anything more, the manager said, striding up to the table. *My apologies to you both. We are closing now so you will have to leave – at once.*

It's them, Fuller pointed, struggling for words. *You should be telling* them –

They say you have been staring rudely and hitting the girl.

She's my daughter, he cried, *you don't understand.*

The man looked incredulous, angry. *Please go now,* he said. *Both of you.*

Adam Fuller lurched to his feet, grabbed his jacket and

started for the door. On the threshold he turned halfway to take Sharon's hand and grasped thin air. He turned fully: she was still in the booth, her eyes anonymous and blank, boring through him. The manager and the young man faced him from the middle of the floor.

'Sharon, come on, we've got to go. You can't stay here.'

She said nothing. The men edged forward, hands clenched.

'Look, tell them, show them you're not Japanese. For God's sake, Sharon, now!'

Go, the manager cried.

But I'm her father! 'Tell them, Aiko – Sharon, look, would you tell them?'

Her eyes were blank as if she spoke no English. Fuller stretched out his arms to her, then froze. *Please*, he wanted to say in some tongue she would understand, *please, we have to go home*, but the two men barred any return and she sat in her stubborn trance, staring, as if he had left already and gone too far for her to follow or absolve. He would have to stumble outside, alone, where each freezing gust would whip the snow like white ash into his eyes and he would be a stranger to everything.

6

A Man Away from Home
Has No Neighbours

The day's last lesson was over. Hashimoto and I were drinking
tea at a small table by the school's main window, which looked
out over broken ranks of factories and warehouses, Love Hotels,
tramlines, baseball diamonds and tenements. In the late afternoon light Ōsaka was dusty and dry and flattened, like a
neighbourhood after an air raid.

'You are a carnivore, yes?' Hashimoto-san eyed me
through the steam rising from his tea-cup. He was my best student by far, and a kind of friend, so I'd asked him to stay and
help clarify something that had come up in the lesson.

'Actually I don't eat meat,' I told him. But I wasn't being
completely honest – I did eat a little now and then, on special
occasions, or when it was offered by a host or visiting neighbour.

'Yes, of course,' he said, 'but I mean "you" in the general,
collective sense. Most Westerners are meat-eaters, is that not
so?'

I hesitated. Clearly Hashimoto-san was about to advance
one of those sweeping racial theories so popular here. Months
before, after a few whiskies, he'd asked if my penis really was as
big as a bottle of Johnnie Walker and if Western women were all
nymphomaniacs. No, I'd assured him on both counts, and he'd

seemed both disappointed and relieved. Now, quite certain I was making a serious tactical gaffe, I admitted that this time he was right: most of us *were* meat-eaters.

He blinked triumphantly. 'We Japanese are not. *We are grain-eaters.*'

I took a calming sip of tea. 'In that case what about the meat you had with your noodles a few hours ago?' I looked for support to Principal Kobayashi, who had eaten with us earlier at the Café New York and now sat at her desk grading papers. But she was engrossed in her work and did not look up.

Hashimoto-san swatted my objection from the air. 'An anomaly,' he said, 'a temporal exception. I am speaking in broadly historical terms. A thousand years ago your ancestors were roasting whole oxen over bonfires, while mine nibbled on cooked seeds, mushrooms and mountain tubers.'

Mystified, I replenished Hashimoto's cup.

'Now, *Sensei*,' he went on, 'surely you would not deny that slaughtering and consuming live creatures is a more violent activity than the gathering of seaweed, pulses and fungi?'

'I suppose that depends on whether you're an animal or a fungus.'

Hashimoto-san furrowed his brow and said, 'You are being facetious. My point is that on a visceral, intrinsic level, Europeans have been habituated to violence and so we must expect them to be more aggressive than their Oriental counterparts.'

'You're a talented linguist, Hashimoto-san, but I'm afraid your biology leaves something to be desired.'

'The opinion is not mine alone, Steven-*Sensei*. It is widespread in Japan, and few scholars dispute it. And with all due respect, *Sensei*, your knowledge of science may be inferior to theirs.'

On the table by my fist a puddle of spilled tea quivered with green flecks, like a pool of primordial soup.

'So this,' I said, 'is what Mr Takaoka was talking about in the last lesson?'

'He did not mean to offend you. He did not mean necessarily that you are violent.'

'I realize he wasn't saying that. It's just ... well ...' I decided to press on, instead of skirting the issue in the discreet style I was now used to. '*All* human beings are violent,' I said. 'Or at least they learn to be.' And I shot a glance at Principal Kobayashi to make sure she wasn't listening; her English was mediocre but I knew her family had suffered during the war and I didn't want her to hear what I had to say. 'The problem with your theory is this: while my meat-eating forefathers were busy butchering each other with spears and daggers, your rice-eating ancestors were doing just the same thing – riding around the countryside with their pretty flags, carving up the peasants, assassinating rival lords ...'

'Certainly, they were, but when the samurai killed, it was always in the line of duty, always out of a sense of *giri*, of obedience to a higher power. I was talking about violence as a natural inclination.'

'That's an interesting distinction. I'm afraid it might be lost on the victims.'

'Nevertheless it exists.'

I picked up my empty cup and put it down again more loudly than I'd meant. To my friend this gesture would probably seem a declaration of war.

'Look, Hashimoto-san, if you force me to do it I can cite all sorts of atrocities committed by both sides in World War Two and you won't be able to explain them away as glibly as you just did the samurai.' The volume of my own voice startled me; I tried to calm down. Hashimoto examined his cup, no doubt seeing my outburst as clear proof of the very theory I was attacking. But what a theory! After all, hadn't Hitler been a vegetarian? Hess? The Khmer Rouge? What would my prize student have to say about the grain-eating pacifists who'd bombed Pearl Harbour? Had they started their day with a nice big steak, or did somebody lace their breakfast tea with animal proteins?

But I couldn't say these things to a man born years after the war, nor could I mention the death-marches and the torture of Allied prisoners and the sack of Nanking when one hundred thousand women were raped in a matter of hours after the city fell. No, it would be unfair to cite these things.

Hashimoto was watching me. He'd pointed out before that as with most Westerners my thoughts were transparent as a child's, and now he said, as if reading from a teleprompter lodged in my forehead, 'You are thinking of Pearl Harbour. And perhaps of other things as well.'

It was no surprise that he'd managed to read me, but I hadn't expected him to say anything outright. Like most embarrassments, national or personal, Pearl Harbour was not to be mentioned in sober conversation. I thought I might as well go on.

'The rape of Nanking,' I said. 'I was thinking of that, too. I guess I don't have to remind you what happened. There've been similar cases in the West and it'll happen again, probably, there or here or someplace else because nothing ever seems to change and people act the same way no matter where they live or how they dress or what kind of food they eat. *One hundred thousand unarmed women.* How do you square them with your stupid theory?'

Hashimoto glanced over my shoulder at Kobayashi, as I wanted to do but could not. Like me, he would be anxious about our words, their effect. I felt a stab of remorse. The ultimate savagery, I reflected, was the dropping of not one but two atomic bombs on Japanese civilians – and though she'd never said it outright Kobayashi had managed to imply her parents had been killed at Hiroshima.

'Yes, well, about the rape of Nanking, as you call it, the

cruelty is obvious and undeniable. But not impossible to explain.'

'Explain it,' I told him, leaning over the table. I heard Kobayashi rise from her desk and pace towards the back of the school.

'A man away from home has no neighbours,' Hashimoto said, squinting as he looked out over the huge city. The sun was going down. 'A Japanese proverb, Steven-*Sensei*. I know you take an interest in our sayings, but this is one with which you may not be familiar. In fact I can see by your expression that you have never heard it.'

'Never,' I said, softly. My remorse and my surprise at his change of tone had disarmed me altogether.

'Even peaceful, unaggressive men will commit atrocities when they are far from home and the eyes of their neighbours ...' Hashimoto went on explaining the proverb with pedagogical care, perhaps feeling that since it was Japanese I would not be able to interpret it myself. But maybe he was right to do it? That night as I rode the subway home to Nagai, as the car rattled rhythmically and lights pulsing through the windows competed with the dark in that way so conducive to meditation and dream, it occurred to me Hashimoto might have wanted to specify a certain meaning because the proverb contained more than one. As my mind drifted over the past hours, and over the last century – or what little I knew of it – I began to see the proverb was explosive, that if you held or touched or turned it in a certain way it would burst open and scatter meaning in all directions, like the white-hot particles of a new galaxy. Like a universe or a grain of sand – a fistful of desert sand turned to glass – it reflected all the past, the present, and maybe the future too.

A man away from home has no neighbours.

Hashimoto-San turned from the school window and almost looked me in the eyes.

'Much, I think, can be explained by this.'

II A WARTIME ROMANCE

Matsuo Kobayashi joined the Imperial Japanese Army in the winter of 1931 and was shipped with his regiment to Manchuria in late spring. He was twenty-three years old. His duty was to help defend a Japanese-controlled railway from the Chinese interference his officers referred to as 'imminent'. Matsuo was proud of his uniform and rifle and of being stationed so close to Mukden, where his father had fought bravely twenty-six years earlier in the Russo-Japanese War. To his parents, who had a farm on the outskirts of Hiroshima, he sent monthly a portion of his small paycheque, along with blurred photographs of himself and his comrades posed stiffly in front of steam locomotives or in the barracks yard or on dry hillsides behind the fort. He did not tell them about Yang, the Chinese farm girl who sometimes brought eggs to the fort and with whom he had fallen in love soon after his arrival, because the Chinese were the enemy and fraternization of any kind was strictly forbidden.

Whenever Yang came to the fort it was Matsuo's job to meet her and collect the eggs, and their exchanged glances soon became shared words. Before long he arranged to meet her in secret. He could hardly contain his excitement but he forced himself to say nothing, even when his comrades teased him or made indelicate remarks about 'the pretty farm girl', for he was quite sure they would not approve of his deepening involvement and he was afraid they would report him.

He had been such an obedient son before. Now he lay awake nights, scheming. By day he sent more of his paycheque home, and vowed that if found out he would confess and offer to end his life, because he had brought shame on the regiment and set a poor example for the men.

The continual chatterings of his conscience caused such tension in Matsuo that sometimes, after making love with Yang

in the hay-strewn ditch behind her village, he was possessed by
a blind rage and imagined strangling her then and there and
freeing himself of his lust and shame. But glancing down into
her eyes, half-open in the moonlight, trusting, he was overcome
by tenderness and then a deeper shame that such thoughts
could occur to him. She knew some Japanese and he a few
words of her dialect; between them they managed to make
themselves understood. In her stilted but strangely lyrical way
she told him her heart glowed like the full moon when he was
near, but watching him creep home over the furrows and await-
ing his return her heart waned to a sliver.

Because Japanese characters are borrowed from the
Chinese and he thought she might understand, he wrote a few
short love poems on army stationery; when he gave them to her
she pretended to read and then praised and thanked him and
pulled him close. Actually she could not read at all, but she
understood his gesture, for the folk tales of her region were full
of lovers who came from far away and courted village maidens
with poetry.

By late summer Matsuo was obsessed with Yang. At first it
had been enough to trade looks and endearments twice a week
when she appeared at the gate with her eggs, and to meet on
certain nights in the field behind her village, but now he crept
from the barracks as often as three times a week to see her.
Though the other men were always dead with fatigue and slept
soundly, his manoeuvres involved considerable risk, for as he
stole through the barracks yard towards the rear fence he had to
dodge a sentry and a spotlight from the guard-tower. But he
could not stop himself. He was often sluggish on parade and
more and more he incurred the wrath of his drill-sergeant
when he responded slowly or clumsily to commands. Yet night-
fall restored a restless energy to his limbs, a feverish tingling to
his belly, an electric numbness in the hands and scalp that
seemed to presage the sweet, freezing blast of oblivion that

swept through him when he made love to Yang. His cries, her cries – they were getting harder to muffle as their love and their knowledge of each other's bodies increased ...

By now it had become customary in the barracks for the wakening men to compare their dreams. They had only a few minutes to prepare themselves for parade, but most of them stubbornly observed this ritual. As they shook and stretched themselves awake, washed, straightened their bunks and dressed, they would holler out coarse commentary on sexual dreams, trying to outdo each other with graphic details or boasting of the traits of dream partners. Gentle domestic idylls in which a mother or father appeared were also common. Some of the men confessed, with uneasy fascination, to violent reveries where they bayoneted real Chinese instead of the stuffed dummies in the barracks yard. Matsuo said nothing. The sexual bravado with which other men armed themselves had always been hard for him to put on, and now he had finer reasons to absent himself from his comrades' exchange: the coarseness of their banter jarred him since he had experienced real earthly love, and besides, it seemed he no longer had dreams to talk about anyway.

He thought probably he had stopped dreaming because of fatigue and the tension, anger and foreboding that oppressed him more and more. Probably, he reasoned, his body saw sleep as its only chance to escape ... But one morning he did remember a dream, and it was horrible. He had been yelling as he raced through Yang's village, swinging his rifle like a primitive club, cracking the skulls of the faceless civilians who had rushed from their huts at the noise ...

'Kobayashi,' a half-dressed soldier leered, 'how come you never let us in on your dreams? Sounds like you had a good one last night – I heard you squealing like a sow. Dreaming of that pretty whore who brings the eggs?'

'I don't dream,' Matsuo spat out, lowering his face to the basin and roughly rinsing with cold water.

'Not the way we do, anyway,' said another soldier, the one whose bunk was closest to the door.

The first soldier cocked an eyebrow. 'What do you mean by that? You mean he doesn't dream of women?'

'Don't think he needs to,' the second one said. 'You don't have to creep out in the middle of the night just for ...'

The man snapped to attention, bowed. The big drill-sergeant, who had entered the barracks as he spoke, paused in front of him and glared. Very softly he asked whom the man was referring to; who had been leaving the barracks in the middle of the night?

★

Colonel Daisaku Morita scratched the scalp under his thinning hair and inspected the boy standing at attention by his desk. Several times in his career he had had to deal with this kind of problem. He had hit upon several disciplinary expedients and now as he watched the boy he turned them over in his mind, as a distracted hand will spin a cup of tea to see how the leaves settle.

His alternatives:

1. Punish the girl so terribly that no Chinese woman will ever dream of tempting Japanese soldiers again. Have the boy go to meet her in the usual place but escorted surreptitiously by his whole platoon. After the boy has had her, let the other men emerge from hiding and have her too, one after another. Have the boy observe everything. After that he will beg to be allowed *seppuku*.

2. Destroy the girl's village so that she will be held responsible and punished by her own neighbours, who at the same time will learn first hand about the fury of Japanese reprisals.

3. Have the boy sent home in disgrace.

4. Have the boy executed before the whole regiment.

5. Have the boy beaten, absolved, and then shipped to

84

another sector of the Manchurian line. After all, what recruit hadn't dreamed of doing as this one had done? The Colonel had to admire the boy's courage, resourcefulness, and tenacity. No, he could never again trust his obedience, but his bravery was beyond doubt and in coming weeks it could prove useful.

On the other hand ...

Colonel Morita sleeked back his thin hair and examined the boy's smooth, impassive face. From far off came the faint cry of a troop-train, arriving.

★

It had been almost two weeks since he had come but he saw at once that she was waiting for him in the usual spot. She was curled up in the ditch, wrapped in a wool cloak, the skin of her closed eyelids vivid in the full moon's light. She was very tired for she did not wake at his approach as she always had before. Perhaps she had given up hope, or no longer desired him ...

But here she was. He knelt beside her and watched the delicate rippling motion of her eyelids, which showed she was dreaming. He kissed the closed eyes and they opened as he pulled away. They did not look startled or afraid but wakeful with recognition, and love, and the certainty he would return.

As he studied her features his heart began to stammer and race. He found it hard to swallow. She wrapped her arms round his neck to draw him down and then held him with such strength that for a moment he felt like a bound prisoner, or like the stuffed bayonet-drill dummies lashed to their posts in the barracks yard. He kissed her repeatedly, his eyes tightly shut. He had come here determined to obey his orders but now his body was betraying him, he felt no sexual stirrings, only fear and remorse and bitter self-hatred. She wanted him, he could feel the insistence of her desire, and it terrified him and made him want to run from her, or with her, quickly, to escape this cruel ambush and free himself of shame. The Colonel had warned him that should he betray his orders both absolution and *seppuku* were out of the question and he would be executed publicly, shamefully, before the whole regiment. 'My heart is full,' she was saying in her strange Japanese, 'I love you –' And he was afraid his platoon, concealed a stone's throw away, could hear every word. Now they would have even more reason to taunt and bait him, though in their hearts they must be envious, and angry too – in fact he was sure he sensed anger, a chafing, rank miasma like poison gas, rising from the ditch where his comrades lay ...

But he could not do it. It was impossible. And he saw now that they would not be able to do it either: they felt nothing for her, to them she was nothing, no one, not even a dream partner, and surely desire cannot be made to take orders. There was no danger here. Disarmed by their own bodies they would disobey, all of them, and they would face the consequences together.

'I love you,' he said in plain Japanese, loudly, so she would not forget the words and his comrades would hear them in their hiding place and they would carry in the crisp autumn air across the fields to the village and back towards the railway and the fort. He stood up so he was clearly visible to his platoon. He drew Yang to her feet and tried to explain what was happening. She looked confused. *Run*, he said, pushing her away towards the village. She came back and he pushed her away again and this time she seemed to understand, she started to run and she glanced back at him as she went, once – twice – and the moonlight flashed off her forehead.

The men of his platoon were yelling. Matsuo turned to face them. Like shock troops out of a trench they burst from the ground with terrifying resolve. Two of them began to scramble after Yang. As Matsuo turned and urged her to hurry, the platoon sergeant drew his pistol, as he had been ordered to do should complications arise, and fired three rounds.

Matsuo crumpled into the ditch where the straw was still warm with the imprint of Yang's body. He did not move again. He never learned that Yang managed to reach the village, where the men were forbidden to follow, or that he was wrong about the well-trained members of his platoon, most of whom would have fulfilled their orders if they had had the chance. He did not know that within two days his regiment would blow up a stretch of track an hour north of the village, blame it on the Chinese (and claim Matsuo as a casualty) and on this pretext invade and overrun all Manchuria within a few months. He did not know, as we do, that the survivors of his platoon, along with several hundred thousand other trained men (including his brother Haruo) would prove years later at the fall of Nanking where thousands of women were raped that *a man away from home has no neighbours*. These are the things that were not known, or could still be denied, just sixty years ago.

To a man with a hammer, the Chinese say, *everything looks like a nail.*

Better that Matsuo never had to learn it.

They buried him in the ditch.

III   TACTICAL MANOEUVRES – A TRUE STORY

Anyone who knows will tell you this is the biggest, finest Love Hotel in Ōsaka. The quantity and diversity of our rooms are quite unmatched, the video selection is encyclopaedic, the staff skilful, courteous and discreet, the location convenient but not conspicuous. If your reasons for using our facilities are the usual – overcrowded apartment blocks, nosy neighbours, live-in relations, rice-paper-thin walls – you'll find plenty of plain, serviceable rooms available at decent hourly rates. And if you're interested in something a touch more exotic – well, anyone who knows will tell you this is the finest place in the city.

There's simply no question: it's only when you're away from home and neighbours that you can truly relax.

Shall we take a look around?

Some people, of course, see Love Hotels as an unfortunate necessity, a symptom of the crowding and domestic inconvenience of modern Japan, but in fact the idea comes from the West, where recent figures show that a skyrocketing proportion of all sexual acts occur in rented rooms instead of at home. The inference we are forced to draw from this finding is plain enough, is it not? Clearly the appetites of today's sexual consumer are dampened by the routines of home and community and aroused by things anonymous, generic, and expensive. Our studies actually show Customer Satisfaction rising in direct proportion to the cost of the room! So that our new prices symbiotically benefit both client and proprietor.

Summer Moon? Yes, that's the name. We chose it to remind potential clients that we're more than just a business. Like any good Love Hotel we provide our guests with amenities as personal and indispensable as the moon is to a lover on a summer's night: consider the romantic atmosphere, the privacy, the freedom from pressure, the quiet, the space to dream. And there's no denying that our Theme Rooms can spice up any marriage or affair gone stale, as they inevitably do ...

Take this room, for example: our 'Cadillac Ranch'. These days it's a big hit with the university crowd. The walls, as you see, are decorated with glossy black-and-white posters depicting various vintage models from the heyday of American auto manufacturing; the big 'drive-in' style video at the back of the room features a staggering assortment of vehicular entertainment, including highlights of last year's Indy 500, exciting footage of road-tests, medleys of the best car ads from the last decade and endless repeats of *The Love Bug*. And there in the centre of the showroom, if you will, the polished, gleaming pink chassis of a vintage Cadillac Eldorado. Were I to retract the convertible hood you would find, instead of seats, a plushly appointed queen-size bed. The mahogany dashboard rising above the pillows behind the mattress has various switches and gauges which control the room's temperature and lighting – including a set of high-beams which shine from the ceiling and illumine the bed at opportune moments – and a soundtrack, which includes hundreds of the best-known automotive hits of the past decades. A 'speedometer' allows the couple to assess their performance in terms of pace and frequency and to compare themselves with previous guests. There is even a species of vibrator built into the bed which, when activated, simulates aurally and sensually the smooth, soporific progress of a Cadillac Eldorado over an American superexpressway. All this for only 10,000 yen per hour.

There are other Theme Rooms, of course. I might mention for example the 'American Dream', a bedroom designed to resemble the inside of a multinational bank. The king-sized bed is nestled within a mock-steel vault behind the tellers' cage at the back of the room and the toilet paper is pleasingly stamped with the currencies of the world's leading industrial powers. The video features various recent Hollywood films – which we find we can choose almost at random. Needless to say (laughs) no security guards are present.

'Grand Central Station', just up this hall here, is another popular one: with its high, echoing ceilings and piped music and travel announcements it could be anything from a rail terminus to the departures level of an international airport. The twin berths are in a sealed compartment as luxurious, we believe, as anything on the Orient Express or the Tōkyō-Ōsaka bullet train. We consider the room's appeal to lie in its promise of escape, of distance from the domestic and familiar.

But in the last few years it's this next room, here, that has generated the most interest in clients both foreign and local. We call it 'Tactical Manoeuvres'. As you can see, the walls are sheathed over with guerrilla netting and painted entirely in camouflage; those hanging vines are artificial, but I think you'll agree they look quite genuine enough. One of the room's many soundtracks offers the martial anthems of every nation in the civilized world while others feature impressively authentic sound effects including gunfire, battle-cries, the rumble of approaching tanks, the roar of jet fighters and all manner of explosion. What? Pardon me? Ah, you don't believe this room is popular! Well, I can't honestly say I see the appeal myself, but believe me 'Tactical Manoeuvres' is doing very well for us and we're not about to meddle with our bottom line.

Some people, I suppose, just come for the videos. Naturally we've got *Rambo* ... *rambō* is everywhere, though, isn't it? (Laughs)★ We have all the Rambo clone films, too. And we have some local efforts – historical numbers like *Ran* and *Nihyaku-san-kochi* – though these days, oddly, our Japanese clients don't seem all that interested in the country's past. Still, there's lots of other material to choose from – we have ten channels that play twenty-four hours a day! But the most striking attraction of the room, as you can see, is this beautiful reduced-scale replica of a Tiger battle-tank, constructed of sturdy, life-like plastic and acrylic and authentically decorated. I can tell you're impressed. Please, go ahead and touch it. Now if you were to climb this ladder and lower yourself into the tank you'd find a comfortable twin bed and above it, where the gunner's sights would normally be, a video screen. There's a sort of dashboard too with the same kind of controls as in our 'Cadillac Ranch'. It's expensive, but you'd be surprised at the number of U.S. Navy officers and men who come up on leave from Kōbe to try it, and then all those Japanese recruits from the bases up north – they could spend a week's pay on a few hours

★ Rambō happens to mean 'violence' in Japanese. The Proprietor is making a joke.

in 'Tactical Manoeuvres' (not to mention the cost of the girl, if she's hired) and most of them are delighted to get the chance. But mainly we deal with tourists and businessmen.

And look – here's the latest. We're importing them from Canada as a novelty: *Camo-Condoms*. That's right, the rubber is actually embellished with a military-camouflage motif, but the really clever thing about them is the slogan here on the wrapper: DON'T LET HER SEE YOU COMING. As you must know, here in Japan we say 'going' in reference to the sexual climax, so the joke is lost even on Japanese who have a little English – but North American clients never fail to make appreciative remarks upon checking out. One imagines a muscular camouflaged guerrilla with a knife between his teeth creeping up on an enemy's woman in the jungle – like Rambo, I suppose! Yes, I think that must be part of the item's allure: here is a condom that Rambo would use ...

So you *are* interested in 'Tactical Manoeuvres'? Fine, that's fine, I thought perhaps you would be. Yes, we do require a deposit, and we need you to sign the register. But where is your wife?

★

You have checked into 'Tactical Manoeuvres' alone. Once the proprietor realizes you intend to do this, he asks no further questions. He has seen everything, everything – and no doubt seeking to spare you embarrassment, he confides that in recent months quite a few people have done the same thing.

You climb down into the belly of the tank and make yourself as comfortable as you can. You try to imagine couples making love in this claustrophobic mock-steel womb, but it isn't possible to imagine. Or perhaps for you it is possible – how can I say?

On one channel you find a movie that looks a little different from the other fare. It is a Japanese film, *Nihyaku-san-kochi*. Numbed, you stare at the screen while wave after wave of soldiers in pillbox-caps and white spats swarm up a hill into gunfire in the murderous moonlight ...

IV NIHYAKU-SAN-KOCHI – THE FILM

So Shoji Kobayashi and Hideyuki Murata will be in the second wave for the first night-assault on 203 Metre Hill. This is something of an honour, though both of them had hoped their company would be placed in the front line; their officer has advised them, however, that in his opinion even under cover of darkness the terrible new guns will demolish the first wave, so for all intents and purposes their attack will amount to the same thing.

A young boy scurries up the trench with an ornamental decanter, half filling the men's mugs with hot saké. 'Three minutes,' he whispers to Shoji, and the decanter, painted with scenes of samurai at rest under blossoming plum trees, quivers in his small hands.

The camera pans away from the crowded trench and focuses on the battlefield: Nihyaku-san-kochi, or 203 Metre Hill, looms above the Japanese lines, its barren flank coldly metallic in the full moon's light. It is a chilly night in late autumn soon after the turn of the century. The crown of the steep hill is scarred by Russian trenches in which riflemen and machine-gunners (most of them in their teens) and their terrible weapons (some newly invented) await the Japanese assault, which they will be expecting after the barrage that has just lifted.

Shoji gulps his saké in one draught and feels it ease the twisted, griping pain in his gut. Unconsciously he presses up against Hideyuki. Through the thick, itching wool of their uniforms he feels the heat of his friend's arm. Hideyuki has finished his own saké and now rests his forehead on the sharp lip of the mug, his downcast eyes a few inches from the earth. He is weeping, or trying not to weep. So as not to shame him, Shoji looks off and concentrates on the moon and tries to compose a *haiku*, as he knows great warriors are meant to do during battle. He can think only of Bashō's famous lines:

> *Ah, summer grass!*
> *All that survives*
> *Of the warrior's dream.*

The order to fix bayonets is rushing up the line, in quick murmurs, man to man, and Shoji thinks of the children's game where a secret phrase is passed round a circle by the whispering players and repeated at the end, by which time it has changed into something quite different, something absurd, garbled, comical – monstrous. Yet he knows that when the lethal gossip arrives and his neighbour turns and gives him the order it will be the same one he expects, and he will obey.

Fix bayonets –

CUT to behind the lines where Count Kiten Morosuke Nogi, the Japanese commander, is composing his own *haiku* as he waits with his officers and scans 203 Metre Hill. It is the key to Port Arthur and for several days he has struggled to take it. So far he has lost 10,000 men. Last night one of his officers, Hashimoto, pardoned himself but insisted on observing that the Count was, perhaps, being rather more stubborn and wasteful of his men's lives than was quite necessary, for now.

Nogi dismissed the objection and reminded the Colonel of their duty to the Emperor.

'*In this world*,' said Colonel Hashimoto, quoting the Emperor's dead father, '*all men are brothers. Why then this constant war?*'

'A moving sentiment, no doubt,' said General Nogi, 'but

a rhetorical question all the same. You are a good man, Colonel, but a dreamer.'

An explosion on the far hillside lit up Nogi's face. He said, 'If men were capable of grasping the full horror of war, every one of them would go mad. But they would not stop fighting.'

Hashimoto was nonplussed by the General's remarks. He wondered if the man's personal losses were unhinging him.

'And the Emperor, General? Is the Emperor a dreamer?'

Nogi thought for a moment, then said, 'The Emperor is a dream. An invention. And, like all monarchs, a dreamer. Kings do not decide the course of history. It is always the soldiers who do that.'

'You mean the generals,' Hashimoto said. 'The soldiers decide nothing.'

'They decide with their lives. They are an extension of us, of me. Like sons ...'

Embarrassed, Hashimoto looked down at the muddy boots he had not removed in three days. 'Then please, General, call off this foolish attack. Or you are killing us both, son by son.'

Nogi turned from Hashimoto and the smouldering hillside. 'I have my orders, Colonel, and officially they come from the Emperor. Good night.'

Hashimoto paced off to the edge of a knoll and stood watching the barrage, like festival *hanabi* – fire flowers – in early spring: sprays of poppy and indigo, Japanese lanterns, molten chrysanthemums bursting out of the dark slopes. *Mottainai*, he mumbled. *It is a waste. Away from his home a man has no neighbours to watch over him and keep him from harm. There is no one to plead his case, none to object to the wastefulness of his death ...*

CUT to the front lines where an officer leaps from the advance trench a stone's throw from Shoji and Hideyuki and rears his samurai sword in the moonlight. It flashes like a line of grinning teeth. Yelling *Banzai, Banzai,* or *A thousand years for the*

Emperor, the first wave of men surges up and hurls itself into the shadows. Then suddenly the whole hillside is flooded with light: two brilliant silver eyes, far bigger than the moon and brighter than a thousand suns, burst open, wide awake, on the summit above them. The confused officer pauses, spotlit, his upraised weapon slowly falling as he tries to make sense of things. There is a clatter of machine-gun fire. The brilliant eyes move, like human eyes, or the watchful brotherly eyes of Buddha, and long tapering swaths of light begin to sweep over the hill. The first wave of men is silhouetted like a row of leaf-shadows on an autumn sidewalk, and now as the machine-gunners pick out their targets the leaves begin to fall. *A thousand years*, a second officer cries, his useless blade gleaming in the harsh new light; the second wave rises from its ditch and advances at double time up the steepening slope, Shoji and Hideyuki unconsciously leaning together, shoulder to shoulder, not seeing they offer a better target this way. Their eyes are nearly closed against the glare of the television lights. *A thousand years for the Emperor*, they gasp, staggering over fallen comrades. Then all of a sudden

CUT.

Sorry, I can't go on with this. Can we see what's on the other channel? Or better yet, let's just turn off the whole fucking machine. But you want to know what happens, right? I sure do. So how about this? Hideyuki was wounded, but he survived. Shoji survived – and so did the whole platoon. They all survived! The whole army went on, miraculous, immune to the blinding light and the whistling bullets and the rockets' red glare, and the Russians disarmed and met them halfway and everyone embraced and sat down for a picnic on the hill and drank each other's health with saké and plum wine and vodka and exchanged whatever gifts they could dig from their packs: green tea and microchips from the Japanese, rye bread, eggs and back issues of *Pravda* from the Soviets, and the officers fumed behind the lines and drew up new orders that no one would obey, and they gave themselves Purple Hearts, promotions and raises, and they mentioned themselves in despatches and they snapped their flint-knives over their knees when nobody applauded. Nobody got hurt at all.

(Much of this actually happened the day before, when a two-hour truce was called to clear away the dead.)

'*Three moons,*' Shoji whispers to himself, spotlit in the field alone, Hideyuki wounded behind him, '*Three moons above the barren hill: the body is a falling blossom.*'

V BETTER HOMES AND GARDENS

Some years after the end of the Russo-Japanese War, Shoji Kobayashi's cousins, the Takaokas, took leave of him at Kōbe. They were bound for America, where other relatives had already gone, and though they had urged Shoji to come and bring his new wife and baby son Haruo, he would agree to accompany them only to the port. In fact he was already planning a move to Hiroshima and the farm of another cousin.

Mr and Mrs Takaoka and their newborn twins, Shoji and Masanori, set sail on a beautiful mid-summer day and docked after three weeks in San Francisco. They found an apartment in the Oriental quarter of the city. After working in a cannery for two years, while elderly Japanese neighbours minded the boys, the Takaokas saved up enough money to buy land in a small valley near Rio Vista, where they intended to farm. The Takaokas had farmed all their lives, and the new land was fertile, but at first they experienced problems because the valley's soil and climate were so different from Japan's. But after a few years, with the help of their neighbours (who were mainly white), they managed to make a go of it.

Their life in the twenties was pleasant and successful in a

modest way and before the Oriental Exclusion Act was passed in 1924 they managed to convince several Japanese relations to come to America. The Act itself was something of an insult, but it did not affect them directly, and like many immigrants, struggling to fit in, they preferred to ignore the whims of their adopted land and avoid trouble. For though at first they had found the open, empty spaces of the valley draining and inhospitable, the idea of a return to the finite rice-fields and jammed quarters of their old Kyōto home was no longer attractive. Shoji and Masanori were growing quickly on the plentiful food and now towered above their parents; once in a while there were troubles with the local boys, but for the most part their neighbours seemed tolerant and not unhelpful.

Things changed in the thirties. The valley was not so badly affected as other regions, but the climate was no longer benign and stable and some of the Takaokas' crops began to fail. Their neighbours, faced with debts and failures of their own, were not so tolerant as before, or helpful. Some of them made it clear the Takaoka twins were no longer welcome in their homes, and when high school 'incidents' involving the twins and certain white boys became common, Shoji and Masanori, who had always been quiet before, were usually blamed for the trouble.

A man away from home, Mr Takaoka concluded one evening over whisky, has no real neighbours.

To make ends meet, Mr Takaoka was forced to take a night job at a factory while continuing to work in the fields with his wife by day. After a year of this taxing routine he grew ill. In June 1937, a month before the Japanese army crossed the Marco Polo Bridge en route to Nanking, he died of pneumonia. His sons cremated him and buried his ashes under a small tombstone at the edge of the fields.

The harvests were much better in 1939 and '40 and the mood of many of her neighbours changed, but Mrs Takaoka grew more anxious about developments in Asia. Still, she was pleased that her sons had graduated from high school and worked now with such diligence on the farm and in the factory – though when Shoji met a Mexican girl there whom he wanted to marry, Mrs Takaoka felt she had to object.

After a brief but heated argument the boy gave in.

In '41 the harvest was the best ever, but that autumn Mrs Takaoka was troubled by forebodings; it seemed clear to her that Japan and America would soon be at war. She mentioned her feelings to the two boys but they paid no attention – they were busy with the farm and with work at the factory, saving money for their future, talking of marriage and of trips to the city to find wives. For their sake, she told herself, she would make a point of visiting the neighbours more often with her gifts of tomatoes, beans, green tea, and pickles.

Soon after the attack on Pearl Harbour, the Takaokas' lives changed dramatically. Because of the valley's nearness to the coast and their presumed sympathy for the Emperor's cause, they were removed from their farm, first to a racetrack where they were billeted in horse-stalls, and then, after a twelve-hour journey in cattle-cars, to a concentration camp in Utah.

The camp was called Argent, but its harsh, scarified environs belied the elegance of its name. Dust-devils hissed in the barbed wire of the perimeter like wind through thistles, and beyond the guard towers a salt plain stretched away for hours, ending on one side with the skyline and to the west at a high range of mountains. At the time, Mrs Takaoka could find nothing to compare it to because she had never seen a landscape like it, but years later she would weep with recognition on first seeing photographs of Hiroshima's remains.

In early spring Mrs Takaoka set to work on a small garden. To coax life from the harsh, resistant soil she composted whatever scraps she could get from the kitchen, collected manure from the chicken pens, and scrounged constantly for water. She had brought seeds with her, and now she planted onions, tomatoes, beans, cabbages, sunflowers, a little corn.

Her sons, formerly so helpful, had become idle and withdrawn and showed little interest in the garden. They loitered each day on the stoop of their lodging and walked the camp's perimeter at dusk, rolling cigarettes as a sun red as the Japanese ensign sank behind the mountains.

In early summer a group of U.S. Army recruiting personnel arrived at the camp and asked for volunteers to fight the Germans. Shoji and Masanori were quick to offer themselves. After passing a brief quiz and check-up and pledging loyalty to the flag, they were accepted. Again Shoji and his mother found themselves at odds, but this time the boy refused to acquiesce, and Masanori insisted on going with his brother.

Dressed in the uniform of the recruit, they resembled grown men.

A few weeks later, Mrs Takaoka escorted her embarrassed sons and a score of other boys to the camp gate and wished them farewell. She allowed her presence to speak for itself and did not shame them further by begging them to be careful. Standing by the barbed wire she watched dust rise in a thickening cloud from the wheels of the truck taking them to the train, and she did not turn back to her garden till all the dust had settled.

That first autumn Mrs Takaoka's harvest was light, but over the next three years she found ways of improving her yield. Her compost heap was now extensive and she encouraged newly arrived internees to use the rich, flowering humus to grow produce of their own. The fresh fruit and vegetables from these 'victory gardens' were a welcome supplement to the camp's meagre, monotonous fare.

Periodically she received letters and photographs from her sons, now stationed in England. They told her they were not being treated too badly, though for a while their lieutenant had refused to believe they were twins because, he said, all Japanese look alike, and they must be playing a joke on him. On leave their movements were restricted but they managed to see a bit of England; her favourite picture, which she framed and hung above the stove, showed the two of them looking festive and rakish, cigarettes drooping from their grins, arms linked as they stood on the platform of a station under a hanging sign that read GATWICK. But they were some distance off and the photograph was overexposed; she had to admit she couldn't tell them apart.

The winter of '44 was a hard one. Icy winds, like the winds from Siberia that blew down over the Sea of Japan each winter, roared over the salt-flats and raised cairns of fine snow against the barbed wire, the camp gate, the pylons of the guard towers. Several of the old folks died in February, among them a fisherman from the coast whose last words were *umi ga natsukashii* – I miss the ocean.

Spring came late that year but Mrs Takaoka's garden was already thriving when news came of the Normandy landings. Soon after, there was a letter from Shoji assuring her that he and Masanori were unhurt and telling her with a disappointment she could not share that their regiment had been consigned to the second wave. This, she reasoned, was a promising precedent, a good omen.

The summer was long and hot and Mrs Takaoka's garden flourished. The gentle, apologetic white woman who taught the camp's school-aged children often stopped by to ask for gardening advice or to share a pot of tea. She never failed to ask about Shoji and Masanori. Mrs Takaoka liked the woman and often forced her to accept an apronful of cherry tomatoes, peas or long beans.

Near Christmas, long after the camp's humble harvest was in and the victory gardens fertilized with a dusting of snow, news came of another battle in France. Hitler, it seemed, had gathered his legions for a last great offensive against the Allies, and the American troops were bearing the brunt of it. Hourly the radio carried guarded reports on the u.s. Army's 'tactical retreat' through the Ardennes and the 'stiff resistance' of encircled troops at a place called Bastogne. Mrs Takaoka listened carefully to these reports, though the nuances of euphemism, which she sensed but could not always interpret, made it hard for her to gauge the situation's gravity.

The day after American New Year, a tall slim man in an officer's coat appeared on the edge of the compound. Mrs Takaoka watched him through her half-frosted window as he marched through the grounds and stopped some playing children, then a hunchbacked old man, to ask a question. He was looking for someone, that much she could tell, and slowly it dawned on her whom he must have come to find, and why. He seemed to look up and peer toward her lodging, then at the window and her face behind it, but she could not be sure because of the frost and the weakened state of her eyes. He was approaching but his features were still unclear. She turned from the window and went to the stove to make tea.

That spring a delegation of smartly arrayed officers arrived in Argent to bestow posthumous awards on the mothers of two boys killed in the Battle of the Bulge. Mrs Takaoka was one of the mothers. As he presented the small, burnished Legion of Merit, the presiding officer assured her that Shoji had died bravely in the service of his country; he regretted that Mrs Takaoka could not leave Argent to receive the medal in more appropriate surroundings, but trusted she understood such things were temporarily impossible.

Mrs Takaoka bowed and turned away, clutching the medallion to her breast.

That evening was clear and mild, but instead of working in her garden as she liked to do when the days were growing longer, Mrs Takaoka took a walk to the camp perimeter and stared west to the mountains. Despite the warmth, her joints ached, and she had to rack her memory for several seconds to recall her age. She opened her hand to look at her son's decoration: it was luminous and star-shaped, like a gem or a talisman, and its keen tips had cut a pentagon of lesions into her palm. The bright scarlet ribbon that hung from it twitched in the breeze. She wished she could place it over the modest stone they had set above her husband's ashes but the farm was days from here by train and lately she had begun to wonder if it would still be hers when the war was done ...

The sunset was no more vivid than usual. The Legion of Merit gleamed like a coin in the ruddy light. For a moment she pulled back her arm in a clumsy wind-up as if to fling the medal over the barbed wire and into the desert, then clenched it tighter and held it to her breast.

Masanori was still alive. She repeated the words several times under her breath, dropping the medal into her apron like a charm and turning back to her garden.

VI ... AND IN EVERY ANSWERING MACHINE A ZEN KOAN

A Japanese businessman shook me awake as I reached my station. He said he watched me get off at Nagai every night and didn't want to see me carried to the end of the line the way a drunk or exhausted commuter might be. I thanked him, stumbled off the train and headed home, my mind still webbed with dreams.

It was late, and a slim metallic moon was balanced over the city. As I walked home past the darkened banks, the pachinko joints, the Love Hotels and bars and stores and on into the empty streets of my neighbourhood, I thought of the apartment I'd left early that morning, how foreign and unsettled it always seemed because I spent so little time there.

Suddenly I wished I had someone – anyone – beside me. Except for Hashimoto and the Principal I had few friends here, yet I wondered if someone might have called while I was out and left a message on my new machine; I thought of voices, a touch hesitant, shy and distorted, their meek invitations wasted on the empty room; I pictured sound waves stirring a few grains of dust on the *tatami* floor. My Japanese neighbours were as busy as I was and I hardly ever saw them – and what is a neighbour anyway if you're never home? Someone away from home has no neighbours because people are neighbours only when you're there. Like the tree tumbling in the forest, like the sound of one hand clapping; when I reached the alley that led to my apartment I turned back towards the lit-up streets and bars around the station.

VII   THE SUN FLAG

'A man away from home,' General Nogi muttered to himself, 'has no neighbours; and away from his neighbours he has no home. Strangers must bury him, and he will sleep in ground his family can never visit ...'

It was dawn. With hands linked behind his back the General paced slowly over the smoking battlefield. His officers followed at a tactful distance, but he was aware of their gaze. Stepping with measured respect over the corpses of his men, he looked up and felt a stirring of pride at the sight of his ensign rippling over the hill. A pale moon surprised him in the morning sky, and he began to weep.

'*A dream in the mind of a dragonfly,*' he quoted under his breath, searching for the right words. But they would not come. From somewhere far off there was a wail of a train arriving or departing and he thought of his sons, one of whom had died earlier that year in the opening assault on Port Arthur, and the other three days ago in the first daylight attack on the hill. In both cases he had given the orders.

He turned to his officers. They were waiting for him to recite the poem a victorious samurai is obliged to compose after battle. He raised a hand, as if for silence, and spoke.

7

A Protruding Nail

deru kugi wa utareru

Midway through a learned sermon on the origin and implications of various Japanese proverbs Mr Sato Takaharu urbanely interrupted himself. His voice bristled with irony as he asked a small girl for her favourite *kotowaza*.

The girl was Kaizaki Sachiko and she was completely at a loss – exactly as *Sensei* had anticipated. He had noticed some time before that she was paying no attention to his lecture and was not taking any notes. She was what the staff of the school, in their wittier moments, liked to refer to as a 'gazer'.

– Sachiko, the looming Mr Sato reverberated. Sachiko, from the beginning of this class, and, indeed, the beginning of term – (a pause for the ensuing round of delighted laughter) – you have obstinately refused to attend to your studies, both in class and at home. Moving you away from the windows seems not to have had the remedial effect I intended. You continue to gaze toward the windows. You are in fact a gazer – (another pause, more laughter) – and idle gazing is one form of negligence I find absolutely intolerable. I shall ask again: what is your favourite *kotowaza*?

Silence for a moment. Sachiko's intoxicated classmates prayed she would say nothing so the titillating harangue might continue. Everyone knew Mr Sato was the hardest teacher in the school, and he himself sensed that students preferred his spectacular ambushes to the study of proverbs they already knew. These students were far too young for his scholarship. He flushed and stiffened as he recalled the university, his demotion ...

– Come, Sachiko, he crooned to immediate acclaim (the laughter choking her, drawing tears to her eyes) – We know you're a clever child!

And in fact she did know her proverbs, even if she neglected to take notes. A clever child, as he had flattered her. It came to her in a fit of inspiration:

– *With flattery even a pig can be made to climb a tree.*

Mr Sato reddened as the class loosed a typhoon of laughter. Flattery, after all, was the device of servants and proprietors, corporate flunkeys and career politicians. The ingenuity of Sachiko's choice was obvious even to her classmates. And it was their attentive presence that seemed to infuriate *Sensei* most; children could be drilled till they learned to retain as many facts as a small computer, but no child needed drilling to remember amusing insults, successful pranks, humiliating confrontations. They were unsurpassable when it came to that. This incident was already stored in their memories. It would cling to his reputation, an unsightly protrusion, like a wad of chewing gum stuck to the blackboard.

Mr Sato strode away from Sachiko's desk and turned on his students, calling for quiet.

Such laughter was completely unsuitable.

This instance of irresponsible hilarity constituted a serious breach of classroom etiquette. Harsh and immediate disciplinary measures were indicated. And Sachiko, on whose (narrow, delicate) shoulders full responsibility for all punitive action ultimately rested, was to leave the room and not return until Mr Sato had duly considered the situation and conferred with her parents, whom he intended to notify at once. Go!

Sachiko obeyed with difficulty, stumbling between desks, impeded by cunningly extended legs and the tears that filled and clouded her eyes. She found herself outside the classroom in the sunlit corridor and heard the door slam shut behind her with the sound Mr Sato's metre-stick made when he slashed it onto the desks of gazers.

The sunlight through the clean glass wall of the corridor blinded her. She paused to wipe tears from her eyes. Behind her she could hear Mr Sato continuing his lecture with a terrifying new zeal:

– And of course the adage you will be most familiar with and which indeed is well known even overseas is one about whose provenance there is still some debate though Murata insists it must have arisen first in the Edo region and adduces as evidence several cogent items we will later discuss. It is fascinating in this connection that the foreign scholars Fletcher and Stromsky argue that almost every language has evolved a maxim of similar import though nowhere perhaps does it enjoy such currency as in our country with the possible exception of several obscure societies which we will later discuss. Will anyone in the class recite this slogan for our collective benefit? You, Mr Inoue, ought to know it. Eh? What was that? Would you do us the favour of repeating yourself audibly?

– THE NAIL THAT STICKS UP GETS HAMMERED DOWN.

– Thank you. Allow me to repeat that.

Sachiko shuffles up the sunlit corridor with the suave modulations of Mr Sato and the cowed, hysterical tone of Inoue Haruo's voice following her toward the far door. THE NAIL THAT STICKS UP. Makes her think of the mistaken nail-head in the frame of the window she used to sit beside. It sticks up a little. She used to stare at it. Gaze. She took a curious pride and comfort in its lopsided imperfection. *Sensei* hadn't noticed it yet and she was worried that her staring at the window might draw his attention to the little flaw. He would call in his superiors who would inspect the deviant frame with a mounting sense of outrage and disgrace. The Inspector of Schools would be notified and a committee appointed to investigate and rectify the error. The Minister of Education would visit the school and apologize in person to an assembly of parents and, should he feel the situation was of sufficient gravity, tender his resignation. Letters would be written in that tone of diplomatic hostility reserved elsewhere for declarations of war. Across the country woodworkers' unions would protest their competence. But heads would roll. GETS HAMMERED DOWN.

And all this time, Sachiko muses, pushing open the door and stepping out into the dirty spring air, he thinks I was looking out the window. Stood by my desk and looked in the same direction to see what I was always gazing at. Factories, streets, garages, smokestacks, cram-schools. It was that nail. He'll find it now. He will. He can't miss it. A crooked little bulge speckled with white paint like the egg of that Arctic bird we learned about in class. I pretended the warm sun through the windows would hatch it. It was like an ancient sundial – as the lessons passed, tiny shadows moved round it and I always knew the time. In winter during the tutorials after school the shadows covered it and it was pale grey like the plum blossoms in Nagai Park that get rained on all March. Sometimes a little snow falls too and when it melts the blossoms are bleached white like the tips of your fingers on a cold morning in February as you walk to school, or on Saturdays to the cram-school across the tracks from the park, with the plum blossoms starting and a little wet snow still falling between the trees ...

Sachiko shuffling through a corner of Nagai Park on her way home, worried about the fate of an unconforming nail. She knows south Ōsaka has not received more than a dusting of snow in a hundred years. She has learned it in class.

... and the snow falling and falling the world white and traffic disappearing the railway tracks covered with drifts

FLIGHT PATHS OF THE EMPEROR

between trains ... snow thickening on the roofs in tall plumes
blocking the tips of chimneys of factories the high windows of
pachinko houses and schools till Nagai Park is white as Hokkaido
    then with my lunchpail through growing drifts of shred-
ded paper, cheeks glowing with cold like the seals like Arctic
hares running north to the frozen shore I learned once there
were packs of wolves there and white bears swim in the sea

8

THE SON IS ALWAYS LIKE THE FATHER

... and the gardener said to the abbot, 'Yes, this tiny tree has seen three
hundred summers, and every year I make it smaller still. Who knows?
In a century, if my sons and their descendants persevere, it may be small
enough to fit inside my skull.' [From THE HISTORY OF BONSAI]

AMANOGAWA AMERICAN ENGLISH SCHOOL, ŌSAKA, 5 JUNE:

This morning on national radio the 1987 Rainy Season was
inaugurated. The sky however remained suspiciously clear.
Principal Kobayashi, who had been warning me for weeks
about the ferocious regularity of the Japanese monsoon, stood
inconsolably at the main window of the school peering out
over the dry streets. Tomorrow, she vowed, her look of disappointment easing into a smile. Tomorrow the rain will be
terrible! You *must* bring an umbrella!

She turned to the window again. Seen from behind, her
ebony hair tied back in a bun reminded me of my mother. As
did her accent, her clipped idiom and the sad, concerted purs-
ing of her lips when she spoke.

*Do not forget! This is not like the rain you have at home! Write
yourself a memo!*

I have no umbrella. I make it a point of honour not to
carry an umbrella – especially in dry weather. As if a further
mark of disparity were needed, I will now be the only soul in
the parched streets without one.

9 JUNE: No rain yet. Even my best students skittish and unco-operative. Each morning the broadcasts warning citizens not to forget their umbrellas become more strident and hysterical. Declaring the week an embarrassment to Japan, Kobayashi begs me to be patient.

Over beer and *soba* in a nearby shop she asks me about myself, where I come from, why I'm here.

TORONTO, JUNE 1979: It had been the first hot day of summer and around suppertime a storm gathered and broke. By dark the thunder had tapered off but a thin steamy drizzle continued to fall. He sat with his mother at the kitchen table and drank Export from the can with smug, overstated gestures; whenever a few specks of foam clung to his upper lip he swiped them away with the back of his hand, as if brushing clean a moustache.

His mother sat across from him, her head and heavy shoulders framed by the dripping window. She was chainsmoking and drinking Metaxa. Her dark hair with grey roots was pulled back and fastened in a tight bun, her stout body wid-owed by an ill-fitting black dress. He knew how tired she was, but the light of the candle flame flitting among the dishes soft-ened her face and she looked better than she had for weeks.

She nodded toward his beer can and said, 'To me it seems you've been rehearsing awhile.' Her accent had thickened, he thought.

With one hand she plucked out a cigarette and reclosed the packet. He gave her a sly look.

'My birthday was only last week.'

'You didn't drink before that?'

'What, besides the wine at communion?' He tried not to grin. 'I guess I've had a drink or two. Maybe on special occa-sions ... Christmas, Easter ... what's the big deal?'

She lit her cigarette and he reached for the packet; her hand snapped down on his like the wire arm of a trap. She loosened her grip but continued to hold him. They were both smiling now.

'Guess you mind if I smoke?'

'You're still a boy.'

'Actually I'm a man now, Mother – by law.'

She laughed at him. 'The law can't make you a man.'

'I'm fully grown.'

'You are too thin.' She squeezed his hand, a small bird caught in a snare. 'Look at these wrists.'

Her grip tightened and he winced, then started to laugh. By law he was a man but she was still stronger. And he admired that strength, yet felt a flash of resentment; he thought he knew what she would say next and she said the words on cue, coughing, puffing smoke from the side of her mouth.

'People grow up too fast these days,' she quoted. 'When I was a young girl in the Peloponnesus ...'

He groaned. 'That was another country, Mother. I mean, Jesus, really it was a whole different century.'

She loosed his hand and he felt relief, as if a painful duty had ended. Her hand recoiled, wilted into a small fist and came to rest between her glass and her untouched food.

'Different in a sense, I mean.'

'He is a man now so he can insult his mother. And like his English father, he swears.'

His father, he admitted, *had* sworn: in the garage under his Mercury, in the basement practising kicks, even at the supper table. And before laughing it off (his bearded, red face brightening, a sun emerging out of cloud) he would freeze, seem startled by his own words, injured, the innocent butt of a ventriloquist's joke. Once during a rare mealtime silence he'd suddenly cursed under his breath, fist clenched, whiteknuckled, then peered out at his shaken family with a betrayed, bedraggled look; his son pictured him hunched over a dark table in a small room somewhere behind his eyes, but could never make out the other diners gathered round him, attentive ...

'Mother,' he shook his head, 'Mother, you swear too – it's just I can't ever pronounce the things you say. Are you going to eat your lamb or not?'

Tragically she pushed the plate away, toward him, and looked skyward, empty palms upturned. Even in the candlelight he could see how the half moons under her eyes had darkened.

'No, you can't pronounce anything anymore. All this talk of flying away to Asia – why won't you go instead to Greece? We have family there, old friends, they would find you a decent job ...'

'And I could meet a nice Greek girl, right?'

'Naturally, that as well. You're making fun of me?'

'Mother, we've been through this already – haven't we been through this? I know how you feel about Turkey, but all Asians are not Turks.'

She rolled her eyes. 'God forbid they should all be Turks, there are a billion people in China.'

'And I won't even be going for a long time, if ever. All I'm planning is to head west and find a job – there's a lot happening there now, Calgary's really booming. I'll see a bit of the country, the mountains, maybe go down to California for a while ...' He paused, swishing the beer over his tongue like some sparkling, imported wine. 'It could be years before I wind up in a Turkish prison cell on drug charges.'

'If your father were here.'

'Come on, you know he lived for a while in Alberta himself, he loves the place.' He was thinking of his father's tales of jobs on the ranches and oil wells when he was young and single and seeing girls whose names – Calla, Myrna, Ellen – he'd loved to run teasingly over his beer-whetted tongue. He'd told over and over of a huge bonfire they built one autumn night to burn off a towering pyramid of straw; of his two-year stint in the army; of an explosion and fire at a wildcat rig in the shadow of the Rockies. His thick greying brows would take flight, his blue eyes flare up and focus as he recalled those reckless, unruly days. *Good days*, he would repeat, *but there's a time for settling down, too.* And he would nod and run his big hand – resignedly? – over a strong but softening belly and the steel-grey hair at his temples, while a bonfire, fuelled with drink, smouldered in his eyes.

'Cheers.' The son quaffed his ale with a Wild West gulp and then tried to crush the can in his fist, the way his father always had. But he was too thin and could only dent it.

He swore under his breath. Under his long hair his nape grew warm, burning. 'Maybe he's out there again now,' he said. 'If I see him I'll give him your regards.'

'You tell him to come home. He's too old for a boy's games.'

'Maybe I'll say you remarried.'

'Maybe I will remarry, there are men at the church who want wives, not even Penelope could have waited forever. Still, I'm sure he will be back. He has left before, he should be back.'

But the son was not so sure.

He pointed out that Diana, his older sister, would be home for the summer, and with her children, too; his mother only shrugged. 'I always get by on my own, don't tire yourself worrying about me. I have the church, my knitting, the *bonsai* ...' Her heavy brows rose stoically and he thought of candlelit icons in the church he attended as a boy – the lugubrious upturned eyes of martyred Christs, of Madonnas whose olive features were solemn and prophetic, who seemed to know already where their sons were bound.

'She's going to be here in a week, Mother.'

'And now your brother living in Detroit, too – Detroit of all places, they have more assassins and thieves there than all of Turkey. Be patient with me, my boy, sometimes it's hard for me to understand, when I was a young girl the family stayed together.'

He brightened, seeing a way out. 'I hear it's the same in Japan,' he said. 'I was reading about the family structure the other day – everyone lives in the same house, even the old folks. Sometimes four generations under a single roof.'

'Four? Imagine, just like in Greece. But with your *papou* dead and now your father gone you don't have to worry about that here.'

He scooped up his empty can and set it down. 'But why would I worry? You know I wouldn't mind if ...'

He broke off and his face darkened.

'Damn it, Mother, why do you have to go and say things like that?'

She wet her lips with brandy, her eyes almost crossing as she peered evasively into the drink.

He tried to calm himself. He clawed an open hand through the fierce smoke that advanced on him from the ashtray, relentlessly, no matter where he moved ...

His father, an ex-smoker, had hated cigarettes too, and one time she had quit to appease him; no doubt she would quit again tomorrow if he came back. *Weak*, he told himself, *weak*, but years later he would change his mind about what strength was, what shapes it adopted. In his mother's heavy form there was a calm, rooted patience, a sturdy assertion of immemorial rights. *Be patient with me, my boy. When I was a young girl the family stayed together.*

After a few seconds he returned to Japan. His voice was mechanical, pedantic, paced by a soothing litany of facts.

'Anyway, things are changing over there too – there are divorces now and the North American nuclear family is the new ideal.'

'A kind of progress, I suppose.'

He felt his anger revive. 'The divorce rate is almost ten per cent in Tōkyō.'

115

'What, you've memorized this whole book? So why won't you go to college here in your own city? Japan, Japan, *ella moreh!* What do you know about Greece?'

'Lots. More than enough.'

'What do you know? Tell me.'

His jaw clenched. 'I know you didn't seem so interested in it when I was growing up.' His own words aroused him, as when you accuse someone of something you know they didn't do and then almost believe they did. But this charge, he thought, was fair. 'You didn't seem to care about Greece at all, or my school or my hockey either, or my friends, but you were involved as hell in other things. How do you think I got interested in Japan in the first place?'

His words had been sharper than he'd meant, but instead of retaliating as she normally would she sat frozen, staring at the unfinished lamb, as if trying to figure something out. Then all at once he sensed he'd made a cruel mistake. Some explosive truth was lodged ticking like a time-bomb between his words and he found himself scrambling among them, trying to find and defuse it before it burst.

Then he understood. For his father's sake, for the sake of the family, she had become involved in new things – first jogging, then French novels, Chinese cooking, sunbathing, tennis, finally *bonsai*. Whenever his father had taken up a new project or pursuit she'd found some complementary field and thrown herself into it with a will he was coming to see as truly Spartan. She hated cinemas, so when his father began to attend French films she started reading, in translation, novels like *Madame Bovary* and *Remembrance of Things Past*. He knew she had never really liked reading so even then he recognized in this gesture a ferocious self-denial that struck him, a supremely self-absorbed sixteen-year-old, as idiotic and beneath contempt. During his father's brief dalliance with tai-chi she'd tried Chinese cooking, when he learned to fly small aircraft she took a driving course, and when on his fortieth birthday he joined a health club and began weightlifting on the poolside lawns she'd forced herself to swelter in the deck-chairs with other wives, despite an upbringing that discouraged all contact with the sun lest it lead to wrinkles or darken the skin like a Turk's.

Such energies – such daily concerted chaos! He'd been stunned as a child visiting his friends' homes at how restful they seemed, how civil and systematic. Where were the crises and accusations, the sudden projects, the loud lavish dinners and claps of laughter and hurried hugs and kisses and looming deadlines? Where was the mad, fertile mix of incompatible cultures? Home for him was not a womb but a crucible.

When his father had hurled himself into karate his mother had joined a *bonsai* club. She began raising the tiny trees on the back porch and in the basement and so far as he knew it was the one hobby she had never deserted – so now for him to tell her that something she'd done to make the family closer was driving him away –

But it was not a question of that. He had to go, could hardly stand the sight of the house, his room, the faded sailing-ship-in-a-bottle pattern of its wallpaper that somehow still recalled bedwetting, his delicate boyhood, the ethnic slurs and slogans and extracurricular beatings of the schoolyard. Yet he sensed vaguely that in time he would come back and see things in a different light, as a loving spouse may sometimes feel the need to spend time away before returning to a stronger bond.

Was that what his father was doing?

The rain continued to fall and trickle slowly down the window. His mother fumbled for her cigarettes. For a moment he felt a surge of hatred for the downturned, defeated face, and he wanted to hurt her again. He was glad his sister was on her way home to inherit what he'd taken to calling 'the vigil' – though it was his mother, he admitted with a blunt stab of remorse, who did the cooking and cleaning and knitted him

117

countless sweaters and had patched his favourite jeans and taken him to the travel agent to book a seat on tomorrow's flight, had baked him *galactoboureko* and *baklava* and bought the Export for his birthday the week before, had made him lamb and Greek salad tonight and would drive him to the airport at seven tomorrow morning –

'I'm sorry I said that.'

'Said what? You said nothing – *tipota*.'

'About Greece and Japan and the *bonsai* and Dad.'

Her eyes narrowed. 'You said nothing about him.'

'He'll be back.'

'*Tipota*.' She seized a fork and as she spoke to him she pressed its tines into her palm. 'Your father ... *never* liked what I tried to do, never, never at all. Whenever he found new interests I would ... always I would try. I thought I was being as a wife should but now I see he wanted something more – more freedom, distance from me. Something.' She bit her lower lip and the corners of her mouth rose, quivering. 'The *bonsai* was a mistake, like everything else.'

He was embarrassed for her, and for himself. He wished he could say something.

'You've done well with them, though. You've won prizes.'

She flicked a hand at his face, as if casting a spell or sprinkling him with water. '*Tipota*.'

'I always liked them, you know. They ... I always liked them.'

'*Nei*,' she said, coughing out a mouthful of smoke, eyes watering, 'so now you have to go see some real ones for yourself.'

'It'll be years, if ever. I'll be home lots of times before then. This Christmas I'll be home.'

'Maybe we can arrange to have your father home for Christmas, too. Though I wonder sometimes if I really ...'

She stopped up her mouth with the cigarette, then

squashed it in the ashtray; he swallowed and coughed and thrust out a hand to push it farther off. Smoke billowed from the dying butt, a spot of light seen from the air, a lone house burning on a plain.

'I'm sure,' he muttered, 'he'll be coming home. Try not to worry.'

'How can you be sure of what he will do?'

He stared down at his hands, his meagre wrists. His wristwatch surprised him. 'Mother,' he said softly, 'I've got to go.'

'So soon?'

But it was almost ten o'clock. His girlfriend Kathryn worked evenings as a cashier at Dominion and he'd arranged to meet her at 10:30 when she got off. She was a puzzled, solemn seventeen-year-old with frizzy brown hair and black eyebrows that sloped outwards, downwards from the bridge of her nose so she had, even frowning or arguing a point, a kind of listless, sceptical air. He was nervous about meeting her tonight. The two of them had things to decide about the future and it seemed to him these decisions were of vast, virtually cosmic importance. *The law can't make you a man*, his mother had said – but he knew something else that could, according to his friends. His body tautened with anxiety, desire.

He sprang up and went to the fridge.

'Not another drink,' his mother said automatically.

Not another drink!

This was the opening cue to a ritual drama they enacted often, using a text unwritten but commonly understood. He starred as the prodigal, lazy, wasteful son, barbarously insensitive to this mother's travails; she was the dutiful *mitera*, the drudge, the sacrificial ewe, her youth and beauty scoured away by the cleaning rag or boiled dry at the stove. Her part came whenever he helped himself to another serving of dinner, of dessert, another snack or glass of milk. Here the script called for her to strike like a Fury. *Ella, moreh, ella! All day I've been stuck in here cleaning, cooking, eighteen years I've been cooking, after eighteen years you're still hungry? The boy won't rest till he eats a mother's heart! Here, why don't I cook him an arm or a leg!* A chorus of wailing Greek women would materialize in the wings as she chanted the ritual lamentations, her hands in tireless, histrionic flight.

The correct antiphonal response was this: he would throw up his own hands Homerically and sharply remind her he was a growing boy and famished and couldn't she spare him a few slops, a crust or two of stale bread, a little water? While the faint initial irritation wore off and he began to enjoy their comedy and his mother's impeccable timing he would sense how pleased she really was that her growing boy was actually *having another.* He would sense it, but say nothing. And now he violated the script.

'You don't really mean that,' he snapped, jerking open the fridge door so its dull wintry light swept over her face, her hair, touching them with frost. 'That's not what you mean at all. Really you're happy I'm having another beer and you're happy when I have another plate of food too, so why bother pretending you don't like it?' He hooked his index finger under the empty plastic rings of the twelve-pack and yanked the last two cans from the fridge. 'Why do you always have to play with me as if I'm still your little boy? I'm all grown up now, Mother. You'll have to start treating me like a grown-up.'

It frightened him, a little, the way she failed to react. Usually she responded quickly when he was stupid enough to talk back. Now she just stared, not at his face but at the beer cans, or past them into the half-empty fridge, as if petrified by its chilly light.

Her face hardened.

'*Skata,*' she hissed, more softly than he'd ever heard the word said before. 'You will be just like him, I promise you.'

In the light of the open fridge, pale cigarette smoke haloed her head like narcotic fumes round the face of an oracle. 'Your sons will treat you the same way, that much I can promise you, the son is always like the father.'

He closed the fridge door, stared at his shoes.

'Look, Mother, I'm sorry I upset you. I really didn't mean –'

'*Thenpirazi. Thenpirazi moreh.*'

'But it *does* matter. And I'm sorry.'

She made the sprinkling motion again with her hand, like an Orthodox priest at a baptism. 'You must go get ready to meet Nancy.'

'Kathryn.'

'I can't keep them straight.' She took a drag on her cigarette and the burning tip seemed to tremble. 'I'm sorry, you were a baby so small you slept in a dresser drawer, we put blankets in a drawer and set it by the bed, now a few years gone and all these women ... You will be careful, won't you, in a city out west?'

He shot her a worldly grin. He ran a hand through the wild rumpled hair she'd tried to 'train' with comb and water when he was a boy. His knees were shaking, his nape burned.

'Go on, then,' she said, her voice stronger. 'Maybe you'll meet your father on the road.'

He hurried downstairs to his basement room and on the way he passed the card table with its shallow, gravel-lined tray and over-arching sunlamp; here his mother worked on her *bonsai* when she brought them in from the garden. Tonight all three were in the tray, as if she had been at work on them earlier: the blue spruce, the oak and the Japanese maple, all set neatly in small rectangular pots among tiny landscapes of rock and gravel and olive-green moss. None of the trees was over a foot high. He had often seen her at work on them on Sunday mornings when he woke up late and stumbled out of his room: she was constantly pruning, clipping roots, bending back the twig-thin boughs and securing them with fine copper wire. Sometimes he would pause, scratching, and pose sleepy questions, and as he grew older these interludes, at first so earnest and edifying, began to give him a distracting sense of pride in his filial forbearance; when he was irritable or hungover they seemed an extravagant concession. As she cropped off twigs, sprayed vinegar on fruit flies lodged in the crux of the oak, or pulled back branches with the copper wire, she would litanize on the history and methods of the art and pass on technical details gleaned in recent lessons. Her explanations, especially of the history, were curiously muddled and improbable; he suspected she hadn't listened with care or had crossbred fact and fancy into an outlandish hybrid, and often, growing older, he would tell her as much.

Each autumn the oak and the Japanese maple turned yellow, orange, or a brilliant crimson, and by Christmas they would shed their leaves. He asked his mother if this would happen if they lived indoors all year under the sunlamp and she said, 'Yes, I am sure it would,' with the mettlesome directness that meant she was improvising but had decided she was right and would not be challenged.

Those three mysterious trees, and his father coming home in the evening, late, after karate practice, still wearing his exotic ivory outfit, his skin pink, bearded, radiating heat and health and a good thick briny father-smell; in time the colours of his belt changing, as if seasonal, from white to yellow to the orange of a rising sun, then to cool ocean-green and finally blue. His father – a blue-belt! – standing by the sink after practice Friday nights plunging his muscular forearms into the dishwater, scrubbing with absent-minded strength so that plates and glasses sometimes broke and his mother wailed and swore in Greek but his father only hummed, sang to himself or to the children in mock-Japanese and recited some droll *haiku* currently abroad in his *dojo*:

> *Dishwashing husband*
> *Later in the evening*
> *Takes up karate.*

(Later in the evening he and Kathryn would make love
and it would be the first time for both of them. They would lie
in the park under pines and maples after the rain had stopped
with cool drops still falling from the leaves onto their bare limbs
and bellies. Kissing her he would be troubled again by those
sceptical, sloping brows, how they undercut the warm promise
of her brown eyes, their gravity. Soon his lust and affection
would make way for other things: a dark sense of initiation and
disbelief, a longing for distance, for an empty pack, a chilly,
impersonal pride.

They would agree to see no one else until he came back
at Christmas and decide then what to do next, but he was to
break his promise a few months later and write a long, extenu-
ating letter she never replied to.)

Stefano, he heard his mother calling, faintly, *Stefano, don't
make your girl wait.*

When he came out of the room she was hunched over the
card table, her back to him, crooked fingers busy under the sunlamp.

'You're getting them ready for another show?'

She did not turn around. Her voice was remote, hypnotic. 'Some *bonsai* can live to be three hundred years old,
many past two hundred. Some have been in families for ten
generations. They are seldom more than a foot high.'

He stepped up behind her.

'Mother?'

'These ones are not nearly so old.' Her shoulders tightened. 'The maple has been giving me some trouble ...'

He could see her hand fumbling with a nest of amber-
coloured wire. The rain beat on the basement windows,

123

pooling in the window-wells. He set his hands on the black fabric on either side of her neck and felt her body stiffen; tossing down the wire she slapped at the maple and knocked it over.

'Please, Mother, don't –'

She spun round and embraced him, burying her face against his cheek.

★

That Christmas when he went home for a visit the gravel tray and the sunlamp still sat on the card table outside his bedroom, but the *bonsai* were gone. He might have asked about them but it was a frantic, unhappy Christmas and he had other things on his mind. On later, happier visits, after his father had returned for good, the empty tray became a kind of fixture – one of those obsolete elements of every house that a family takes for granted and only strangers notice. So that years later, when he started to feel like a stranger himself – albeit a welcome stranger, a cherished guest – he saw the table with fresh eyes (it now looked like a Zen garden) and wondered about the trees.

Gone, his mother shrugged when he asked. And she offered him more whisky and seed-cake and told him to sit down and tell her and his father what it was like to be living in – where was it now? Vancouver?

That night after his parents had gone to bed he found the trees. His mother had stored them in the cold-room on an old trunk under shelves of pickles and preserves; here too, he saw, she had hung several of the Byzantine crosses she'd kept above her bed when his father was away. Neglected for years in the cold, sunless room, the oak and maple had died, their tiny leaves fallen, clenched in brittle clusters on the rocks and moss among grizzled roots. The trunks and boughs were now freed of their wires and were leafless, arthritic and shrunken, delicate as a bird's skeleton or an old woman's upturned, empty hands. At least the blue spruce maintained the illusion of life; it was a

124

hardier tree and would have outlived its deciduous cousins by months, even years. Maybe it had drawn enough moisture from the damp air to survive until recently, for its tiny needles, still clinging to the boughs, were not yet brown and continued to exude a faint cool odour, like frankincense at Communion, or pines and cedars on the dry hillsides above Sparta.

As a gesture he might have watered them, but there was no faucet in the cold-room and no cup by the bathroom sink. All he had (and it would do the trees no good) was the half-empty gin-flask he always kept in his room on visits home. Not that he drank from it much. The liquor was a memento, a sign, a distillation of the sharp-tasting essence of another place – a reminder that his real life had gone west and now moved among the grown-ups of a distant city.

14 JUNE: Kobayashi and I sit between classes drinking tea and listening to the sound of the monsoon pummelling the roof and crashing into the parched Ōsaka streets. The welcome, long-awaited sound began suddenly halfway through the last lesson and my students, usually so stiff, cramped and cautious, broke spontaneously into back-slapping and cheering and manic applause. A male student, eyes darting nervously, hands clasped in the way that warns you a carefully researched and rehearsed remark is impending, announced, 'This is the most overdue Japanese monsoon rainfall in almost one whole century.'

I suggested we take a break and go to the windows to watch.

We decided to let the class end early and now Kobayashi reclines in her chair, languid, sipping her tea with a serene, beatific expression, not unlike the Buddha in certain Japanese prints.

'Of course the farmers will be relieved,' she says. 'I see you did not bring your umbrella.'

The storm surges to a brief crescendo and I shiver, thinking

125

of my return tonight from Nagai Station past the wooded park. Usually there are couples on the benches and a few families still out walking, men practising judo, their eyes and teeth glinting like fireflies in the dark, limbs ghostly, while singers in kimono rehearse mournful old songs under the pines. Tonight the park will be deserted to the rain and the cicadas. Pools will be deepening by the path and a few strangers will hurry by on their way home, umbrellas brandished, wet faces turned down and away.

9

ON STRIKES AND ERRORS IN JAPANESE BASEBALL

I wasn't there. My father wasn't even there. But let me see if I can remember.

At 8:10 on the morning of 6 August 1945, a single airplane appeared in the clear skies over Hiroshima ...

That isn't it. No. *Ikenai*, it won't do. The cadences are too familiar, possibly stolen, and I've a gut feeling the time is incorrect. Did the airplane appear a few minutes earlier? Hell, I'm not even sure about the date; August 6 is my father's birthday, it's quite possible my mind is playing tricks on me.

It does that sometimes, especially when I'm alone here in the school – as if I'd been teaching too much or going gradually, discreetly insane. Who was Charles Manson speaking for when he said his father was the Second World War? Not me, thank God, I'll never be that crazy.

So then. On the afternoon of 6 August 1945 my father leaned over a glittering birthday cake and to the cheering of friends and parents extinguished all eleven candles. Auspiciously the locomotive of the Ontario Northlands, pulling out of North Bay Station at that moment, let out a lingering moan. A small grey dog darted over the soft lawn and leapt into my father's lap. My father passed round to his friends the eleven birthday candles, half-melted, sticky at the bottom with icing

127

and sweet adhering crumbs, and invited them to eat.

Then who'd like the first piece, my grandfather demanded, lifting a glittering knife into the air.

It looked that way: a thin blade suspended in mid-air, glinting. The fragment of some shattered mirror. Or a missile, spent and barely moving, soon to plummet to earth.

Sometimes nowadays the satellites appear at noon over Airport Hill in North Bay, Ontario, and as they reflect the sun they too look that way, though of course they are hours off in the stratosphere and their intentions are benign and dependable.

Above I wrote (or stole) something about an aircraft appearing 'in the clear skies over Hiroshima.' But were the skies really clear? I'm no historian or meteorologist so in the interests of historical authenticity I consulted Principal Kobayashi's set of encyclopaedia. She brought it in for our students, *The International Junior Encyclopaedia*, a 'reliable source of information for children and students of the English language'.

I couldn't locate the information I wanted. There seemed to be no entry referring directly to Hiroshima. There was no allusion to Hiroshima in the sections on ATOMIC ENERGY and no section at all on NUCLEAR POWER and its development. The passages discussing Japanese history did mention the bombing but didn't provide the precise chronology I'd hoped to find. It was mystifying. When I was a child my father told me *Everything there is to know you can find in the encyclopaedia*. But something was missing from this one. An event had virtually disappeared, been neatly uncoupled from the absolutes of time and space – set adrift. As if it were being consigned to the orbits of pure abstraction, myth or dream, flickering beliefs held once in a remote past better forgotten.

By whom? It was plain the episode would be hard to realize, for me at least; I wasn't there.

I noticed in passing there was no entry dealing with the

Rosenbergs – a reflection perhaps of the editors' conviction that the Rosenbergs, like Hiroshima, had already been dealt with effectively enough.

I turned finally to the expansive section on World War II. Leafing through it I scanned in a few moments the careers of miscellaneous empires, democracies, regimes and reichs. Then the pages began to stick. It seemed some kind of drink had been spilled over the bottom portions of the book and the stained paper was stuck together. Pages ripped and shredded as I tried to part them.

Some student had been here before me. A faint sweet odour rose from the torn pages and with it the sense of another presence, a child beside me on the couch, invisible, peering over my shoulder. I turned towards the metallic glitter of the tin can he held, and holds, a canister of cherry pop or Coca-Cola that suddenly explodes and spatters the classroom with its corroding fluid, shatters the glass of the bookcase as the encyclopaedia, illegible anyway at the key points, drops from my hands to the floor.

The children begin to pass the small grey dog round the table, faster and faster – like a hot potato! It yelps and bats at the air with its paws.

Stop at once, my grandmother cries, you'll hurt the poor animal.

She smiles.

But you've already had seconds, James. Is everyone else finished his cake? Who'd like a little soda?

On the eastern edge of the city Shoji Kobayashi emerged from his corrugated-iron and plywood hut with a lilting, almost martial scream. He had smacked his forehead, as he had done nearly every day for the last seven years, on the rough lintel above the door. His wife's customary laughter pursued him from inside the shed. Out through the door and into the cool, windless air where an odour of chives and lilacs hung. Early morning. The fragrant little field was bounded on all sides by streets and tenements, entire city blocks, though Shoji Kobayashi could recall a time when that had not been so.

Picking a rake from a set of tools by the door he started slowly for the west side of the field where the rows of earth were being rested, raked in long lines like gravel in the Kyōto rock garden he had gone to once as a boy. He had walked halfway across his field – a matter of a few steps – when he first noticed a faint whining sound, vaguely annoying like mosquitoes over the *futon* at night, finally insignificant, not the droning low-pitched roar of massed bombers in formation. Shoji Kobayashi looked up and saw an airplane high above him in the clear skies over Hiroshima. Momentarily he was transfixed by the craft's gorgeous silver gleam in the fathomless blue of the sky. And it occurred to him that the airplane resembled a small fish he had seen briefly in that Kyōto garden he had gone to as a boy – a beautiful silver carp that darted under a bridge in a dark pool. Now, as he watched, a smaller silver gleam, like the lone spawn of that faintly remembered vision – a fish vanishing into the shadows under a bridge – floated slowly down from the aircraft.

It was just then that he heard his wife's voice calling him. Ah then, the tea was ready so soon. Well, the gardening would have to wait. He turned and started back through rows of chives toward the hut.

My grandmother collected paper plates and cups and excused the children. *There is no excuse for you, John*, one of his friends teased my father, who laughed along with the others at this familiar jibe. Suddenly one of the older boys, Arnie, broke from the group and began to chase the small grey dog round the yard. Come on, he shouted, let's corner it. But the other boys ignored him. The dog leapt a low hedge and disappeared, its frantic yelps soon fading away.

For a few seconds the boys stood silently, restlessly uncommitted. It was one of those childhood times when the boundless freedoms of summer become ponderous and exhausting, the contours of reality take on an atomic complexity and one nears an explosive insight: there is a vacuum at the core of things, a flattened yard full of hours and silence where no one plays any games at all. But you're only a child, so the explosion that would hurl you and your world ready-or-not into adulthood never quite occurs. So that something always happens to distract you, just then.

It was my grandfather who came out of the house and asked the boys what they wanted to do. He was a great organizer, my grandfather, a vigorous deliberate man, a sergeant decorated twice in what he always referred to as the War to End All Wars. But for a moment no one answered him. Then came a spree of proposals which soon petered out into boyish bickering. Three or four of the boys wanted to play football but the others argued it was too hot. And it *was* very hot, the sun punched down through gaps in the maple leaves and focused on the small group in the middle of the yard. *War*, cried Nick, and all the boys shouted their approval; but no one would agree to be a Jap or a Hun so the idea had to be dropped.

Someone suggested tag but everyone knew that was a girls' game.

It was too early in the year for street hockey.

Baseball? It was up to my father to choose, he was the birthday boy. He was also a very good fielder so he opted for baseball and the boys hurried into the cellar to find gloves and bats and a ball, then ran off together toward the park. It turned into a race and my father sped into the lead, baseball bats and all, and, I'm sure of it, led the others by half a field by the time he reached the diamond.

This time it's my boss looking over my shoulder. She's just arrived. She can see I'm not preparing for my next lesson but what I actually am doing she can't be sure, my handwriting's almost illegible. Which is just as well; she's hinted her family suffered pretty badly in the war.

Now she walks away from me and toward the unshattered bookcase – which she opens. I'm afraid she'll find the volume I damaged, we damaged, a man and a boy far removed in space and time, joined through an act of historical desecration. An historical act? Kobayashi-san returns with a beginner's guide to English grammar. Really I shouldn't have worried, she doesn't consult her reference library any more than our students do. For young Jews and Germans, History is alive, an organic, groping thing, tentacled and inescapable. For Japanese youth it is largely forgotten – a fabulous nightmare from which their parents shook themselves awake. Now the waking hours are filled with robust, progressive industry. Economic success as a wholesome amnesia. Kobayashi-san's school is so very successful she has, she says, no time for music or television or books, no time at all – though she does take in the occasional ball game. I can appreciate that; the busyness, I mean, the forgetting. Once I said to her, 'Those who forget the past are condemned to repeat it, sure, but those who dwell on and in it make it present again for the rest of us. Make a present of it to the rest of us.' Something like that.

Kobayashi-san, do you know what hour of the day they dropped the bomb on Hiroshima?

Of course I didn't ask her that.

Some facts to consider.

The people of Hiroshima – indeed, the Japanese High Command itself – did not believe we ('the enemy') would bomb Hiroshima. It was after all a small relatively unimportant provincial city. Volume eight of the *International Junior*

Encyclopaedia, under the heading MODERN JAPANESE HISTORY, mentions it was 'a military base', but concedes that 'such installations as existed were of no real strategic importance'. Moreover Hiroshima was, along with Nagasaki, one of the main Christian centres of Japan; if the allies had so far spared the nation's cultural capital, Kyōto, they were not likely to attack one of the focuses of Christian faith in the country.

So when the single silver airplane appeared, a shard of glass or metal to some, to others a carp in a pond's dark water, to some a reconnaissance flight or the Second Coming or a lone seagull flying inland – no one rushed to the bomb shelters. Perhaps it was Sunday and members of the city's Catholic parish were flocking to an early service. In vacant lots and yards on the city's edge children raced and kicked cans and played baseball and soccer ...

And this: North Bay is a small economically unimportant city on the edge of southern Ontario. It was incorporated as a city in 1925 and a recent census puts its population at 56,001 – a curious roadside figure that often makes children in passing cars exclaim *Who is the one? I wonder who the one is.*

Dad can't answer that.

At one time travellers had to pass through an imposing archway billing the city the GATEWAY TO THE NORTH, but in the year of my grandfather's death the highway was changed and now runs between a mounted jet bomber, and, aimed straight for the heart of town, scratched and swarmed on by local children, a Bomarc missile. Summer brings tourists, but not in the numbers the lakes to the south attract. There are many unemployed. The scenery is beautiful. At one time the city was a junction point for various railroads, a centre for freight and east–west passenger traffic, but since the war its importance as a rail port has declined.

It would be piquant if, as a kind of 'sister-city' to Hiroshima, or Nagasaki, North Bay were the Zen Buddhist axis of North America; but of course it is not. The place is important to me because my father grew up there and my uncle, one spring day when the ice had just gone off the lakes, was drowned there, and my grandmother and grandfather grew old there and passed away ... Yet North Bay is important to others as well. Under the shrugging wooded shoulder of Airport Hill are concealed various military installations 'vital to the security of Canada, the U.S.A. and their allies.' So that North Bay, a small economically unimportant city of 56,001 souls, is most certainly a coloured light glowing on the maps of our fanged and drooling enemies. Subject to the flick of a switch, the quick pressing of a crimson button. Contingent. The histories I invent for my father retroactively erased, no silver sliver appearing in the sky but a nightmare whistling, a flash and fiery tail then flat silence, the lakes roiling, giving up their dead, the hills levelled and green leaves smouldering on the earth like postcard autumn.

But surely this rhetorical flight is no more sentimental than the notion that the enemy (us again) would not bomb churches? Surely. I spin round to the rippling toll of the telephone ringing. Do not ask for whom. The boss answers.

Kobayashi-san: Satomi Tatsuya wants to cancel his lesson. He is – *anō* – *byōki*, sick, *chotto*. Just a little. We'll close the office, *neh*? Here I hold tickets to a baseball game. *Ikitakunai?*

Ah, Gakk'cho-san, dōmo arigatō .

In the third inning, or maybe the fourth, my father made a diving catch that left the other boys gasping. James, the biggest kid in the neighbourhood, had driven an easy pitch deep into right field. The crack of bat on ball was unnaturally piercing. The defeated pitcher, Arnie, dropped to his knees on the mound and covered his ears.

The other boys stood shocked. They punched their mitts with their fists or scratched themselves idly, gazing into the sky where the ball described a stunning trajectory and at its zenith became as faint as a satellite or the first star that appears at dusk.

It seemed to hover above the fielders, as motionless as they. Except my father. He was sprinting for the back fence with such rash determination that everyone in the park now turned to watch. James, a heavy boy, was sluggishly rounding third base and still the ball was high above the distant running figure. James lumbered over home plate and plopped down in a dusty puffing heap. But no one cheered, no one watched him.

They were all watching my father.

So James followed their eyes into the dazzling light over the outfield where his impossible hit was finally nearing earth, slowly, like a red sun setting, and seeing another body moving to intercept it at the same apparent speed he realized their conjunction was inevitable. My father's tiny form was seen to vault up over the fence and twist in midair backward like an Olympic jumper of thirty years later, then to vanish like a blip on a radar screen, dropping; and the ball also vanishing.

Everyone heard the far-off yet distinct sharp leathery smack, so satisfying and unmistakable. James loosed a torrent of oaths. My father appeared at the fence with a gloved hand raised high above his cap in salute, a small white figure shimmering mythically in heat waves off the brilliant fields.

Baseball was played in Japan as early as the 1890's, but it was not until after the war when the American army of occupation began to challenge the local teams and introduce new techniques that baseball achieved the popularity it now enjoys. By 1948 there were amateur leagues all over the country! In 1963, less than a century after the game's adoption, a Japanese all-star team defeated the New York Yankees 6-4 *in a game played in New York City! Believe it or not!*

(From Ridley's *Believe It or Not*, Mainichi *Daily News*, Ōsaka, July 8, 1987)

...needless to say baseball is now our nation's most popular sport. There is even a group lobbying to have the colours of our world-famous flag reversed so it would feature a white sphere – a baseball – superimposed on a blood-red background.

Thanks for that trivia tidbit, Ono-san. There's a good crowd here today in Ōsaka stadium, I'd say, oh, at least eighty thousand, the real figures often differ from the official. At any rate today's game features the slumping Hanshin Tigers and the Hiroshima Carp, who are unbeaten in their last five starts. Now you'll recall the last time these two teams met, the decision was in favour of the Tigers to the tune of 9–3 so you can bet today this red-hot Hiroshima squad will be out to even the slate.

Down to you, Ono-san.

Thanks, Asami-san. And here's some more statistical trivia that might be of interest to our viewers ...

It's an easy sport for a foreigner to watch, the afternoon races by. Most of the terminology is taken directly from American English. Out, run, strike, error, there's been no effort to trans-late. The lettering on the jerseys is *romaji*, roman, a break from the constant *kanji* and *hiragana* and *katakana*. Why, even some of the players are Westerners, big hairy tobacco-stained types dis-carded by the A.L. but still able to hit home runs with the slightly smaller Japanese ball. In fact the only thing that doesn't ring 'true' is the name of the Hiroshima team; while most clubs have chosen typical Western names – Braves, Tigers, Lions – or some suitably fierce Oriental variation (the Dragons come first to mind) *Carp* seems a comical misnomer, the invocation of a scaly and placid mascot that would doom any North American franchise to rapid insolvency.

The Hiroshima Carp.

'Steven-san, that Hiroshima *gaijin* always hits home runs.'

'Sure. But the game's almost over and the count's against him this time.'

The count is in fact one and two. And the score after eight hard-fought innings is Tigers 3 Carp nil. But the bearded colossal import hunches over the plate, slugging humid air with practice swings and scuffing the dust with one cleated foot like a bull about to charge. Casey. It's a classic scenario, bases loaded and the last batter needing a home run to win his team the game. The crowd is standing, tense and hushed. A couple of wide pitches and the announcer cries *full count*. Kobayashi-san is silently tapping her knee with one hand and with the other hand clutching her programme. The slim, very agile pitcher winds up and fires a fastball so powerful he recoils and topples off the mound on release, crashes to the diamond, disappears in a cloud of startled, rapidly rising dust ...

... and it's a hitter's pitch, much slower than expected, seeming almost to float over the plate. Flushed and bulging, James is seen to smirk slightly then grimace as he hauls his Louisville Slugger through a whistling arc. This time there will be no mistake. The wood and punished ball connect at the optimal spot and the report is like a gunshot, artillery pieces firing a barrage, a stadium audience clapping once in perfect time after the anthem. O say. At once they all lose sight of the ball. The sky is brighter than a thousand suns, the colour of pure radium, blinding. The outfielders see nothing in the dazzling blue but light. Motionless in the hot field they stare upward and shield their eyes, helpless, antiquated like foot soldiers under a formation of fighter jets.

Shuffling round second base James aims a triumphant leer at my father, who slouches in the sun helpless and obsolete as the others. At home plate he is mobbed by a cheering circle of teammates. The game is won. The ball, it seems, has disappeared forever, atomized by the boy's fabulous strength.

Then my father is seen pointing up into the air.

Edging slowly backwards he shouts and with his raised glove indicates something the others seem not to see, something in the sky, *Look at it gleaming* he shouts, *Look at it, there, it's starting to drop it's coming down, oh look can't you see it, see —*

10

How Beautiful upon the Mountains

TŌKYŌ : From now on, Japanese who are too busy or live too far from family grave sites can pay to have professionals visit and clean the graves and burn incense in their place. The new service, provided by Clean Cemetery Co., has been in high demand since it became available last month. [From THE JAPAN TIMES, December 10, 1987]

NORTH BAY, 1985:

After the funeral my father said to me, 'As long as she was alive I felt my home was here.'

My grandmother is buried on a bleak escarpment near the airport on the edge of the city. The day after the funeral I drove out again with my brother and sister, and afterwards, drinking coffee in her favourite restaurant, we found we'd all felt the same thing while standing above her grave: hunched together in the icy air we'd wanted to gather her in, to retrieve her from the frozen turf and hold her, take her somewhere warm. But none of us had spoken. In the restaurant my sister wondered aloud if we'd feel different about things in summer, when the wind would be mild, the graves green and the headstones festooned with wreaths and fresh flowers – but we all live a long way from North Bay now, and none of us went up the next summer, or the summer after that.

My sister's fingers flitted over the arborite as if hunting for the cigarettes she'd given up years ago. She asked us if we thought we'd be able to go up in the summer.

'I should be able to find time,' I told her. 'Dean?'

'It's a long drive from Detroit,' he said. 'It's a long way from anywhere.'

My sister cupped her palms around her coffee mug and shivered. 'I don't like to think of her never having visitors. You saw those graves behind her? Nobody's been out to them in years.'

'You'll miss the lake, Dean,' I said.

'In Detroit we got the river.' He tried to grin. His eyes had a raw, invaded look – it wasn't long since he'd set his childhood behind him, the fledgling of the clan; he thought he'd escaped us, and that part of himself we would always keep alive. Now these reminders, this baring of a nostalgia he should have been too tough for.

He blinked down at his coffee. His eyes, as relatives had been telling him for years, were his grandmother's.

'Anyway,' I said, 'I should be able to find time. Maybe I'll fly up with Dad – he still comes up now and then.'

'Maybe I'll come with you,' my sister said.

We must have imagined our grandmother was eavesdropping, or that Carla, the waitress who'd always served her, would tell her everything we'd said the next time she came in. Because we all live a long way from North Bay now and it's not easy to go up for a weekend. Not the next summer, or the summer after that.

On a sunny morning in October 1947 the principal of my father's school marched into a classroom accompanied by an officer from the mountain airbase. The principal instructed all boys to rise and stand at attention. The officer, his chest gleaming with badges and winged decorations, saluted the principal then turned to the boys and told them to follow on the double; he cracked his black boot-heels on the tiles and swaggered from the room. Frowning, the principal levelled a long arm toward the door and urged the boys to hurry. At first they had to run to catch up with the long-striding airman.

The boys filed down the main hall of the school through a gauntlet of ravenous eyes – their younger schoolmates, gathered at the classroom doors, envious, applauding, or else leering and full of taunts, depending on the rumours that had hatched among them. My father heard them speculating as he passed by.

They get the day off to go visit the airbase.

Lucky buggers. Must of done something to help during the war.

Yeah, like what? Collecting garbage? Cleaning toilets?

I say Herman Weiner's a Nazi spy after all. And the others must of helped him.

They're all gonna be taken out and shot.

The boys were trooped single-file into a camouflaged bus past a hawk-nosed driver who started the engine and steered them from the parking lot before they were properly seated. The officer from the airbase rose and stood at the head of the aisle. Smoothing his moustache and sweeping the cap from his bald head he called for silence and began to brief the excited boys. At 0400 hours this morning, while the city slept, an RCAF Hurricane fighter on a training mission had for no apparent reason crashed into hills behind the airbase, killing the pilot on impact. The boys had been granted a brief discharge from their scholastic duties (here the officer paused momentarily, as if for a smile he could not quite execute) – a brief *reprieve* so they might help the Air Force gather evidence pertaining to this strange accident. The boys would be required to search a densely wooded mountainous sector for pieces of the aircraft. No souvenirs, it went without saying, were to be looted from the site.

The speeding bus hummed and crackled like a wireless with the boys' excitement, but James Merritt, the biggest boy of all, urged them to be wary.

The sector's densely wooded, he winked. *We'll have to look out for Kraut snipers.*

The other boys smirked and giggled or shaped their hands into Lugers and fired them out the window at make-believe foes. But Herman Weiner's smile was forced.

It's the Japs I'd watch for, he said. *The Japs and the land-mines. Blow your balls off.*

James Merritt leered at the other boys, then glared at Herman. *We all know there's no Japs around here,* he said. *But even one Kraut's too many as far as I'm concerned.*

Before the boys could join James in laughing, my father interrupted and told them he'd seen some Japs the year before while driving in the hearse with his cousin Hal, the undertaker. My father liked to remind the boys about his cousin as often as possible, and for their part they seemed to respect and even fear this connection, as if Death were the boy's personal acquaintance or a not-so-distant relative who might be expected to guarantee the safe conduct of his kin. And since North Bay was smaller then, and the hearse had to moonlight as a back-up ambulance, my father held another enviable and exotic post: second cousin to the city's spare ambulance driver.

The day he saw the Japanese, my father was driving up the mountain with his cousin to pick up an air cadet hurt in a brawl with a veteran pilot. *An odd one, that pilot,* his cousin said. *Hear he's always getting into trouble. The war, I guess …*

What do you mean? My father wanted to hear more of what had happened to the pilot, but his cousin couldn't tell him very much. There were rumours about bad experiences in combat, how his fighter squadron had flown on costly raids with the bombers over Dresden and Cologne before being transferred to the Pacific in the last months of the war. But no one knew the details. *Maybe he flew with the* Enola Gay, my father said – but cousin Hal told him the *Enola Gay* had carried out its mission alone.

At a level crossing he and Hal passed a party of Japanese workers standing by the road, resting chins and folded hands on the grips of their spades, smoking cigarettes with languid, half-closed eyes. *Japs*, his cousin told him. My father still recalls how they looked at him through the hearse window with dull apathetic faces, like men watching the funeral procession of a stranger. They were perfectly still, as in a group photo. Suddenly one of them, much younger – a boy no bigger than my father – grinned at the hearse, a cigarette drooping from his lower lip as he smiled; and before he could stop himself my father smiled back, the reaction as automatic as returning an enemy's fire.

Those were the first foreigners he had ever seen.

But they're not even foreigners, he told the boys in the bus. *Not really. My cousin said. They're fishermen from* B.C. *and they were born there and brought East for logging and to work on the railroad.*

Once a Jap, always a Jap, Herman Weiner said – and in spite of himself James Merritt had to agree.

The bus laboured up an incline then began to pick up speed as it pitched breakneck into a valley. The driver geared down and the engine roared but the bus continued to accelerate, the chassis rattling and wind hissing through hidden flaws in the metal and it was just like flying, all the boys agreed. None of them had ever flown. The bus shuddered to a stop at the base of another hill and the officer from the airbase leapt up and ordered the boys to follow him out.

The year I turned eleven my father took a course and learned to fly – small planes, Mooneys, Cessnas and Pipers, Beechcraft Musketeers. He bought into a second-hand Musketeer with seven others so that every two months, technically, the plane was his for a week. But he only had time for it on weekends. And one weekend it came my turn to go up with him.

We were planning to fly to North Bay – my grandmother's

heart problems had started earlier that year, and besides seeing her my father wanted to drop in on his cousin Hal and a few old friends. He'd charted a course that would take us north-northwest over Nottawasaga Bay and Christian Island then due north over the Magnetawan to the French River and northeast over Lake Nipissing to the city.

I grinned and wriggled in my seat as the engine caught and the propeller melted into air. I was to see this stunt per-formed again in the future, but the sorcery of that vortex where steel became sky, where things invisible could kill you and cut you to pieces or haul you birdlike through the heavens – for me that magic never disappeared. I pored over our map. I'd been appointed navigator and now tracing the flight path my father had drawn and savouring the exotic syllables of Iroquois names I felt important, much older, involved at last in the distant, bil-lowing adventure of adult lives.

And it was just us – for the whole weekend I would have him to myself, my father, the guardian who now depended on my navigation, my co-pilot.

I had never flown before and at first it was even better than I'd imagined. The Musketeer seemed to bolt over the runway like a racing car along a dragstrip, there was a bellying sense of lift then a sudden weightlessness as we took flight; I held my breath and waited for schoolbook laws to strike us down. The wind-shield was a planetarium of open space and in the midday light the full moon hovered like a destination. Gravity tackled me to my seat as our engine fought the thinning air. And all the time my father seemed calm, unaroused, his features as still and impar-tial as the dashboard's face of glowing dials and gauges; it took me years to see that he would always compose himself, as he did until the end of the funeral, whenever he knew I was watching.

The city, our home, had fallen away beneath us so that all I could see was a flashing cinematic backdrop of densely ranked towers so unlike the common, squalid concrete boroughs we passed through on our drive to the island airport. This was another city altogether, a fabulous and magical sprawl, like New York, where my father had gone to work for a year, like Cologne or Bombay orŌsaka. Beyond the receding skyscrapers Lake Ontario sparkled like a tropical gulf and already Lake Simcoe was visible ahead, sleek with sunshine, shot through with highlights of coral, indigo and amber.

I had never flown before and now I saw that the earth showed a different face to all creatures of the air – to birds, to angels, to gods and pilots. It was the face of a foreigner, and I could not take my eyes off it.

'You like the view, son?' My father glanced down at me. 'You're looking a little green.'

And as I returned his gaze I felt the pain lift off: a headlong, swooping nausea that would hold an air-show in my belly for the next half-hour till we turned back and made an emergency landing in Buttonville. In the future it would make all flight an agony, and at one point impossible, so I would learn that even the most innocent of escapes had its price – and that ecstasy is soon followed by nausea.

'Not in the cockpit!' my father cried, as the stunt-plane inside me executed another impossible loop.

How beautiful upon the mountains, Uncle Hal declaimed in his resonant, responsible mortician's voice, *How beautiful upon the mountains are the feet of him who bringeth glad tidings, who publisheth peace ...*

My mother leaned against me in the pews and whispered, 'This sounds a little cheerful for a time like this. Didn't we hear it last month? The Christmas service – you and your sister home –'

I shrugged, trying to hear the rest of the words. *Who bringeth glad tidings, who publisheth peace.* 'It's fine,' I whispered. 'Really. Maybe she requested it.'

For eye to eye they see the return home of the Lord God to Zion.
'I think this is a Christmas reading,' someone behind us said.

And so it turned out. Uncle Hal had confidently recited the wrong passage from the Book of Isaiah. After the funeral my grandmother's only surviving friend was furious, but I heard my father say to my mother *I'll have to add something to my will about that. Have them read the same thing for me, will you?* And my mother, who had been so stolid until then, embraced him and hid her face against his shoulder.

After the funeral my father said to me, 'As long as she was alive I felt my home was here. Where my mother was.'

Whenever a blast of wind hit the building we felt its frame shiver, as if an earthquake or a bomb were levelling some distant place; with each gust a slight draft drifted in from the walls. The reception was almost over. It was getting dark beyond the windows but there was still enough light to see my sister's children making angels in the snow.

Wing Commander Morris Kimmett stood stiff as a flagpole beside the camouflaged bus and drafted the boys into six companies of five men each. Each 'man' was then issued a camouflaged burlap tote-bag. One member of each company was appointed leader and assigned a small whistle of military issue and a topographical map. The latter was merely a precaution, Kimmett advised them, as the area to be searched was fairly small and had been cordoned off at 0800 hours by Air Force personnel using fine-drawn phosphorescent night-wire.

Wing Commander Kimmett led the boys through a gap in the wire and instructed them to spread out and begin their search. They were to meet at the crash site – a scorched hollow at the heart of the sector – at 1200 hours – or exactly one and one half hours from the present.

James Merritt had been appointed squad leader and it took no more than five minutes for Power to corrupt him absolutely. When Herman Weiner refused to hand over a charred scrap of metal he'd just found, James used his wobbling bulk to bodycheck the smaller boy into a birch tree. Herman sat crumpled against the trunk, trying not to cry.

Goddamn Kraut, James said, subduing a smile. *I order you to stand. On the double. Stand and salute me! I'm your commanding officer!*

As Herman faltered to his feet the boys were distracted by a sharp cry; apparently someone in another squad had made an exciting find. Scowling, James huffed a shrill blast from his whistle and ordered everyone to fan out.

And don't come back, he chided them, *till you got something to show.*

My father soon lost contact with the others. He wandered uphill through a pine grove, scanning the forest floor for things unusual. Suddenly there was a beating of wings above his head and as he glanced up, afraid, he glimpsed through the boughs a low-flying arrowhead of geese, like the great B-29 formations he had seen in the newsreels. He was relieved. This flock would be the last of the season, he thought, to go south.

Looking down again his heart leapt when a ray of sunlight set off a small metallic object on the ground – a bottle cap. And for a moment he thought a piece of the bottle, lying nearly, was a chip from the plane's shattered windshield. Then he saw something protruding at eye level from the trunk of a pine: a small sharp sliver of iron, like the bit of shrapnel that had wounded his father in the Great War and was now mounted at home in a trophy case under a parade of chevrons, pins and decorations.

My father tried to pry the scrap from the tree but it was too deeply embedded. He decided to walk in the direction it was flying when it hit the trunk. This was shrewd, he thought, and his cunning and stealth as he crept forward without a sound made him feel like a crack commando. Squeezing between two large pines he entered a thick bramble of raspberry bushes speckled with fruit the birds had missed – berries gone black, withered and hard, like tiny globs of congealed blood. He could not advance, so he knelt and peered under the bushes. And from the far side of the bramble two eyes peered back.

Later he wondered if the scream he heard then actually was his own, though the other boys swore it came from elsewhere in the forest, and for better reason. Yet no one ever owned up. My father recalls opening his startled mouth on a dry, mechanical throttling, and then a terrible shriek coming from somewhere to fill it.

Hurtling back through the forest a few seconds later he almost crashed into Herman Weiner. Herman's eyes widened when he saw my father's face. *Hey,* he said, *that wasn't you screaming a minute ago, was it? You don't look too good.*

Let's get out of here, my father said.

No, come to think of it the scream came from over there. But something *must have happened to you.*

Herman –

So what did you see? Geez, you look awful. Did you find the pilot's head or something?

Something, my father said. And he thought again of the eyes he'd seen, almost human, fierce yet leery like human eyes, narrowed to anonymity, aglow with an alien, hypnotic light. They'd seemed hungry yet patient at the same time, like the eyes of a predator crouched in ambush – as if they'd been waiting since the day he was born for him to enter the forest and kneel down and peer under the bramble. And he'd thought he knew every animal that lived in the region.

They heard James Merritt's irascible whistling and found him and the others in an open space, squatting in warm sunshine on an outcrop of granite. James was surveying his map with a concise, critical expression. *I know exactly where we are*, he announced, looking up from the map and strafing the surrounding brush with his eyes. Then he saw the approaching stragglers, shuffling quickly like troops in retreat, burlap sacks slung over their shoulders like homeless men.

Weiner and John, report! What have you got to show?

My father, still shaken, had nothing to show, but Herman had found a small singed piece of fuselage with writing on it. The boys knelt around the scrap but could make out only a few words, apparently painted on in a shaky, unofficial hand: MERCURY III — FROM HERE TO

— the rest had been melted and blurred by the furious heat of the explosion. It looked like scribbles in an alien alphabet, the scrabbling of small birds in the dirt.

So he called his plane 'Mercury', one of the boys whispered.

That scream, Herman Weiner said, emboldened by the success of his find, *what was it all about?*

One of the boys raised a finger to explain but James cut him short. *Just rumours*, he sniffed. *We can't pay attention to rumours.*

A hand! cried another boy before James could stop him. *Someone in another group found a hand in a glove!*

And that's not all, another boy said.

From somewhere farther up the slope Wing Commander Kimmett's whistle, with its characteristically lower pitch, began to shrill. So they were to reassemble already. James ordered the boys to fall in and look smart and keep an eye out for more scraps, and as they trudged through the forest toward the whistle's repeating shriek they found more and more pieces scattered among the pine cones and stuck in the trees and they dropped them like Hallowe'en candies into their clinking sacks. They could see they were drawing closer to the source of the fragments. Now the birch trees they passed were streaked with brown swathes and in the crotch of an aspen whose bark had bubbled on one side from the heat they found a tiny nest, empty save for feathers and a few particles of shell. The nest was utterly charred and fell to pieces at my father's touch.

It's like a puzzle, Herman Weiner said, bending over to pick up another metal scrap. *When they have all the pieces they can put the plane back together and they'll know why it crashed.*

I think my father must have wondered then whether the assembled scraps could tell them everything, as Herman Weiner and Wing Commander Kimmett seemed to think. At any rate, I wonder. These days the mountains are pocked with the relics of fallen shuttles and jetliners and because the pilot is always first to go we never hear the full story. The jungle digests faulty wiring, rotten struts. Flight recorders plunge into the depths off Okinawa or settle, like small steel coffins, into unmarked desert graves.

Wing Commander Kimmett stood at attention in the heart of a sizeable crater and beckoned the boys in from the forest. My father had thought there would be plenty of wreckage in the crater but there was almost none, and it was rumoured variously that helicopters had lifted out the bigger chunks that morning, that foreign agents had spirited them away before dawn, or that the heat of the blast, like an atomic explosion, had instantly vaporized everything.

But most of the rumours at large that moment and in the following weeks concerned *the hand in the glove*. Drawing shallow breaths, his thin cheeks plausibly pale, little Dawson Parker swore he'd found it by a rock – a black scorched crumpled thing, like a fallen crow. No one else had seen it, but his squadmates backed him up, and though at first no one believed them when they explained how Kimmett had promptly confiscated the hand, the boys found it useful in time to abandon their incredulity and recount the tale to all who would listen, so that now if you go to North Bay, anyone over a certain age will tell you with conviction about the Hand in the Glove.

(At the time it was also rumoured that something had been found in the hand – a photograph, some said of a child, others thought of a parent or else a woman, *a foreign woman* – but back then North Bay was a sober, sensible community, and while the Hand survived by virtue of its solid fleshly weight, the other rumours soon went the way of all romance.)

As he collected the tote-bags Wing Commander Kimmett asked the squad leaders if they had seen during their searches anything worthy of report. James Merritt shook his head No, but Herman Weiner cried out *John did! John saw something scared the living daylights out of him!*

Dawson Parker blushed. His squad leader, Arnie Lukits, sneered from across the crater. What could beat a real live hand? *Shut up, Weimar*, he called. *Go back to Deutschland.* So that Herman Weiner, giggling nervously, had to turn it all into a joke.

You should of seen his face, he snickered, contorting his own features grotesquely. *Said it was a Jap hiding in the jungle who hadn't surrendered yet.* And almost everyone was ambushed by laughter then – even my father. Even James Merritt, demoted to childhood by a boyish grin, gave his Air Force whistle a festive toot.

Wing Commander Morris Kimmett surrendered them a smile.

After the funeral my father said to me, 'As long as she was alive I felt my home was here. Where my mother was. As long as your mother is alive, you know, you never really feel the place you're living is home. There's always somewhere else you can go to.'

How beautiful upon the mountains are the feet of him ...

I left my father with Uncle Hal and strolled through the reception hall to say goodbye to the last guests. Hal was trying to cheer my father up; he'd just poured him another Scotch and over my shoulder as I walked away I could hear him reviving memories of their rides in the ambulance/hearse when my father was a boy. Did he remember that time an Air Force Colonel from the States fainted on the runway and they'd raced up in the hearse to take him back to town and he'd come to just as those big black shiny doors swung open and they tried to stuff him inside? Hal's hoarse voice rises at the familiar climax, as if trying to include me too though I am walking away. 'And then – you remember? – he starts shouting, "For Christsake not yet, you bastards! For Godsake not yet!" '

I'm wondering if this old standby is really appropriate when along with Hal's studied chuckling there comes a strange unexpected burst of familiar laughter. My father. I can hear how he tries to suppress it and I'm relieved when he fails. 'For Christsake, you – you *bastards!*' I hear him reciting the words as both men laugh harder and harder, hysterical now and uncontrolled, a series of gentle explosions, the whisky and a shared past ablaze inside them. *'For Godsake,'* I hear, *'not yet!'*

I embrace my sister, my brother – both drunk. 'Sad place to end up,' my brother mumbles, looking away, betrayed again by his grandmother's eyes.

'You used to love it here, Dean.'

The walls and floor shake slightly as jets from the base pass overhead. My brother-in-law and my mother are silhouetted against the window, smoking, watching the children play by the road. The snow outside now seems the only source of light: the sky is almost dark, and it's getting difficult to see inside the hall. Someone should turn a lamp on but nobody will – the dimness in here, the last light of this funereal day, is all that still connects us with the absent woman. If the lights come on we'll be able to see each other clearly, and her face will not be among us.

Now and then, even these days, my father plunges and awakes, shot from the clouds of a peaceful sleep by those marksmanlike eyes, tumbling to earth like an exploded shuttle. The dream never varies but he will not describe it, so we are forced to imagine how the eyes look; and even if he told them in detail, or if I did, you would see a different pair, another creature behind them.

More than ever you are haunted. You live in a centrifugal atmosphere, an age of airline passengers, scattered families, flight paths and far-off destinations ...

My grandmother's eyes were inlaid by the time of her death with the layered stone of an adamant, familiar landscape. Over time the slate blue of her eyes was seamed and subtly altered by the Shield's grey projections, the quicksilver tint of the sky, the quivering light-waves of the deep lake she swam in as a girl and sat watching as an old woman.

'A sad place to end up,' my brother mumbles, thinking of the long dismal winters and the bleak graveyard with its frozen ground – but the ground, however cold, was known to her, and would have recognized her in return. I think a parcel of clay behind a subdivision of Ft. Lauderdale condos would have been colder.

Where will my father end up? My mother? Or for that matter, me.

Ft. Lauderdale?

Mt Pleasant?

Ōsaka?

The loons and geese of Trout Lake fly south in the autumn but don't try to tell me they die there. They have to come home for that. Birds aren't stupid. They have principles. They understand the mechanics of flight.

But then who can really blame us for scattering? Dean wasn't the last of our family to light out for points west – Vancouver, Hawaii, Japan. The skies swarm with ultrasonic waves and satellites and international aircraft bringing rumours of the beautiful invasion, the exotic and now-accessible enemy who becomes a neighbour. How does anyone stay another night in a small town, a small city, a farmhouse on the prairies?

My grandmother never left North Bay, and took to the air only in death. My grandfather left only for the war, which must have been a kind of reprieve for him and his friends, an opportunity, as war has always been, for men to run away from women. And after that too-long, muddy, blood-spattered flight, he never felt an urge to leave home again.

What eyes he must have seen! The story goes that he entered an enemy trench and killed an officer with his bayonet, but it is not recorded whether he looked the dying man in the eyes, whatever colour they were, or what he saw in them if he did.

Home is wherever you're used to the eyes around you so that habit disarms their menacing heat. Home is somewhere below you on the dark plains – a dry nest, blazing.

The breast of a lover is home. A scar, a photograph.

Home is if your mother still lives, and where.

My father and I have discovered that two Gravol and a banana milkshake will settle my stomach enough that we can fly for several hours at a stretch. This is two years after the first flight and many more before the funeral; I've entered that brief and falsely promising phase before the onset of adolescence. Suddenly I'm old enough to wonder why people feel as they do about things, but not yet too self absorbed to care.

Over the gargling of the tiny engine I ask my father what first made him want to fly, and for a moment he seems unsure how to answer. When he finally does, he focuses straight ahead through the windshield as if we're on a crowded highway and he must watch for oncoming cars.

'I suppose it started with the search', he begins, 'for pieces of that crashed fighter. I told you all about that ...' He pauses for a moment and scans the instrument panel. 'But it wasn't the search itself – that just showed me how dangerous it is to fly – it was what we found out after.'

'What do you mean?' He hasn't spoken about this before. I turn to face him but he continues to stare straight ahead, his pale eyes in profile translucent, illegible.

'I told you about the pilot, didn't I?'

'Sure. He was going out with the sister of someone you knew. And he was weird, right?'

'Not weird. A little ... erratic. Very quiet, and sad. And aggressive when he drank, I heard. No one seemed to know where he was from. People said he'd had some bad experiences during the war, something about the bombing raids, but no one knew the exact details. I remember wondering at the time, you know, what was he doing up there, flying a fighter plane in the middle of the night? But then I guess I must have thought that was a regular part of his training.'

'He didn't crash the plane on an official flight?'

'Well, *he* seemed to think it was official. He left behind a complete flight plan. And he mapped out his route in detail.'

My father nods, widens his eyes, changes expression while he speaks as if addressing someone face to face, instead of the windshield and the sky beyond.

'So where was he going?' I say.

'No one really knows. No one had heard of any of the places on his itinerary, and he'd drawn his route on a map he'd made himself. But it wasn't of any real place – he'd made it all up. And the names were nonsense too – invented.' My father grins lazily and shakes his head as if wanting me to see it's not worth dwelling on, but I know by his evasive manner that the story intrigues him too, puzzles him, won't leave him alone. 'And so he went up at four in the morning and crashed a few minutes later into hills behind the airbase ... Look at that, son.'

Glancing down I'm caught off guard by our altitude, the

STEVEN HEIGHTON

sheer, sunlit fabric of space parachuting away from us, the dizzying tug of the ground; sometimes you wake for the briefest spell and remember that flight is miraculous, impossible.

'Do you see?' My father nods toward Niagara Falls, the American side just now coming into view. Directly below us the escarpment runs – sinuous and ragged, the shattered spine of a crashed jet.

'Beautiful, isn't it?'

'Did anyone ever say,' I ask, 'what the name of his destination was?'

My father casts me a quizzical look, then turns back to the windshield and the invisible steel of the propeller. 'Well I don't suppose anyone really thought much about the actual names. They were words he made up – maybe he'd been drinking, maybe he had a dream. Most people thought he was already half-crazy. I guess the names didn't mean much to anyone else.'

'And they never found anything when they put the plane back together? Couldn't something have gone wrong to make him crash?'

'I suppose it could have, yes. But the things we found didn't help them much. They decided he crashed because his instruments malfunctioned in the dark – but I don't know if they had any evidence or not. I don't suppose they would have had to tell us either way.'

My father banks the plane sharply so I can look straight down into the falls: a riveting spiral of fierce white, like a hurricane's eye on a weather map. I want to ask him again what it might have been that he saw that day in the forest but I know by the way he's controlling the plane – with brusque, manly, martial gestures, as if piloting a fighter jet instead of a Musketeer – that he's tired of talking and wants only to fly.

We descend steeply for a few moments and when we level off, Lake Ontario fills the windshield like a gulf or an ocean, dazzling, unpredictable and vast. Sometimes he flies lower than

156

he really should over our neighbourhood, almost buzzing the apartment blocks, a barnstormer, and for a moment I pick out our house and point down at it like a bombardier and tell him I can see my mother, and perhaps I really can – she's hanging laundry in the back yard or standing on the porch with her hands on her hips staring up at us, her face shorn of features by distance and the summer light, like an old photograph, fading. My brother and sister (is it really them?) are falling over themselves as they race our passing shadow up the sidewalk, waving yet running frantically as if we were something to escape. We call this 'strafing home'.

As we bank sharply to the east I begin to imagine that other flight, how it might have been. I've never stopped imagining. How would it feel to light out before dawn for a destination no one else would know – and everyone, perhaps, has imagined? In the chill dark of 4 a.m. you climb into your cockpit on the mountain. Your engine snarls and bites into the cold. To gust over the runway and feel the air sudden beneath you, a weightless irresistible wedge rearing up like a summit as you climb, the early wind and the sun and all that's familiar falling away as the prop cleaves crystals of ice and dim continents unroll beneath ... to fly eye to eye with the darkness, and see.

11

SLAUGHTERING DARKNESS: THREE TALES OF CHINA

We began, like all the others, with a vision ...

If this is what we have evolved toward,
I have to laugh
     – Gary Geddes, *The Terracotta Army*

Here is how it must have been.

When the villagers who were digging the well returned from lunch they found that soil in the bottom of the half-dug pit had settled, exposing a stony prominence, broad and grey and mottled, like the petrified egg of a dinosaur.

The first villager shuddered and refused to climb down into the pit. Clearly this was a skull, he said, and it would be better to dig in another spot. After all, what was a skull doing buried in the middle of nowhere? He turned from the pit and wagged his upturned palms at the empty fields stretching away toward the tomb under Mount Li. Long ago someone was murdered, he said, and buried here in secret. Or perhaps tales of the emperor Ch'in Shih Huang Ti were true, and hundreds of his retainers had been buried alive around his tomb. In which case, the first villager said, we must go elsewhere before we disturb more of them.

The second villager had been smirking throughout his friend's speech and now he laughed openly and leapt with his shovel into the pit. This is no skull, he grinned, poking at the speckled bulge with his foot. Anyone can see it's a piece of pottery. Get down here and give me a hand.

A third and fourth man clambered into the pit and began helping the first one scrape sand and soil from the mysterious object. Which did look like a skull, as the first villager had thought, or like a baby's bald head, crowning, squeezed into the waiting hands of a doctor. But it was neither of these. As the three villagers worked slowly and gingerly in the cool pit, first a forehead then a pair of eyes emerged from the soil; as if brushing clean the face of a grimy child, the second man knelt and gently dusted dirt from the open eyes of a clay statue.

The first villager squatted on the rim of the pit with his back turned to the others. He sucked fiercely on a cigarette and stared toward Mount Li, where even now the archaeologists from the capital would be busy with their excavations.

Clearly, he said, we have found another buried tomb. We must dig elsewhere.

Don't be a fool, the second man grunted from the pit, where he was prying steadily with a small hand spade around the figure's broadening shoulders. Don't you understand? We'll be as rich as kings.

The dead should be left alone, muttered the first man, crushing the stub of his cigarette into the earth.

We were told to dig here, the fourth man said.

Rivers of mercury, chanted the third man. *Jewelled coffins, ivory pillars and Tibetan gold* –

The dead have no use for such things, the second man reasoned. Keep digging.

A geyser of earth sprayed up from the pit like an underground explosion; the first man angrily brushed particles from his hair, his face. He turned on his haunches and glared down at the men in the pit, who were kneeling in a tight circle, their darkened faces peering up at him, hands scrabbling invisibly, like midwives or a team of surgeons on a battlefield.

It's bad luck, said the first man. What's buried should stay buried.

We have our instructions, the fourth man said.

I. Andrew gripped Sheila by the elbow as he led her into the crowded, dingy Kunming post office. She was only a few months pregnant but already he treated her with a kind of frenzied courtliness she seemed to find both charming and inane. The pregnancy was accidental, of course – everyone had warned them about conceiving while they were living and working abroad, especially as Sheila wanted to travel on their brief vacation to the more primitive parts of China. But the Tibetan frontier was closed because of unrest in Lhasa, and landslides had cut off another province she'd hoped to visit, so their travels were confined to safer and less exotic areas. Andrew was relieved. They were too old now, he laughed, to go rough it in a war-zone – yet even in quiet Kunming he was worried about Sheila's health and the child's. The food in a few places, savoury though it was, sometimes made them ill, and he couldn't help wondering what effect it would have on a developing constitution.

The post office was grimy and cramped and full of bitter fumes from coal fires burning in the street past the open windows. Under the low ceiling the sluggish air, marbled with cigarette smoke, was lit up by a stale, unwholesome light. Andrew held Sheila tightly and inched forward through the crowds: Chinese men and women in the listless blue and khaki uniforms of the provinces, tourists bloodying their fresh new outfits with sweat, gangling backpackers in tank-tops and army pants and flamboyantly-coloured tube-socks, all spilling against each other in dense, dissonant waves, like ripples in a cistern. Around chipped wooden tables others were sewing souvenirs into fine cotton shrouds and writing on the finished packages the names of their cities: London, Paris, Jerusalem, Oslo, Ottawa ...

The five queues leading to the tiny wickets wavered and jack-knifed like the long silken tails of a festival dragon. Old Chinese women butted and shoved their way toward the front of the lines. The heat was overpowering.

'Maybe we should forget the postcard,' Sheila said, putting her mouth next to Andrew's ear and almost shouting. 'Just call the embassy instead.'

'You know what that's like.'

'They might not even get this by the time we get back.'

'We'd better send it anyway. I told them I'd let them know when we were coming back.' And by way of complaint he reminded her he was expected to host a group of visiting pale-ontologists before his holiday ended and he went back into the office for the year.

Sheila frowned and nodded slowly, then let her head slump forward in apparent frustration: their holiday was too short, the country far too vast ... Andrew found himself glaring into the severe, startled eyes of a pale Chinese man who'd pushed up against them in the queue. There was a flash as something thin and metallic was jerked back into a baggy pocket. Andrew thrust out at the man with one hand. With the other he groped at Sheila's tote-bag. Over the clamour of the post office he heard a faint clatter of coins and small objects spilling onto the floor. He saw two frayed lips of fabric at the bottom of the bag.

'What is it – Andrew?'

'Your bag. *Damn –*'

The man broke Andrew's grip and charged between two frightened tourists in safari suits. Someone in the crowd behind them began to scream. Andrew lunged and managed to touch the man's back but he bulled his way onward, head and shoulders stooped like a boxer, toppling a shrunken old woman as he made for the exit. A Chinese soldier in the queue shoved him hard but he stayed on his feet and reached the door. Andrew heard Sheila shouting at him to turn back – *nothing's gone*, he thought he heard – but somehow he couldn't stop. He burst through the door a few steps behind the man, who began to accelerate like a practised sprinter. After a few steps Andrew saw he was beaten. He began to slow down. But as the thief glanced back to find if he was safe, a tall policeman appeared in the street in front of him and he was quickly tackled.

Andrew approached, breathing hard. He saw the thief's face again and now the severity was gone: the man cried and whimpered as he was hauled to his feet and roughly searched. He stared with glazed, defeated eyes at Andrew and the gathering crowd. The policeman barked out some kind of order.

A young woman, no doubt a student, stepped out of the crowd. 'The soldier tells me to say that this criminal has no money at all, so you do not have to worry. He says that all people who trouble foreign friends will be punished.' And as Andrew nodded thanks to the woman he saw something surge up and break the calm surface of her eyes – it was the anger he'd expected of the captured thief. She hated him, he saw that now, hated his clothes and his comfortable belly and his flushed, fulsome middle-aged face, and for a moment he could not blame her; years before, he had looked at older people in the same way. And now that he'd exchanged his sandals for polished patent-leather shoes it was this face – the face of committed, contemptuous youth – that unsettled him most.

He was flooded with remorse. The thief was being led away, penniless, consigned to some untouchable fate by a foreign bureaucrat's conscientious pursuit of Justice. But he'd been startled, he reminded himself, he had seen a knife, his wife was pregnant and he was under a lot of strain –

Objection overruled.

But would anyone else have acted otherwise?

Irrelevant. And inadmissible – for what could the thief have stolen from them anyway? Some loose change, a few pens and trinkets, and their undeveloped film of the stone forest and the buried army at Xi'an.

Sheila stood in front of him, shaking, cradling her small ruined tote-bag against her breasts like a baby. He wondered how much she had seen.

'We should go to the police station,' she said in a slow, deliberate monotone, as if hypnotized.

He nodded and let out his breath. 'I suppose you're right.'

'Really, I don't want to see – why did you have to go off like that? It's not like you. I was all alone in there, trying to pick things off the floor.'

He took a few steps forward and tried to embrace her. 'What things?'

'Nothing. The guidebook and some souvenirs. Our film's disappeared.'

The stone forest and the buried army. For an instant he saw them again – the huge, tapered stones like monoliths or the teeth of a prehistoric monster, the disciplined ranks of warriors filing into the earth.

'I suppose we should go to the police,' Andrew agreed. 'The new camera's all right?'

'It's fine.' Sheila's words were muffled, her face buried in his hair. 'But why did you have to chase him?'

'I'm sorry,' he mumbled, shaking his head. 'Sheila? Come on – if you're ready we can go right now.'

II. By early afternoon they had uncovered the shoulders of the hidden statue and cleared from its face the encrusted grit and soil that had masked it. The first man, still squatting on the edge of the pit, cast a quick superstitious glance at the figure: its clay face was life-sized and life-like, its thick moustache uncannily detailed, mouth set in a benevolent, almost amused expression. The lowered eyes were serenely contemplative. This was a patient, avuncular face – the face of a man with grown children who has come upon a faded, long-lost photograph of himself with his newborn son in his arms and is regarding it wistfully ... And yet there was something vaguely sinister about the figure's position in the sand, as if it were a criminal or a captive buried to the shoulders and left in the sun to perish.

The second man pointed a slippered foot at the statue's lowered eyes. For two thousand years, he declared with uncharacteristic sonority, this man has been meditating in the earth.

I don't think he was alone, the third villager said, turning from the corner of the pit with a spadeful of debris – the remains, apparently, of another figure, mingled with dust and small stones full of sea-fossils. Who knows, he added, how many statues we'll find!

The fourth man began to smile.

Perhaps this is the image of a priest, the second man continued, in a much louder voice. Perhaps – he turned on the fourth man. What are you grinning about, he demanded.

This statue, the man said, labouring to suppress a smile, reminds me of my Uncle Yang from Wuhan.

The second man shook his head paternally and frowned; his friend was not often so frivolous. Their discovery, he tried to explain, was a serious matter, and expert help would have to be called in; he asked the third man, who was visibly reluctant to leave the site, to go at once to the archaeologist's kiosk at Mount Li.

The first man, teased by the others and broiled by the midday sun, finally agreed to come down into the pit. You say he's a priest, he grunted, kicking at a bulge of earth till it dissolved and the metallic glint he had seen on its surface elongated into a rusty spearhead.

What would a priest, he said, have been doing with this?

They saw now that the figure's arm must bend under the surface to grip the spear.

Clearly he is a warrior, the second man pronounced. You

have to admit, though, that he looks like a priest, or like a scholar or sage – anyway like a man of peace.

I wish we'd never found him, the first man interrupted. It's a load of bad luck, if you ask me. We should just cover him up again.

Nonsense, the second man said, it's too late for that. Anyway, who knows what else is buried under here? We've done something of real importance today, we should all be proud of it.

It's bad luck, the first man repeated. He lit a cigarette and nodded at the silent warrior, then inhaled and gazed up at the meagre, brilliant circle of sky above the pit.

What's buried should stay buried, he said.

III. Late in the fifth month of her pregnancy Sheila went through a bad time. She woke exhausted every morning and could hardly eat. Beijing University gave her some time off and every day when I got back from the embassy I would sit beside her on the bed and we'd talk, or I would read to her from a book of Chinese tales I'd picked up at the foreign language shop on Wangfujing Street. At one point we thought of going home, but towards the end of the month she felt stronger and able to return to work and we decided to stay.

At night while she lay on her back, eyelids twitching, fingers clenched, I would ease down the blanket and examine her ripening belly. In the pale, lunar light filtering through the blinds it was smooth and rounded as an egg, or a mound of moonlit earth.

Sometimes my attention seemed to get on her nerves and one time she lost patience. You're smothering me, she said, I'm not an invalid. Get out and do something for a change, we won't be here much longer.

One Sunday while she slept I went to a restaurant we knew in the old part of town and met Chun Jian, a student at the People's University. He was one of those firm, frustrated linguists who stride resolutely toward a table of foreigners and seat themselves and demand permission to practise their English. When I saw him coming over I guessed his intentions. I had other things on my mind and at first I was a little cold with him, but I had a soft spot for students, like the ones Sheila taught, with their gallant, hapless efforts to master the languages of countries they might never see – so I listened to him, and after a while I began to speak.

'Do you plan,' I asked, 'to go overseas at some point in the future?'

'Abroad? Yes, I hope so. Yes, certainly, that is my dream.'

For all his initial boldness Chun Jian found it hard to look me in the eye and whenever I felt my own gaze was making him uneasy I looked away. Today the restaurant was full of students drinking beer, talking in low voices and smoking. It was drafty and cold. I thought of Kunming with its sunny tea-shops where the old folks would sit admiring songbirds in tall cages they took everywhere; Sheila had wanted to look for work there but I was used to the capital and my job and I talked her out of the change.

In unison Chun Jian and I offered each other cigarettes and burst out laughing.

I learned that Chun Jian's father was a major with a regiment in Tibet and that his mother had died soon after his birth, so he had never known her. He had an older sister, also at the university, but she was far more conservative than he was. I assured him my sympathies were with him. I mentioned the activism of my own youth but his interest and a sudden tide of nostalgia made me infuse it with far more immediacy than it deserved, and I realized later he probably thought I was speaking of things recent. He told me more about his own life and his convictions. His shy, evasive eyes grew lively and unguarded as he spoke and his words seemed to gather momentum; I had the distinct impression he'd never told a foreigner so much about himself before. Perhaps in English his life story seemed new to him, necessary, exotic and rich, the way a stranger's life would seem.

Listening to him I felt younger and less defined, as if the world was still waiting for me to make important choices. I was drunk with fraternity and virtue – like those times in Ottawa when I went out with jaded friends and by midnight the bars were too cramped and mean for our towering potential and we plunged invincibly into the streets and were suddenly dwarfed – sobered up – by the freezing weight of an arctic night. But this was different. We'd had nothing to drink but tea – and still I felt like a source of renewal, and change.

It was an exciting time to be alive and young in China, Chun Jian said. Important things were happening, changes were on their way and though the reform movement was still young and vulnerable, nothing could stop it for long. Guests of the country were fortunate to be here at such a time. This period would be one of the great ones in the history of China, like the years of the Long March, or the days when Ch'in Shih Huang Ti unified the nation and erected the Great Wall ...

After secretly vowing to read about Ch'in, whose story was told in a later section of the book I'd bought for Sheila, I told Chun Jian that my wife and I had visited the Great Wall and Mount Li, the Emperor's burial site, and were deeply impressed by his resurrected army. Chun Jian was delighted to hear that I had a wife. He wanted to know if we had any children.

'One's on the way,' I said.

'Pardon me?'

'We will have a child soon.'

Chun Jian beamed. 'I am happy for you,' he said. 'So many of the foreign friends I talk with do not have children and do not seem even to want them. We Chinese can not understand this. Here there are laws to prevent us from having more than one child. Yes, of course I see why these laws are made, but ... it is difficult for me to explain. I am happy for you. Children are the future. I hope to have many.'

After two hours Chun Jian and I shook hands warmly and exchanged addresses, though I decided, for reasons I did not understand till later, to give him the address of the place we'd be returning to in six months time. We promised to write each other and I left the restaurant with a brimming, fluid warmth in my chest – a feeling I had often as a young man busy making friends with the world but which comes to me less and less as time passes. In my office at the embassy the people of China were figures I was employed to balance, unpronounceable sur-names and fuzzy police-style mug shots on endless applications, but now, for a moment, as if I were a child again, the layers of habit and apathy and self-protective camouflage were peeled back and I was drawn through another's eyes into a strange world that was somehow familiar, like a field, a hillside or a city street you know you've seen before but can't place.

I went home with renewed confidence in everything. It hardly mattered that for the sake of Sheila's delicate mood I had to strain my feelings into a bland, palatable mush. During my first marriage I had forced myself to do it so often it was second nature to me now.

A month later I saw Chun Jian again – this time marching in a snowy street with a few other students. I had no idea what his placard said. But I remembered our first meeting as an almost perfect episode of human contact and suddenly I realized I was not going to greet him, that in fact I wanted to avoid him, and I found myself backing off and crouching down behind a news-stand to light a cigarette. I felt bad about it, later on. Like a wanted man I'd stolen a quick glance at the marching students and the signs they were brandishing and for a moment I thought Chun Jian looked over – but I couldn't be sure. After a few seconds he and the others were absorbed by the crowds.

In filtered light from the streets long after dark Sheila's belly rose and fell with her tense breathing and I listened with my ear against her skin to the muted, insistent drumbeat rising from beneath.

IV. THE TALE OF CH'IN SHIH HUANG TI: In 246 B.C. a thirteen-year-old prince was crowned ruler of Ch'in, a small kingdom in what is now central China. For the first few weeks of his reign the students and scholars of the capital made light of his youth and resurrected old jokes about adolescent kings and how unlikely they were to focus their attention on matters of government when their hearts still belonged to their mothers, and every waking thought to young girls. But the boy soon proved himself precociously mature. His enthusiasm for bloodshed and power were conspicuously adult, and within weeks of his coronation he decreed that a huge and magnificent tomb should be prepared for him. While a force of 100,000 conscripts toiled to raise a great tumulus above the plains near his capital, and while artisans forged his copper sepulchre and carved from imported oak the snarling dragon-ship which would bear him through eternity, another army of conscripts was on the march among neighbouring kingdoms, vanquishing the forces of rival monarchs and toppling their thrones. In the words of the historian Ssu-ma Ch'ien, Ch'in Shih Huang Ti *was like a silkworm devouring a mulberry leaf.* After twenty-five years of war he became the first emperor of a unified China.

Now that he had at his command a vast and populous kingdom, the Emperor brought serfs from every part of the country to labour on the tomb at Mount Li. Soon 700,000 men were slaving and dying as the colossal monument rose into the air. *The deeds of my life and the memory of my death shall humble the very mountains,* the Emperor declaimed. *In two thousand years the kings and warriors and peasants of this land will still walk in the shadow of my tomb, and I shall never be forgotten ...*

Work on the tomb progressed. In the dark subterranean passageways where workers lived and died, the dragon-ship with its coffin of bronze now sailed across a flawless scale-model of China, the Yellow and the Yangtze and all the other great rivers of the land being carved out in microcosm and furnished with mercury and caused to flow into a miniature ocean. On the vaulted ceilings above this tiny world the firmament was charted in skillful detail, so that it seemed the hand of heaven itself must have guided the craftsmen. Nothing that the Emperor had required in life was absent from the tomb. The interminable wicks of the candles floated in tall terracotta vats of whale oil so that they would burn forever, like the sun, and never leave the Emperor in darkness ...

And it may have been in the year he consolidated his empire, while criminals and prisoners of war and banished scholars began to erect his Great Wall, that he ordered his finest artisans to shape him a guardian army of officers, infantry and charioteers to march behind him into the silent kingdom. As if, having come so far with the sword, he was unable to conceive of a peaceful afterlife, an epoch of rest. As if he were young no longer but already aged, bent and bitter, filling up with his death like a brackish well, drop by drop, relentlessly ...

v. It was a long labour and when I asked her afterwards how it had felt, she said, 'Like a piece of stone inside me that nothing would move. Like something that hated me, wanted me dead. I've never felt that kind of hatred before.' But I know that feeling must have disappeared when she held Clara for the first time.

A few months later we were home, Sheila once more attached to the university and I in another well-paid clerical position I would soon come to regret. But what was the alternative? I'd grown to rely on a certain income and the things that had engaged me in my twenties and even into my thirties – political and social issues, education, the anti-war movement –

those things wouldn't help with alimony or a mortgage or with sending kids to school in the future. It amused me in a sour way, how my old friends and I avoided each other if we passed in the street and if we had to talk were always quick to let on that our sympathies were still respectably liberal. But if everyone betrays an idea does the notion of treachery have any real meaning? I'm not sure. I only know I was glad the Andrew of twenty years ago wasn't standing outside the office waiting for me as I left each day at five.

From my office window the blue hills of the Gatineau shimmered in the winter air. I slouched behind my desk, another remove from the daylight, dwarfed by snowdrifts of Important Paper. It might be a long time before Sheila could arrange another overseas placement – and by the time she did I would probably be used to the new routine. But I had Clara to come home to and my feelings of futility seemed to relent, like a wound anaesthetized, as soon as I picked her up and held her. She made me sentimental, optimistic. When I looked into her crinkled, ancient face, eyes half-closed as if meditating, mouth nuzzling at my chest, searching for a nipple, I couldn't help feeling there was some hope for the future. And I remembered reading once the only reason men could wage war was because they'd never had another body, a man's or a baby's, inside their own, or suckled a newborn child, and if they had they would never be able to send waves of half-grown adolescents through mine-fields or into machine-gun nests. Women, I read, could never wage war, but Sheila told me that was a stupid lie and it wasn't just women with barren wombs who would press the Big Red Button in a matriarchy. She said the political romanticism of my youth had evolved into a sentimentality about women – I'd treated her like a piece of fragile china when she was pregnant and now I thought that only men carried violence around inside them like blood.

Sometimes she accused me of getting old, of getting boring, yet she always did it when she seemed bored and tired herself, and I would tell her as much. She was still in her thirties but after Clara's birth the doctors made it clear she would not be having any more children. That was all right. We had Clara. It wasn't a bad marriage.

The morning Clara became ill we got a letter from Chun Jian but I didn't read it then. We left almost immediately for the hospital, where Clara was admitted for tests. Sheila stayed with her overnight and when I came home, late, to our unlit house, the letter was waiting for me.

Chun Jian wondered if I remembered him. He hoped our son or daughter was well. He asked if I had been seeing and hearing a lot about China in recent weeks; exciting things were happening and he wanted to share them with me. The students were organizing, he explained, they were going to demonstrate and force the government to consider their demands for 'important social changes'. *Old men, old men,* Chun Jian wrote, *some terrible thing happens to old men in power. I am not sure I know the reason why. Perhaps they think that holding to their power and the old ways will help them cling to their life. I do not understand. But, I know they must be forced to change and when we are old men it will be the duty of the youths to arise up and challenge our complacency. Do you agree with this? What do they say of Deng Xiao Ping in your country? We hear he is very sick and may die any time.*

Please write to me soon. I wish to hear your opinion of what is happening here ...

His generation, Chun Jian wrote, had new ideas about peace. They wanted to put away the rifle and the sword. *Bury the hatchet, is your English phrase.* And I thought of how impossible it would be to do so as long as there was sickness in the world; at that moment I felt capable of performing almost any act of violence to ensure Clara's security. Old age is a kind of sickness, I thought. It wasn't so far off, either. I nursed a cup of coffee and smoked till dawn, then dozed on and off till it was time to go back to the hospital.

VI. In his later years the Emperor Ch'in Shih Huang Ti was beset by nightmares. Though he was not yet an old man his intrigues and insatiable ambitions had aged him prematurely, and he suffered incapacitating migraines and haemorrhoids and various digestive disorders that the ablest physicians in the land could not assuage. Work on his tomb was nearing completion, and though he no longer liked to leave the relative safety and opulent comforts of his capital, he heard with satisfaction his messengers' reports about the great progress being made upon the tomb and the underground army. In the meantime he continued to strive toward the objectives he had set himself in his energetic, visionary youth: the committee of scholars he had appointed to superintend the codification of laws and the standardization of written characters had met with exemplary success, and his engineers were steadily enlarging the web of roads and system of canals he had ordained to link and solidify his kingdom. And at the centre of the web, on the still axis of the whirling heavens, the aging Ch'in Shih Huang Ti squatted among his spoils and victims, like a spider.

For as the decade of his rule elapsed, the Emperor's progressive measures were increasingly overshadowed and stained by the blood of his subjects. The weekly reports from the north-western frontier told not only how many miles of new fortification had been built but how many slaves had been killed in the process, and it always included a request for a corresponding number of replacements. During a particularly hot mid-summer, two miles of rampart and three guard towers cost his engineers two hundred head; at least half the victims were buried alive under the boulders of the wall, their bodies fused with the stone of the Emperor's misgivings, skulls ground into a greater impulse, their blood and marrow the mortar his security required.

173

His purges of the intelligentsia, especially Confucian scholars and their students, increased in scope and ingenuity as the decade wore on. He had lost patience, he declared, with the pettifogging dissension of the intellectuals, their subversive lectures and endless scribblings and unflagging petitions; how were they to know what it had meant to march as a young man at the head of a tired, hungry army and face countless enemies and defeat them and draw together a vast nation under the aegis of a new order? Thousands of volumes were dragged down from the shelves and burned, the ashes interred, their authors likewise buried alive or sunk in pits up to their shoulders and decapitated. Others were sent to the north-western frontier where they vanished into the lonely plains or under the boulders of the Great Wall. For the Emperor had become obsessed with walls, with barriers. He slept in tiny chambers barred from the outside world by up to six consecutive padlocked doors of the sturdiest oak, yet he woke from nightmares in which a sinuous, cancering darkness flowed over the borders of his kingdom in the form of Mongol hordes, or the bodiless faces of enemies long since slain, who mocked him now with their serene imperishable beauty, for they had died young and never aged. And in the middle of the night, bathed in freezing sweat, he would send out messengers and demand more frequent despatches on the progress of the Wall.

After the first attempt on his life his fear became chronic. An old friend had surprised him by concealing a dagger in a rolled map of China and in the moment when the map was unfurled, exposing the luminous blade, the Emperor had seen his kingdom transformed into a treacherous, unpredictable entity, a diagram of his coming demise.

At night he saw bearded scholars in advanced states of decay rising from the earth and marching on his capital. As they neared they chanted treasonous slogans and devised shrewd arguments and proofs with which they would turn his subjects against him. He now possessed two hundred and seventy separate palaces and each night he slept in the sanctum of a different one, always alone, for any concubine who witnessed his impotence and was unable to allay it was executed – and one by one he had had to kill them all.

He had developed a nervous twitch in his dagger-hand and his beard was white as a centenarian's. He found it difficult to eat even his favourite foods for lack of appetite and fear of poison. During the day he summoned to his court renowned sorcerers and magi and promised them half the riches of his kingdom if they could recite the names of all his enemies and bring him a vial of the elixir of life.

A famous oracle from the far west told him of islands in the Eastern Sea where old age and sickness and war were unknown, and though Ch'in Shih Huang Ti sent a fleet bearing young people and artisans as a vital offering, no one returned from the islands with a remedy for his disease. Some say the islands were Japan and those young people its founders.

For two years the capital had seethed with gossip and speculation about the Emperor's health, and finally, as if in compliance with the constant rumours, he became gravely ill. The end followed quickly.

For every clay soldier in my buried army, the Emperor wheezed on his deathbed, *I want ten young men and women buried alive with me. The most beautiful and brilliant in the kingdom!* And he whispered: *Now light the candles in my tomb.* Then his guards and physicians saw the light fade grudgingly from his pupils, like two smouldering coals sinking into the deep; and after he had fallen into his eyes, and his eyelids, like the lids of coffers, had been decently closed, the gathered witnesses quietly agreed His Lordship's dying request had not been made in earnest, that he was delirious or dreaming, that his words must be suppressed, and they turned from the deathbed full of plans and stratagems for securing or enhancing their own power.

VII. For a week Clara glided in and out of fever and the doctors were helpless to diagnose her or to offer relief. Her tiny face was bright red and she grimaced as if consciously straining. I kept thinking she was about to wake and cry out.

I took my summer holiday now and Sheila was still on leave from the university so we could spend most of our days at the hospital, in the waiting room or beside Clara. She looked even older now, a wise little man, but her bead-blue eyes stared up at us, when they were not closed, with blank unrecognition.

Sheila was frantically withdrawn. At times she snapped if I touched her – though at other times she would cling to me with a crushing, relentless strength. I'd told the doctor about the problems she'd had in China and he speculated that while we were there she might have picked up some sort of blood disorder and passed it to Clara *in utero*. But he wasn't sure, and his tests turned up nothing. He was sorry. He imagined, he said, we must be following the events of the last week in Beijing with great interest – though of course it would be hard for us to think of anything now but our daughter ...

At the end of the week we came home after a full day at the hospital and Sheila lay down without a word and fell asleep. We hadn't said much to each other for the last couple of days. I turned on the television, volume off, and sat smoking on the bed while an eerie, underground light guttered through the room and over Sheila's upturned face. It was not flattering. I thought of my first marriage. Nothing ages a man or woman faster, I thought, than giving life.

The news came on. I hadn't watched it in over a week and though I'd seen the headlines and glanced at a few of the stories in the hospital waiting room, I had no idea how serious the situation in China had become. Numbly I'd acknowledged that at any other time the students' courage and the swelling of the crowds would have excited me, but I had not been excited by them, or even very interested. Now, it seemed, the impossible had happened: as I watched the silent, murky footage I saw tanks forging through the heart of Beijing, students and older citizens scattering frantically as a makeshift monument the students had raised – it looked like the Statue of Liberty – was toppled by some military vehicle and crushed to pieces.

I leapt off the bed and knelt by the television. I turned up the volume so the anchorwoman's steady voice was just audible ... *as many as one thousand killed by troops of the People's Liberation Army ... hospitals jammed with dead or dying students and civilians ...* And on the screen the appalling spectacle went on, the tanks grinding inexorably through the square, the ramshackle barricades crumbling, students and old women scurrying in terror. For the first time that week, perhaps, I was not thinking of Clara. I was thinking of Chun Jian.

He stands with a handful of others behind a line of wooden boxes drenched in kerosene. From the edges of the square there is a rattle of automatic weapons, screams of fear or defiance, the earth-and-gut-shaking bass rumble of advancing tanks.

None of them has believed this could happen. Within an hour all but a few of their number have filed bitterly from the square but this small group has elected to remain, believing that the People's Army will not fire on unarmed students while the whole world looks on. He sees now – they all see – that this faith was misplaced. The old men, the old men behind guarded doors in the Zhongnanhai, a stone's throw from the Forbidden City, they must all be watching, he was right to distrust them and to fear their fear – their terror of the future, of the young, their headlong refusal to die – in their very death-throes they will clamp the young and their changes in a firm, withered embrace and pull everything down with them.

Chun Jian imagines Deng gasping in the palace, feebly crushing flies around his deathbed. The tanks thunder over the empty square towards their barricade. He hears shouts and a sudden crash and spinning round sees their statue on the far side of the square tumble and shatter. Constant, concerted gunfire from the violent storm whirling in the streets around them. Chun Jian takes his cigarette and tosses it with

studied composure onto the barricade. A jagged wall of flame leaps up.
For a moment it obscures the approaching tanks and soldiers but he
knows it will not stop them for long.

He and the others link hands and line up behind the barricade,
chanting, feeling the angry singe of the fire on their smooth faces. Over
the darting dragon-tongues of flame they see the tanks nearing and sil-
houetted between them the boyish shadows of men picking their way
forward, rifles levelled, and now and again a white flash of light in the
darkness and the crack of a rifle. Light, and then more light. And
beyond walls of overwhelming noise, the silence.

VIII. It took the police a long time to produce a translator, and
when one finally arrived he was little help. No, nothing had
been found on the prisoner, but it was impossible to release
him.

'But if you found nothing,' Andrew said softly, 'couldn't
you just let him go? We realize you're just trying to do your job,
but I'm afraid that, well, my wife is concerned that if ...'

'There's no need to punish him,' Sheila cut in. 'What if he
has family? He looked like such a poor man.'

The drawn, rumpled translator waved a grey hand in the
air to stop her. His fingers were shaking. On either side of him
uncomprehending policemen stood at attention and scowled
professionally.

'Excuse me,' the translator snapped, 'but that is not your
business. We shall treat him now. There is so little crime in our
country, but we must not let criminals walk in the streets.'

'We realize,' Andrew said, coughing, 'we do realize you're
just trying to ensure –'

'He didn't steal a thing,' Sheila said, brushing Andrew's
hand aside.

'He will steal again. We are endeavouring to protect you.
And excuse me, please, but this is not your business.' And he
turned and muttered something to the policeman on his right.

In her broken Chinese, Sheila urged them again to let the man go.

'No,' the translator repeated in English. 'And I must require you now to leave.'

IX. You wonder sometimes how Clara's illness will mark her. For all illness leaves its scars. Will she be like your first wife, timid and reserved because (her mother always said) of a childhood disease that left her too weak for the family's suppertime banter or the spirited games of the neighbourhood children? Clara's illness came and went unexplained, within a single week, and it left no visible sign. You wonder, though, if she will be shyer, less credulous than other children, knowing in some secret part of herself that everything is infirm, that the equilibrium of the ablest, most distinguished bully in the school is subject to a casual nudge, the evolutions of a summer holiday, a vice-principal's most senseless whim.

But she's healthy now, and walking, and beginning to say things that can make you sink to the floor sobbing with laughter, because she's so candid and fresh and clairvoyant, so unpredictable. Sometimes you wonder if she'll still see clearly in twenty years and if you'll hate her for her contempt.

All right, one more story to help you sleep, then it's bedtime.

Clara's eyelids flutter uncomprehendingly as you read to her from the book of tales you brought back from China. Her small pink ears, you think, are like sea-shells – inside them your words are a hollow roar and your own name and *Sheila* and *Chun Jian* and the name of the first emperor of China fold together in a calm, meaningless stream of sound, like the chatter of fossils in an undertow ...

Already she's asleep, but you read on.

Many have wondered about the buried army of Xi'an, and some have seen its creation as a gesture, a sign for posterity, a promissory note to unborn generations. For surely in his last years Ch'in Shih Huang

Ti grew tired of the killing, sick of suspicion and fear, and dreamed of the islands in the Eastern Sea from which his cargo of beautiful, brilliant youths did not return; perhaps he too wanted to summon a paradise out of the bones and rubble of war, and thought the time for ruthlessness was over, the days of armies done, peace and heaven provided for by centuries of tumultuous suffering. And so he hid his army with him under the earth that would soon no longer feel the tread of marching feet, the flow of blood, the lonely embrace of fallen soldiers ...

The third villager returned from the archaeologist's kiosk with several other workmen, all carrying spades. All right, said the second man, let's dig this fellow up.

Tonight, he added with authority, I'll call the curator of the museum in Xi'an ...

Before dusk they had completely disinterred the first warrior and the heads of several others. The first man had long since wandered off, muttering bleak predictions, and in the darkening pit the new workers squatted and scanned the clay faces, like parents searching for their own features in a forebear's portrait or in the eyes of the young.

12

THE BEAUTIFUL TENNESSEE WALTZ

Jason, Ōsaka, 1983

I fell out of love with my friends at the American Dream. We all knew the honeymoon was over. To them I was no longer exotic and alluring like the refinished Chevys in which patrons of the Dream drank malteds and Manhattans and cans of Budweiser – because with each meeting my Japanese improved toward fluency, and I began to say things they considered out of character. I told them I did not regret, as they sometimes did, having been born after the fifties and outside of America. I explained that in English the word 'dream' meant not only reverie, promise, hope and ambition, but illusion. I became more and more of a disappointment to them.

And they to me. From the beginning I'd been subject to their mild, well-meaning condescension, but I reminded myself where I was and let them be masters in their own house. Then I began to mature. I learned their language as quickly as a child, and like any clever child grew smug and distant toward my 'elders', began to sense their deceit and doubt their infallibility. More and more I saw how their condescension disguised a paralysing reverence for everything Western. This wasn't their house, after all, but a crass parody of my father's world, a pastiche, a cut-rate cathedral of imported icons.

'I suppose you must be comfortable here,' they would say. 'We want very much for you to feel at home.'

'Well,' I told them, 'it's not quite what I expected.'

They tried to reason with me. 'Japan is changing,' they would say, 'like everything else. This is the future. These days young Japanese are thinking more internationally.'

I told them that in theory that was a fine thing, but their bar looked pretty American to me.

Ah, so the style was authentically American?

After a fashion, I said. But in fact its decor oppressed me, like their endless questions – and my own impatience and ingratitude. At first we had seen each other as spiritual guides to remote Promised Lands, then discovered our maps were obsolete, our purposes at odds. We were falling out of love, but at first we would not give up. I pestered them with queries about Mishima and the Emperor. I patronized them, and they patronized me. They continued to insist I must be American.

Though my friends saw themselves as modern and Western and Americanized (and in many ways they were) the ritual and delicacy of our last meetings proved to me how deeply the old values had been instilled. These rowdy, irreverent students made falling out a kind of sacrament. Their compliments on my Japanese became strident, almost liturgical. They stopped mentioning my 'quaint obsession' with the old culture, and when I ordered saké (only old people and foreigners drink saké) they smiled beatifically and said nothing. There were parting gifts, of course, but only one really mattered: the skeleton key of language. I was glad to take it with me.

I began to frequent the little coffee shops in my own neighbourhood – a shabby precinct of squat, crowded apartment blocks, corrugated-iron roofs, tangled fire escapes and aerials – where I shared a kitchen and a six-mat room with Fumiko, a college student who waited tables on the weekend. At first my infatuation with her lent a halo of glamour to our dingy surroundings, and I could almost imagine how things had looked before the war, when this had been one of the more elegant sections of the city.

I learned about the old neighbourhood from Mrs Yumeta, the owner of a local coffee shop. She explained that the area was rebuilt immediately after the war when good materials were hard to find. Food was scarce too, she added. After the last bombing hardly a building was left and you could see a long way over the smouldering rubble. Back then most houses were flimsy. Only the Western-style buildings survived. If you bombed us again, Mrs Yumeta laughed, much more would be left standing ...

A few coffee shops, I thought, would have to be among the survivors. Like Kamakura with its little shrines, the neighbourhoods of Ōsaka seemed to have a café in every block. Mrs Yumeta explained that they'd appeared with the Americans after the war, and in the names of many I saw a lingering reflection of those times: Yan Kee Café, American Life Coffee Spot, Lik's Café Américain, the Idaho Caffeine Palace, even an American Dreem. But these shops did not have 3000 yen cover charges like the bars. Their interiors were dim and tranquil. When I got tired of rice I could order little sandwiches on spongy white bread. The middle-aged or elderly proprietors liked to sit with me and talk, and often they refused to let me pay for my meals or drinks. Finally I was able to get by on my paycheque.

Every Sunday, while Fumiko waited tables in Umeda, I visited two or three cafés. There were so many in the neighbourhood that I rarely had to visit one twice, which was ideal since I wanted to meet and talk with as many Japanese as possible. Most of them belonged to that pivotal generation that had seen the old Japan beaten and radically altered by the West. These aging proprietors were a living bridge between the old and the new, East and West, the virginal, untarnished culture and a rapidly evolving hybrid. I believed they would help me embrace the Japan I had read of and idolized.

My education proceeded. I heard of famines before the war, bitter poverty and the privileges of caste, military festivals, endless lines of soldiers parading across the memory as in a yellowing newsreel, and the Emperor Himself appearing one sunny spring day in a cortege in Nagai Park as blossoms fluttering down from plum trees were crushed to red pulp under the royal tires. The school curriculum was very different then. The Emperor was a deity whose unbroken lineage began with the God of the Sun. Of course no foreigner could lay claim to such august descent. Foreigners were gangly, unwholesome and vicious. They rarely bathed. They smelled like rancid butter.

'Of course we laugh at these things now,' Mrs Yumeta told me on my second visit to her shop. The New American Café was conveniently situated three minutes from my door and five minutes from the park, but the reason I had come a second time -- and continued to come religiously in the following weeks – was Mrs Yumeta's aggressive hospitality. While many of the other proprietors would not accept my money when it came time to pay ('*Sensei*,' they would say, referring to my status as a teacher of English, 'you are the first foreigner to visit our shop, you have honoured us, forgive me but it would be impossible to accept your money'), and while others brought unrequested snacks and hot towels to my table, Mrs Yumeta asked me to accept several expensive gifts after my first visit. A fine silver pen, a lacquer mug. 'So you can have your own cup when you return, *Sensei*. And with the pen – you can write to your friends about the old Japan, and my story.'

Of course it wasn't just gifts that made me return, or her need to have me listen; I had other reasons to seek her out. During the week my plans and my illusions continued to fall apart, as if the seismic tremors rumbling through the city in recent weeks were undermining everything. For a long time I'd found consolation in Fumiko, because seeing her I was still reminded of the courtesans of the Floating World whose portraits I'd always loved; they were inhabitants, I thought, of an orderly, coherent circle, where myths and meanings were commonly understood. But as I came to understand Fumiko's words I found her less and less consoling. Now she would say things that seemed out of character. Hairline flaws began to taint her beauty, like cracks in a museum mask. Sometimes I snapped at her. For the first time I understood what it meant to be foreign.

Sundays I took refuge in Mrs Yumeta's shop.

Mrs Yumeta was heavy and small and when she walked she stooped as if expecting the low ceiling to collapse at any moment. Like the walls and the two circular tables by the door her face was cluttered and messy, a collage of wrinkles and erratically applied make-up. (The walls were covered with posters of American show bands of the '40s, old calendars, framed portraits of Bogart, Bacall and Hepburn; she explained that she'd studied and loved traditional Japanese flower-arrangement but a coffee shop must have exotic decorations.)

The two small rounded windows by the door reminded me of her eyes. The panes were tinted umber like the colour round her iris, an unwholesome, tainted shade, as if she never left the smoky shop for the relatively fresh air outside; the shop's light, a muted amber, was matched or mirrored by her complexion so she looked like a figure in a sepia print.

I sat at the table nearest the door and farthest from the stereo. Mrs Yumeta had a slight hearing problem ('the bombing,' she explained) and played her music loudly. Old American Favourites, she said, rummaging through a heap of old magazines and unopened mail for the record jacket. 'Some people were interested in the big bands before the war, and American movies too, but it was ... unsuitable for people to show such a feeling.'

'Western things were seen as a bad influence,' I suggested.

'That was the official idea,' she said. 'I think the generals had already decided on war and didn't want us involved with foreigners in any way.'

Mrs Yumeta slowly exhaled a chestful of smoke until the little shop seemed filled with it, like a dim lobby during an intermission. This was the time I watched her finish a whole pack of Larks without rising from the table.

'I became interested in the music after the war. Near the end my husband – he'd been an officer in Malaya but he was wounded and sent home – my husband said to me, "If the Americans win"' – (in Japanese there is some ambiguity, she may have meant *when* they win) '"they will be the new masters. The *Sensei*. Everything they do we will have to admire, not despise." He said it with great contempt, and disappointment. He was much older than me.

'At the end of the war I was ready to change with the times. The people who couldn't adapt died off ... those who hadn't been killed in the bombings. Listen – this one's my favourite.'

I recognized the song. I remembered my mother singing it, half facetiously, on various occasions. Probably I'd heard it a few times on nostalgic radio shows:

> *I was dancing with my darling to the Tennessee Waltz*
> *When an old friend I happened to see;*
> *I introduced him to my darling and while they were dancing*
> *My friend stole my sweetheart from me ...*

Mrs Yumeta would always break off whatever she was telling me to sing along with the droning, scratchy, primitive recording. I *remember the night and the Tennessee Waltz, now I know just how much I have lost* ... She had no English but she could sing the words perfectly. She could even mimic the wistful, drawling quality of the unknown singer's voice. ('I must find you the record jacket,' she repeated.)

One time, the last time I visited her shop, she rose when

the song started and spread her arms wide and sang as if performing for a full nightclub or auditorium –

Well I lost my little darling, the night they were playing
The beautiful Tennessee Waltz

– and I recalled her polite disappointment of a few months before when she first learned I did not know the words by heart. I could not even satisfy her request that I demonstrate the waltz. 'You're like the young people here in Japan,' she taunted me amiably. 'You've forgotten everything.'

Mrs Yumeta was a skilful narrator. She revealed her knowledge in tantalizing fragments, gliding forward and backward in time with what seemed a meandering senility. But I knew she had some purpose in mind. Perhaps it was only my imagination, or wishful thinking, but it seemed she was drifting toward something final and momentous.

'My brother was a poet,' she told me. 'While he was still attending university in Kyōto his first book was published. I didn't really understand the poems, many people called them eccentric, but I was proud of him. Critics praised his book, they said it combined the most interesting aspects of Western poetry with the great Japanese tradition. My brother worked hard to translate it into English because he wanted to have it published overseas.

'Soon after he finished the translation he became convinced that the authorities were having him watched. At the time we thought he was being ridiculous, but the next year when the government decided to remove Western literature from all curriculums he spoke against it at the university and was arrested. Within a month he was shipped to a labour camp in Manchukuo.

'For about a year we received letters and poems, then a message came from the government informing us he had died

187

suddenly of typhoid. I suspected this was untrue but could do nothing. My husband, who by that time was a colonel stationed in Kyūshū, had been disgusted by my brother's actions and terrified they would discredit the family and ruin his career, so when news arrived of my brother's death he seemed relieved. Still, when I begged him to take a post in Manchukuo to find out exactly what had happened he agreed to try – partly, I suppose, for his own reasons. But he was not a bad man. He felt sorry for me.

'Unfortunately the authorities refused his request and sent him to Malaya as soon as the fighting began there.'

I asked her if she still had a copy of her brother's book; she told me her copies had all been destroyed in the bombing. 'So much was destroyed,' she said. 'We were all left with nothing. I felt my past had disappeared entirely. Photographs, gifts, letters ... I was lucky enough to inherit money from wealthy relations of my husband who were killed in Kōbe. So I have been able to make a new life ...'

She lifted her hands in a kind of priestly gesture to indicate, or consecrate, the new world she had made. I wasn't sure if she was being ironic – the shop was small, musty and sepulchral, as if no one had entered since the day it was built. Mrs Yumeta's fingers began to waver, like a bandmaster's, to the beat of an instrumental piece that was quickly becoming familiar. By the time of my last visit I could hum along with most of her favourites.

When her favourites ended she always returned to the past.

War. Her mother and father died early in the bombings. Her husband returned from Malaya in 1944 with a shattered arm; until the end he was forced to wear a cast and sling. (He had been hit, she insisted, with a large stone hurled by an American prisoner-of-war, who had unfortunately been shot for it. *Wasn't that an unusual kind of wound for a Japanese officer to suffer?* Ah, but the prisoners were being mistreated, everyone was willing to admit that now, and men driven half-mad by hunger will do rash things. *But why Mr Yumeta?* Many guards suffered similar injuries, she said, though few had the good fortune to be sent home. Her niece came every day for a month to sit by his bed and comfort him.)

Children. The couple had one child – a girl – but she'd died in infancy before the war. And in the closing days of the conflict an exhausted Mrs Yumeta had miscarried.

The occupation. The American soldiers she met after the war *were* loud but not especially smelly or vicious as she had been taught. One, in fact, had become something of a friend. Mrs Yumeta often remarked on our uncanny resemblance.

Childhood. As a girl she had fed the birds in Nagai Park, and as a young bride she had fed them in the garden of her husband's home. (Taking a bag of bread crusts she went to the open door and stood at the threshold to demonstrate.)

Yes, exactly here it must have been. This shop was built over the ruins of the old house. These birds – you would think they were the same ones as ever. *Neh?*

On this occasion I was drunk, a little dizzy, so I did not move from the chair. I had been drinking a lot on recent visits. I watched Mrs Yumeta stand in the doorway tearing strips of crust and tossing them out into the bright chilly air. It was mid-fall and the last of the summer heat had vanished; for a moment a fresh draft penetrated the shop. From outside an impatient squabbling, birds struggling over the bread.

'When he returned from Malaya my husband was able to tell me things he couldn't say in his letters. The year before, my brother had suddenly appeared in the company of intelligence officers and a group from the Ministry of Propaganda at a POW camp near the place my husband was stationed. They were having him speak to the prisoners, in English, about the decadence of Western customs and ideas and about the hopelessness of their cause. This was meant to persuade them to lend their services to the Ministry, which would then let them warn their compatriots by radio about the futility of further resistance. My husband said my brother seemed cooperative, even zealous, and apparently had not been beaten or drugged. Of course there's no telling what might have happened to him before, but at the time the only thing that seemed important to me was that he was alive. I wanted to rush out and announce to the neighbourhood that he had seen reason and was not a traitor after all – you remember I told you how it was for me, alone here, when my brother was first arrested, then interned. But my husband would not let me talk to the neighbours. He seemed very strange, I wondered if the injury had somehow affected his mind. He suffered terribly from nightmares. And he told me things I could hardly believe – that the war was going badly for Japan, that it would soon be over and when the Americans won they would be the masters here. He told me he was deeply worried about my brother's activities; he himself had gotten involved because when my brother realized he was stationed nearby he'd honoured my husband by suggesting he help the Ministry, as he put it, 'persuade the prisoners to cooperate'. My husband would never tell me exactly what he'd had to do in the camp, but he was anxious, he said, because in his capacity as a – an investigating officer – he'd heard prisoners' warnings about what would happen to all such men after the war. He admitted that what he was most afraid of was his relationship to my brother. He seemed certain my brother would come in for special treatment when the war ended. In fact he felt sure the whole family would be destroyed and its fortunes confiscated. And he was right – my brother died during his trial in 1946 and my husband's family were killed in the final bombing of Kōbe.

   ' "I myself have done nothing unless told," he insisted, and at the time I believed there could be no stronger justification for his actions, whatever they were.'

She lit another cigarette and looked away. I had a feeling she knew more about her husband's activities than she was letting on, but I said nothing; her words were beginning to strain under the weight of their confession, and I felt I should grant her whatever freedoms she required for a swift, painless passage through her story.

Suddenly she changed the subject and despite several broad hints would not return to her past. We discussed the problems of small businesspeople, which were the same all over the world. She complained a little, as she often did, about the young people who frequented her shop on school days. They were arrogant and impolite. They were allowing the cultural tradition to die out. They seemed to her like – foreigners.

I left with a package of expensive Kyōto sweets, promising to return the next Sunday, but problems at home kept me away for several weeks. My relationship with Fumiko had been crumbling for some time and on the night of the fall's most serious tremor it dissolved completely. Then, a few days after she left, the principal of my school said he had had complaints from students about my behaviour. I was arrogant and condescending, they claimed, about things Western and things Japanese. But I love Japan! I protested, I revere the culture! *Gakk'cho-san* said nothing. Nobody is ever fired in Japan. He waited politely for my resignation, and after a few moments I gave it.

The next Sunday, jobless, virtually broke, I returned to Mrs Yumeta. I found myself wondering when I would hear about her husband's death, which had grown more and more implicit, a pale thread woven subtly but visibly into the fabric of the story. I began to sense his death would be the climactic chapter, as it seemed to have been in Mrs Yumeta's life; I couldn't help speculating on the kind of conclusion and revelation it might bring. But that Sunday I learned nothing.

A few days later I had a shock. On my way home after

191

another unsuccessful job hunt I stopped at the Café Pittsburgh for a bite to eat, and the white-haired gentleman behind the grill asked why I'd never patronized his shop before. I explained that I usually went to Mrs Yumeta's. He couldn't hide his surprise.

'You are the only one who ever goes there,' he said. 'You and the odd stranger to the neighbourhood.'

I agreed I was usually alone there, but wasn't Sunday a quiet day in all coffee shops?

Not in his, he said. But then Yumeta-san had never done any business, even during the week. Neighbours avoided her. She didn't need their business.

As he leaned over the sizzling grill a vein of sweat trickled between his eyes. I could tell he'd been drinking.

'She is a strange woman,' he whispered. 'The war. They say she killed her husband. Some kind of minister in the old government. I hear he had a bad leg and during the bombing –'

He withdrew across the grill, grinning with shame as the Japanese sometimes do. Probably he thought he had embarrassed me by mentioning the bombs.

'Rumours,' he said, shrugging. 'Who can say for sure?'

★

It was late November. The weather had turned gloomy and cold. That morning, briefly, snowflakes delicate as sifted flour had blown out of the northwest. Japanese winters come down from Siberia, Mrs Yumeta explained. The winter of '45-46 had been a cold one. She had sheltered two families in the newly built coffee shop until spring ...

I was broke. The schools had either heard of me from *Gakk'cho-san* or weren't hiring. I had nothing left but a ticket to Vancouver. I told Mrs Yumeta I had to go home in a few days – there had been a death in the family, something unexpected – and as I spoke I couldn't help relishing the sense of advantage such news confers. It hardly mattered that it wasn't true. If my stories could not tantalize Mrs Yumeta at least they could surprise her. I assured her I had not been close to the deceased who, according to the Japanese euphemism I politely used, had simply disappeared.

I regretted she might have to end her story prematurely, as I would not be able to return.

Mrs Yumeta lit a cigarette and looked shrewdly over my left shoulder, as if she'd expected me to say something of the kind. I began to feel impatient. I sensed I was being kept in the dark for reasons even she might not fully grasp; suddenly I was tired of being teased with fragments, as I had been since coming to her country. So when she began to speak, in what I took to be a deliberately evasive way, about her husband's career in the military and his stiffly patriotic views, I broke in and with very Western directness asked what exactly had happened to him.

'My husband?' she said. 'Yes, you must want to know ...'

Her favourite record was playing. The opening bars of 'In the Mood' erupted from hidden speakers at an urgent, alarming volume, like a siren in the room's still air. She smiled sadly. 'Poor Mr Glen Miller,' she said. 'A perfect American. Like my husband, he died too soon.'

Mrs Yumeta broke off and looked away towards the door. From outside there was a muted commotion – the birds congregating for their daily meal. She stiffened as if about to rise and go to them, then leaned towards me across the table. She frowned and fumbled for a cigarette and for the first time I was almost sure she was performing.

'The fire-bombs started to fall just after midnight, when most of the neighbourhood was asleep. The sirens didn't start till after the first bombs had exploded. By the time we got out into the street everything was burning.

'My husband began to rush around trying to help people

193

whose clothes had caught fire. There were many like that. He was naked, he had removed his *yukata* to smother the flames. I remember he struggled with his cast and he was badly flushed and sweating. Together we helped a neighbour – an old woman born around the time of Perry – out into the middle of the street away from the flames. She was dead by the time we set her down.

'This seemed to finish my husband. He wept and clutched his bad arm, he was ashamed of his pain – then suddenly he was reminded of something. He leapt up and shouted that he had to go back into the house. I begged him not to, I screamed at him but he wouldn't listen. When I tried to grab him he pushed me away. I insisted there was nothing we needed so badly but he turned from me and ran back into the burning house. I tried to follow but a neighbour held me and would not let go. A few moments later the roof collapsed.

'In the morning all we could find of him' – Mrs Yumeta paused and raised her upturned, empty palms about the table, in a gesture that struck me as indecently dramatic – 'bones. Really there was nothing left. And of course no trace of whatever he went back to find. About that I have always wondered ...'

Her tone was suggestive. The photograph of a lover? His uniform, perhaps, his decorations ... Her upturned palms still hovered above the table, conspicuously empty. Whatever he had turned back to save had disappeared with the rest of the old world, with *bushidō*, geisha, colonels and their swaggering dreams, the cryptic smiles of a billion Buddhas ... *In a gust of wind the white dew on the autumn grass scatters like a broken necklace* ... The coffee shops and American bars that sprouted from the debris must have gleamed with a pledge of reformation, wholeness, survival. In the smell of brewing coffee there would have been a bracing freshness that promised change, like the scent of a shifting wind. But the new story had never got past

194

its introduction. The old one was not yet finished and never would be. *I have been left hanging,* Mrs Yumeta's expression seemed to suggest.

'This shop is built on his ashes,' she said finally, letting her hands fall to her sides as a melodramatic riff moaned from the speakers. Everything seemed staged, but her tears welled up suddenly, prodigally, and I felt guilty and cynical for my detachment. But I have reason to doubt her, I thought, remembering the old man in the Café Pittsburgh ...

Like Mrs Yumeta I was trapped between worlds. There had been a time, I supposed, when it was easier to believe in things. Now I was paralysed, unable to leap forward into faith and compassion or retreat into sarcasm and incredulity. I could picture myself asking the immense question, Did you kill him? and imagine her look of disbelief, then feel her conviction that I have made an error, some quaint and terrifying mistranslation – but no, she has heard correctly. *No,* she is saying: *no, I didn't kill him. It was you.*

The story, I discovered, was not quite over.

The morning after the attack, for the first time ever so far inland, sea-birds had appeared in large flocks and swooped low over the ruins. Afraid they were scavengers looking for scraps of flesh, the survivors had tried to drive them off, but the birds continually returned, screeching and flapping, alighting on broken rafters and shards of scorched metal ...

Mrs Yumeta smiled and looked away. The Japanese consider it rude to dwell on their misfortunes. She glanced at her watch and spoke gamely: 'They'll all be gathered by now, the birds, it's time. And listen – it's our old favourite.'

And it was. Mrs Yumeta stood and spread her arms wide and began to sing, then took me by the hand and drew me to my feet. 'Come,' she said, 'this is the last time. You're American, show me how to waltz.'

Somehow, to my surprise, I did.

I remember the night of the Tennessee Waltz, now I know just how much I have lost …

We turned and glided through the sluggish air of the little café. Dust swirled up from the floor and settled on racks of unused cups and piles of old magazines. As we danced I could feel her cheek trembling at my chest; her mouth was pressed against it so that when she sang out, without understanding, 'my friend stole my sweetheart,' the words seemed to resonate inside me.

'You're a good dancer,' I told her, the song ending. 'There. I really have to go now.'

As Mrs Yumeta drew the back of her hand over her eyes I politely looked away. Her face would be a lurid mask of drying tears and smudged make-up; it was better that I didn't see. And now, years later, as I remember leaving, I see myself taking leave of a different Mrs Yumeta, much younger, a bride, a fiancée who does not turn away or hide a face blurred by tears and flattened with time; when she reaches through the room's dim air to turn off her music, so the birds are suddenly audible, the arm is slim and supple and glides with a whisper of silk sleeves over skin.

'There,' she says – the voice smooth and youthful – 'there, you can hear them. They always come. They are as punctual as you were, *Sensei*.'

Taking her bag of crusts she walks me to the door, then presents me with a small jar of homemade pickles she has somehow concealed on herself till then. 'Ginger,' she says, 'and mountain herbs. The art is almost forgotten.'

She pulls open the door: a mob of gulls, cranes and herons fills the narrow walk, cawing and flapping, edging forward. A light snow is falling and the feathers of the gulls, grey with soot, seem to whiten before our eyes. I smell brine, a hint of the Inland Sea. The road is a scribble of fading footprints. As Mrs Yumeta tears and throws out crusts to the strange birds I kiss her smeared cheek and tell her I hope to come back when everything is cleared up at home; but the one Japan I would have returned to is dead, or murdered, and I am no longer certain it ever lived.

'Goodbye,' she echoes me in Japanese – *sayōnara, sayōnara* – though the old word does not really mean 'goodbye', but *Well, if it must be so, so be it.*

13

'A Man with No Master ...'

AMANOGAWA AMERICAN ENGLISH SCHOOL, ŌSAKA, DECEMBER 1987:

A few days before Christmas, when my teaching job was due to expire, I was kidnapped by the Japanese mafia.

I heard the front door of the school swing open a few minutes before my one-o'clock lesson. I turned from the coffee machine with a counterfeit grin, ready to greet an early student; two *yakuza* stood in the doorway. The stocky one wore mirrored Ray-Bans and the tall one's tiny eyes stole from side to side, taking things in. Roach-brown leather jackets, pressed black slacks and pointy, patent-leather shoes. Permed hair, of course, though the tall one had only a few curls left on his polished skull.

'*Konichi wa!*' I blurted out. 'Interested in improving your English?'

The sunglassed one glared up at his partner who glared at me.

'Ah,' I coughed in clumsy Japanese, 'forgive me. I see you don't speak English. Perhaps a beginners' course, then?'

The tall bald one unzipped his jacket halfway and took a few strides into the room. He rubbed his fingers over a small pockmark on his cheek. A bullet scar. Tattooed on his hand and wrist under a Seiko quartz was a long thin samurai sword, crimson.

'I'm afraid,' I spread my wet palms, smiling, 'I'm afraid you

198

gentlemen may have made a small mistake. Perhaps you're look-ing for the pool hall? Or the *pachinko* house up the way ... Next block, both of them.'

'No mistake,' snapped the bald one in guttural Japanese. With one slick motion, as if drawing a knife, he whisked a cig-arette from inside his jacket and jabbed it into his mouth. 'We have come for Principal Kobayashi. Is that her in the back?'

'You're just hearing the television,' I bowed. 'Miami Vice.'

Ray-Ban's sullen mouth showed interest: the bald one nodded down at him, then cleared his throat.

'You – usually wear that hat when you teach?'

I removed a scarlet toque and dangled it in front of me by its flossy white pom-pom. The two men stared.

'The theme of the next lesson,' I shrugged, grinning fee-bly, 'is Christmas in Canada.'

Ray-Ban shoved past me, heading for the TV.

'This is Japan,' the bald one snapped, 'and the mistake is yours.'

There was a fierce cry, a crash, and the TV went dead.

★

Like a samurai steed careering through the shifting tides of a Kurosawa battle scene, the sleek black Toyota Crown surged forward, frantically accelerating whenever a break appeared in the herd of tiny honking cars, shuddering to a stop at red lights and whenever the deadly press closed in along Motomachi Dori. Ray-Ban-san was driving. The bald one, still smoking, turned from the front passenger seat and held out his pack.

'What are you going to offer me next,' I heard myself babbling, 'a blindfold?'

'*Eh? Nani ...!*'

'Sorry,' I managed in Japanese. 'I'm sorry. But if you wouldn't mind telling me – I mean, if it's not too much trou-ble – where are we going?'

199

Ray-Ban geared down dramatically and the bald one's answer was swallowed by the engine's braying. His full lips had not opened but I knew he'd said something because his cigarette had wagged up and down like a stern, condemning finger. I glanced at his scar.

'... *school*,' I caught now, '*has made ... foolish mistake.*'

'Pardon me?'

'... *costly, too. Very ... and unethical.*'

We screeched to a stop.

'But I told you I don't know anything about it!'

'Of course not,' the cigarette bowed. 'You are merely the foreign *sensei*. Your principal is responsible and she will have to pay for this mistake.'

Ray-Ban revved the motor and my pulse raced.

'Please,' I said, 'where are we going?'

'The other school warned her one time already. They did not want to call us but you left them no choice.'

We roared off and Ray-Ban cackled as the Crown thundered through the intersection.

'I THINK I'D LIKE TO GO HOME NOW,' I found myself saying. 'IF YOU'D JUST DROP ME OFF? THE LIGHT UP AHEAD WILL BE FINE.'

'... *unfortunate for you that your principal was not ... school when we arrived ...*'

'THAT LIGHT WAS YELLOW!'

The bald one asked me if I would like to calm down. '*You have nothing to fear,*' his cigarette bobbed – the barrel of a carelessly held handgun. '*But ... have to keep you with us until ... contact your principal. We could not ... warning her about meeting us. She ... might call ... police.*'

I admitted she might.

We braked and he tried to smile, his bullet scar squeezed to a dimple. 'You have nothing to fear. As soon as we reach her, you will be returned to the school.'

' "Set free", you mean.'

'Your Japanese is very good,' he assured me, 'for a *gaijin.*'

I accepted a cigarette. My hand was shaking. The Toyota charged under the green light and swerved round a traffic island on which a single officer stood. '*Omawari, neh?*' the bald one smiled; it was the slang term for 'policeman', and meant 'thing idly standing around'.

We braked for a light near the north gate of Umeda Station. As the bald one passed me his lighter I glimpsed the red sword tattooed on his wrist. *Katana*, I thought – and fumbled the lighter.

'I hope you will not be fired,' Katana-san growled sympathetically, 'for abandoning your English class.'

'I'll just tell them I was kidnapped.'

'Yes,' he nodded quickly, 'they will understand if you say that. In Japan everyone knows all about us.'

He paused.

'You – usually take this long to light a smoke?'

Ray-Ban gripped the gear-shift with adolescent zeal and the motor shrieked and snorted. We covered the intersection then veered off the street down a sudden ramp into a dimly lit basement garage, jarring to a stop seconds later. The two men leapt out and Ray-Ban ripped open my door. He barked out some harsh staccato command.

'We will phone the school now,' Katana-san said as I followed them through a doorway and up several flights of stairs, 'and I will speak to your principal. You did say she would be back after lunch ...?'

I nodded, trying to catch my breath.

'*Sensei,*' he confided, clutching my arm, 'you look terrible. Perhaps in future you should get more rest!'

Under his watch, the tattoo-sword was lined with scarlet characters that dripped like blood from the blade.

★

I waited with Ray-Ban on a blue suede couch in a dingy, air-less sitting room. The end tables were crammed with dirty cups and glasses and dog-eared piles of pornographic *manga*.

'It's Snoopy,' Ray-Ban recited in English. From behind his glasses he nodded at the TV, tore open a can of Budweiser.

A Charlie Brown Christmas in Japanese: Charlie's voice plaintive and befuddled, like some of my students, struggling and overworked; Lucy roaring like a samurai field marshal. I looked away. Above the droning set hung a woodcut of *ninja* in training and an autographed still of James Cagney.

'Bad news,' Katana-san reported, swaggering into the room. Ray-Ban finally grinned – I hoped at something on the screen.

'I am sorry to tell you that your principal is still out of the school, so we will have to keep you with us for some time.'

'But she told me she'd be back after lunch – she's always on time!'

Katana-san glanced at the television. 'I spoke to one of your students,' he shrugged. 'Your principal did come back after lunch. And when she found you had abandoned the class, she left at once to find another teacher.'

'But I *didn't* abandon the class, you – kidnapped me!'

I caught myself. Ray-Ban cackled and slapped his knee three times; Linus was on stage delivering the Christmas passage from the Gospel according to Luke.

'You have nothing to fear,' repeated Katana-san, smooth-ing the unruly wisps on his polished skull. 'And *kidnap* is a very *strong* word, do you not agree? I feel it would be better for all of us if you did not use such a strong word ...'

Ray-Ban giggled, then aimed a large black pistol at the TV set and changed the station. A car chase, it looked like – the last few seconds of 'Miami Vice.'

'Especially when you talk about us hereafter,' Katana-san

resumed. 'We would like to let you go, of course, but we have to be certain you will not say ... unfair things about us to the police. Unkind things ...'

'Really, I – can't imagine what you mean.'

Ray-Ban fired another round at the TV and a *sumō* match appeared.

'So say nothing,' Katana-san nodded. 'That would be best. We rarely have problems with the police here and everyone is happier that way.'

A huge wrestler rolled like a beachball from the *sumō* ring. Ray-Ban fired another round. MTV – Madonna. BLAM. 'Miami Vice.' BLAM. *Peanuts* again.

'You have nothing to fear. I explained to the student that you were called away by an emergency, so, if you go back, you will not have lost face.'

'*If* I go back? Emergency?' I swallowed, coughed.

'I said you had a heart attack.'

'I'm twenty-eight years old!'

Hurt, Katana-san stared at the floor, smoothing his wisps, then glanced at the TV. Linus was summing up.

'A *mild* heart attack. You have nothing to fear, Japanese people will believe anything about foreigners. And you did look pretty bad coming up those stairs ...'

'I *feel* pretty bad' I bleated, clutching at the arm of the couch, 'I feel *terrible!* I've been kidnapped by *gangsters!*'

Ray-Ban offed the TV with a single shot and turned to me, glaring.

'*Sensei,*' Katana-san rumbled, 'I think we already agreed about not using words like that. Am I wrong?'

I stared at the dark stain my palm had left on the couch.

'We have been very patient with you so far. We are trying to be ... *obliging.*' He stabbed his face with another cigarette. 'Hospitality is an important part of our ... our cultural heritage here – our code.'

I peered up at him. His bullet-scar dimpled into a smile. 'Let's go for lunch,' he said.

★

Ray-Ban, slurping beer, gawked through his glasses at the TV set mounted over the long counter. From the corner of my eye I made out the opening scenes of *Seven Samurai*.

'How long does it take to make one phone call?' I fretted in English. Ray-Ban ignored me. The aged proprietor, a skeleton in grease-stained apron and paper cap, mumbled to himself in Chinese as he flipped over our sizzling *okonomiyaki*. His wrinkled forehead shone with sweat and every few seconds he clutched a hand towel and swabbed it dry.

'*Mō ip'pon!*' snarled Ray-Ban, slapping his empty beer can on the counter. The old man quickly replaced it.

Katana-san emerged from the gloom at the back of the restaurant, his face a black flag.

'She is still out,' he shook his head. 'And the students are gone now, too. I got an answering machine. I called her home number as well. Another answering machine.'

'I ... don't suppose you might have left some kind of message?'

'QUIET!' Ray-Ban spun from the TV and glared.

Suddenly I was annoyed. 'You know, something like, "Hi, this the Mob. We're holding one of your teachers hostage and we intend to extort several hundred thousand yen from you at our earliest convenience. We can be reached at the following number ..."'

'I sense your irony,' Katana-san growled, seating himself close on my other side. 'Perhaps with foreigners this is a sign of nervousness?'

Ray-Ban guffawed and rattled his beer can on the counter. With one blow, I saw, a samurai had just cut his hairy opponent in half.

'You look pale again, too. Tired. Perhaps with a little food ...?' Katana-san gestured expansively at the grill where our *okonomiyaki* were browning. The old proprietor swabbed his brow and glanced up at us with a nervous smile.

'And beer – perhaps that would help. Suppose you take a beer.'

I nodded, weakly. 'Could you – make it something stronger?'

'A Kirin for me,' he barked, 'double Suntory for the prisoner.'

I looked at him. His scar dimpled again.

'A joke!' he said, draping his arm round my shoulder. 'Granddad here doesn't know more than a few words of Japanese, just brand names and numbers, that's why we always come. I was making a joke!'

I felt myself smile.

'Besides, the *okonomiyaki* are very good. True, the old man is Chinese, but he has run the shop for a long time. Did you know this place is over forty years old? I know you *gaijin* are interested in our history, so think of our ... our little *outing* today as a kind of, well – a kind of historical tour.'

'Hmmm. I hadn't thought of seeing it that way.'

'You must try.'

The old man piled the steaming greasy pancakes onto plates and set them before us, along with my whisky and two more beers. Ray-Ban ignored his meal and stared up at the TV.

'A wonderful film,' Katana-san mumbled, nodding at the screen, cheeks bulging with beer and food. 'I have seen it many times. You – uh – would like another whisky?'

'If possible. Please.'

'You're not touching your lunch.'

'*Kill him,*' snarled Ray-Ban, beating a thin metallic knell on the counter.

'He knows every scene,' Katana-san explained, swallowing.

'The film is an important one for us ... Probably you think of us as uncultured people ...?'

With his eyes the old proprietor signalled at my glass. I nodded gratefully.

'... and it is true that I, for example, have never been to the university. But I enjoy a good meal, a bath, the *sumō*' – he stuffed a chunk of *okonomiyaki* into his mouth – 'and I do try to read as much as possible.'

'*Arigatō*,' I thanked the old man.

'... Mishima, for example, and many of the Japanese classics. And I have read *The Godfather* – you know it? – three times, in translation.'

'Ah,' I sighed between slugs of whisky, 'that's good. Wonderful.'

'But better in English, I suppose ...?'

Something on the screen made Ray-Ban laugh. I smiled again. The knot in my gut was dissolving in whisky, chest growing warm.

'... I really must try to read that original ...'

'Maybe,' I mumbled, covering my mouth, 'maybe we'll bring in a special course for mobsters.' I chuckled. 'Criminal English 101.'

Katana-san blinked and pursed his lips, then released a hearty laugh and brandished his empty beer can at the proprietor. 'Now you feel better,' he beamed, 'I can see it! Not so pale. And such fine Japanese!'

'*In the belly!*' urged Ray-Ban. '*Like a dog!*'

Katana-san guzzled beer and jammed his mouth with the moist, delicious-looking pancake. For a moment he could not speak and sat back chewing, cheeks puffed out, stabbing the air with his chopsticks.

'*Mmmmmbb*,' he finally coughed out, 'in some ways, you know, we are the only warriors left. The only real Japanese. The older people ... the older people are like robots with their factory jobs, working on and on, so obedient – like peasants – and as for the young students you teach, well, you know how ... how *frivolous* they can be – like small children. You know, in a way our people keep alive the warrior's tradition. Like the forty-seven *ronin* – you know them? – or your Robin Hood. We are outside the law, certainly, but we are always fair. Why, just look, that other school called us instead of the *omawari* when your principal broke the rules of fairness!'

'You still haven't told me what she did.'

Katana-san dispatched my remark with a slash of the chopsticks. He signalled for another round. His eyes were glassy, vague, as if focused on some faraway object.

'Nothing,' he declared, shaking his flushed head, '*nothing* is better than to live with intensity and honour. For some people, my friend, an ordinary life would be far too ... too ordinary! Unbearable! We are the warriors of our time and our code will always be more important to us than the laws of the land, which change with every government. We are like ... like the *ronin* – warriors without a master.'

I nodded and looked down, unsure how to respond; I tried to read the time on his watch.

'Of course this is difficult for you to understand.'

'Of course.'

'There are not many of us left.'

Shouts, screaming from the TV. We had to pause. The rattle of musketry rose, then fell. After a few moments I said, 'That inscription on your tattoo ... I've figured out a few of the characters – "man", "without" – but some of the others ... your watch is kind of in the way ...'

'HOLD THEM!' howled Ray-Ban, shoving aside his untouched food. A sudden rumble of drumming hoofs; Katana-san had not heard me. He spun round and raised his beercan to toast the warriors in the television.

'No,' he said at last, turning back to me, 'there is *nothing* like living with that kind of honour.' And his earnest eyes seemed to issue a challenge. The drug deals and knifings my students always spoke of – I was not about to bring them up.

He blushed. 'Come now, *Sensei* – you must eat!'

'You're not going to hurt Kobayashi-san, are you?'

Ray-Ban turned to us at once. Katana-san gazed up at the TV, nodding and reaching into his jacket, exhuming a cigarette. 'I suspect,' he said, 'that is very unlikely. *Very* unlikely. We prefer to leave civilians alone. The injured party has simply asked us to … secure a token of your school's regret for its … its unethical mistake. It should be a very simple transaction.'

I finished my whisky in one gulp.

'It is really too bad we cannot reach her yet. Things will move very quickly once we get through. We carry out this sort of business all the time.'

'Of course.'

He lit his cigarette and exhaled. 'You have nothing to fear.'

Ray-Ban laughed again and turned to me, nudged me in the ribs. The old man bowed over the grill and set a plate of fortune cookies before us. I had never seen this done before in an *okonomiyaki* house.

'True, it is unusual,' Katana-san said, 'but times are changing – even here.' He crumbled his cookie, shook his head and frowned. '*Yappari, nah!* The fortunes are in English, too!'

I unfurled my own:

SOON YOU WILL BE CROSSING THE GREAT WATERS

Wonderful.

'TRANSLATE,' Ray-Ban barked, thrusting his slip at my chest.

'*Soon*,' I improvised, '*soon you will meet with a … a slow, very painful, and untimely end.*'

208

He snatched the slip from me and held it to his glasses. Katana-san passed me his own.

'*He who lives by the sword,*' I translated, '*dies by the sword.*'

He grinned. 'I know more English than you think,' he told me, signalling for the bill.

Unsteadily we rose. Katana-san muttered something at Ray-Ban who still slouched on his stool, motionless, gaping up at the screen. A scruffy barbarian had just fired his matchlock at an unarmed samurai, and missed.

★

Katana-san, flushed, explained that he and his men went to the *sento* each day at five sharp and since he'd still not reached my principal there was no need to break with tradition.

'Besides,' he belched, holding the door for me, grinning, 'a foreigner can always use a bath.'

Dating to well before the war, the *sento* was situated in the heart of thriving Motomachi Mall; Katana-san explained how the huge shopping centre had spread around and absorbed the bath-house a dozen years before. 'It is our favourite *sento*,' he said. 'When they built the mall they wanted to tear it down, but we – we let them know we considered their plans a little, well ... *unwise*. For historical reasons ...'

We passed through an antique wooden door and the *sento* assistant – a wire-thin student with granny glasses – dropped his comic book and shot from his chair and bowed deeply, repeatedly. Without straightening up or raising his head to look, he motioned with both hands toward a further door. Katana-san did not offer any money.

We stumbled into an empty change room. Under the harsh fluorescent light the tile on the walls and floor looked new, as if recently replaced. In one corner a miniature Universal Gym and in the other a Coke machine, couch, two chairs and a TV ...

Outnumbered, armed only with swords, the Seven Samurai continued to resist the barbarous onslaughts of their scruffy, firearmed opponents. But I'd seen the film before; I knew their time was at hand.

'We strip here,' Katana-san said, slurring the words a bit. 'I bet you have never been before to the *sento*!'

'Today's been a first in a lot of ways.'

'For me too,' he smirked. 'I have never yet seen a foreigner naked. Not in person, that is. Naturally I have seen a lot of films ...'

Ray-Ban was standing stark naked in front of the TV screen like a patient receiving some New Age therapy. His back, turned towards us, was a rainbow palimpsest of tattoos. There were wings on his shoulder blades, an eye on each buttock, and along his spine a milk-white Snoopy on horseback slaying with a purple lance an Oriental dragon.

Katana-san had a black handgun tattooed on his muscular belly and around either nipple two slightly faded Rising Suns. And, on his penis, a faint inscription, pale blue.

'What are you staring at?'

'I can't make out the third and fifth characters,' I said. 'It's not Bashō, is it?'

'Bashō?'

'I've always admired *haiku* poems,' I smiled. 'Their brevity.'

Hurt, Katana-san seized my clothing and stuffed it with his own into a locker. There was a sharp metallic clanking as he shoved the jumbled clothes to the back of the box, tossed in his Seiko and slammed the door.

'Follow me.'

As soon as we entered the steaming bath-room the five or six elderly men soaking themselves in the far tub thrashed youthfully from the water and scurried past us to the change room, eyes downcast, hands daintily dangling white washcloths over their loins.

'The owner must love you guys. Does this happen every time you come in?'

Ray-Ban laughed with surprising warmth.

'We take care,' Katana-san said, smoothing his curls, 'to go to a different *sento* each night of the week. We would not want to hurt anyone's business. The school, the *okonomiyaki* house, the *sento* – these businesses are as important to us as our own.'

The tile in the bath-room was faded badly, much older than outside, but had been kept meticulously clean. The light was softer, the bulbs worn; we seemed to be moving back in time. Squatting on low wooden stools, we washed at the antique taps. Katana-san's tattooed sword was smudged and faded on the wrist where his watch had covered it, but I made out two more characters: *sensei* – master – and *shimpo* – progress. *A man with no master moves forward ...*

'*Oide*,' Katana-san nodded, leading me to the first tub. We clambered in and I gasped at the water's heat.

'Always heard it was – dangerous to take hot baths after drinking.'

'Oh, this is not hot at all,' Katana-san beamed, his head lolling back on the porcelain rim of the tub. 'There are two more tubs to go, each hotter than the last.'

'Maybe I'll just – cool off a bit first. In the change room –'

'We would prefer you to stay with us, please. I will telephone your principal again when we are through. Come now, *Sensei* – relax and enjoy yourself!'

The second tub was piercingly hot. My skin prickled and I was dizzy, short of breath; Katana-san's scar was a gory red, his damp skull bright as a buffed helmet.

'I've heard this kind of – kind of water is – terrible for the sperm count —'

Ray-Ban glared at me and moved to the next tub.

'– blood pressure too –'

'You know,' Katana-san calmly observed, 'nowadays

211

people lack the will to endure pain. I believe that our people are ... are *survivors* because they have that will. The will of the warrior!'— his finger burst like a sword from the steaming water and wagged in admonition – 'with the strength to live with intensity.'

He rose abruptly and goose-stepped into the next tub.

'And, of course, some discomfort ...'

The third tub, smoking, churning with bubbles from the air jets, was a cauldron at rolling boil. After I'd lowered myself in I could no longer speak. Suddenly everything was clear: with liquor the *yakuza* had lulled me into a false sense of security and now after I'd passed out in the boiling water I would be left to drown. Pink, lifeless as a steamed lobster, I would be hauled from the tub in a few hours and my death put down to foreign inexperience and stupidity.

SOON YOU WILL BE CROSSING THE GREAT WATERS.

'*Mā, jūbun da neh!*' cried Katana-san. *Enough is enough!*

I rose with difficulty, reprieved.

'Time for a sauna.'

Five minutes later, basting on the wet, scorching bench between my captors, I was sure my drunken fears were well founded. I was trapped. The sauna was tiny, dim, a muffled box, the pine walls stained and warped and soon to decay, I was sure, with moisture. The brazier in the corner, topped with rude, steaming slabs of granite and glowing from beneath, was a primitive firepit. I was trapped in a cave, a burial site. No one would hear me when I cried out. The men were silent. Waiting. Katana-san, it was true, seemed to be dozing – leaning back, hands folded on his chest like a marble knight on a tomb – but I sensed Ray-Ban was wide awake.

I pointed out how dark it was in the sauna and asked him if he would like to take off his sunglasses. He didn't respond.

Just as I touched the floor and reached for the rotting

212

handle the door swung open with a fresh cool draft. Hashimoto, my best student, stood naked before me.

'*Sensei!*' he shrieked. 'Such a surprise!'

I heard startled grunting behind me, violent movement. Hashimoto's eyes and mouth formed O's of wonder as the dead warriors awoke, sprang from the shadows and gripped me by the arms.

'*Tomorrow's lesson,*' I got out in English – '*explain to you then.*'

'*Nan'tte?* What was that? What did you tell him?' Ray-Ban shook me by the arm and I saw red. I turned and shoved him, hard. Katana-san grabbed me from behind.

'Stop! Stop it!'

'I'll get help,' Hashimoto cried, scuttling over the wet tiles toward the change room. I broke free and tried to follow but Katana-san caught me at the door. I watched Ray-Ban dash into the change room and charge at Hashimoto, who had managed to grab a hand towel. 'CALL THE POLICE!' Hashimoto yelled as he flew past the assistant's booth – but the assistant was gone.

Towel in hand, Hashimoto reached the front door and streaked out into the mall. The door swung closed on the screaming of shoppers. Ray-Ban stopped himself at the threshold and spun round, fists clenched.

'He will call the police!'

Wearily, Katana-san blinked his bloodshot eyes. 'I don't think he will have to.'

'The *gaijin*' – Ray-Ban neared, finger outstretched, face sweating – 'the *gaijin* is a problem!'

'It does not pay to bother the foreigners. Get dressed.'

'It will be no bother.'

Katana-san turned to me, frowning. My knees shook and I was glad for his grip on my arm. 'You have nothing to fear. We have our code. We have never yet hurt a foreigner' – he tilted his head, squinting, and by the harsh fluorescent light I

saw that his bullet wound was really an old smallpox scar –
'Well, there *was* that one time … My assistant here was involved,
in fact. But since then I have been watching him. He is very
useful to us, you see, but not … not altogether …'

Ray-Ban had already forgotten us and was closing in on
the TV. He seemed to be mumbling. He flexed his back and
Snoopy's lance skewered the dragon, which bled sweat and
water. The final stages of *Seven Samurai* flickered over the
screen: struck by a musket ball, the slender, weary knight collapsed, hurling his sword away from him as he died.

★

Motomachi Mall swarmed with Christmas shoppers pushing
carts full of crammed bags and sparkling parcels and worn-out,
cranky children. Everywhere young girls, dressed up as elves,
timidly passed out flyers. Some of them looked shaken. From far
off, under the great clock set over the mall's far entrance, the jan-
gling drumbeat and faint glitterings of an approaching parade.

'This way,' Katana-san growled, devouring a cigarette.
'The *sento* boy saw him running this way. And we can call your
principal from the pay phones up ahead. If we get her to pay
damages at once, the *omawari* will not want to do a thing – not
after the fact.'

He checked his watch. I glimpsed the sword again and
recognized another *kanji*. I tried to focus on the inscription,
translate it, stay calm.

A man with no master moves forward like … like …

Ray-Ban gripped me by the arm. The two men's heels
slapped double time on the tiles and bystanders, furtively watching, made way. 'If you say anything …' Ray-Ban hissed in my
ear – and I could smell the stale Budweiser on his breath.

'There,' Katana-san pointed hastily, glancing back at me
over his shoulder. On a billboard between a Nintendo shop and
a Benetton's I saw one of Principal Kobayashi's posters:

ENGLISH LANGUAGE
MADE NOT EXACTLY EASY BUT
HELPFUL FOR YOUR BETTER LIFE.

AMANOGAWA AMERICAN ENGLISH SCHOOL
ŌSAKA, 521–3651

Unmistakably it was tacked up over another poster.

'In several key locations,' Katana-san raised his voice over the growing jangle of the parade, 'your principal has covered up the advertising of a rival school with her own. That is strictly illegal, and so we have been called in to gain reimbursement.'

We were approaching the pay phones at high speed. A salaryman glimpsed us, hung up, turned and sprinted off.

'Let us hope I can reach her now.'

... moves forward, fearless and very fast, like ...

We came to a halt. Katana-san ground his cigarette underfoot and jabbed his calling card into the machine.

Like time, I said to myself, *that must be it. Fearless and very fast, like time. A man with no master moves forward, fearless and very ...*

Ray-Ban squeezed my arm. I turned to him, glaring, then froze: reflected in his dark lenses were countless tiny screens, all of them in turbulent flux. I spun round and stared past the phone booths at the TV shop that now commanded his attention. Absently he freed my arm and shuffled off like a blind man, bound for the store's towering window; he stopped before it and stood frozen, his body haloed with light. The televisions inside were stacked five storeys high and a dozen across and as far as I could see in that two-second span each screen held a different image, from cartoon mice to calm anchormen, from preening rock stars and pious talk show hosts to Clint Eastwood cleaning a gun and the Prime Minister pointing a finger and *sumō* and soccer and ads for ginseng-tonics and well-aged whiskies and the spiralling Wheel of Fortune ...

Katana-san had covered his ear with one hand and leaned deeper into the glass booth to escape the clamour of the nearing parade, the beat of drums and cymbals, the frantic farting of the tubas. He seemed to be arguing, shouting. Ray-Ban was frozen under the window. I turned away and walked a few steps, still faint, then began to run. A few seconds later I heard shouting from behind. I sped up. I could see the parade ahead – I'd almost reached it now – the first float led by a team of cardboard reindeer towing a fat waving Santa on a Styrofoam sleigh. I passed the float at high speed, weaving through crowds, making for the huge clock-face that stared from over the far entrance. Ranks of people applauding the parade now watched me. Parcels flopped from fumbled bags, and a Christmas elf, already shaken, set eyes on me and dropped her flyers and fled.

'*Come back!*' I heard Katana-san yelling. '*Please!*'

Applause and shouts of approval at the passing floats echoed from the high ceiling of the mall. Bands marched between the floats, playing Christmas carols, and a rabble of schoolchildren appeared, singing along, dressed up as samurai and geisha. More cheering and applause – but up ahead and behind me those sounds were mixed with shouts and cries of alarm. '*Sensei ... sensei, please! ... come back!*'

I knocked over a full shopping cart and a second later almost tripped on a hand towel. I kept running. I swept past the long applauding ranks and through a multinational gauntlet of stores and ads in ten tongues and flashing signs and people staring in that vast mall boundless as the world, past papier-mâché dragons and *sumō* wrestlers sparring on a cardboard ice floe and men dressed as penguins and polar bears and three pious bearded wise men and a dozen *ninja* —

Someone screamed directly ahead. Three policemen charged straight at me, holsters slapping at their thighs.

Instinctively I stopped and froze. Some of the floats had halted too, and the marching bands and bears and *ninja* were piling up behind them. Musicians had lost their place. The jumbling bands made a deafening cacophony.

I knelt down and the cops raced past on either side as if I were a ghost. I glanced back. The two warriors had stopped, spun round and were now in full retreat from the Law. Inexplicably I hoped Katana-san would escape.

Raucous laughter now, shouts of surprise, as a last float hove into view: a shining turreted Japanese castle tinselled and decked out with flickering lights, the name of a local college emblazoned on the walls and round the moat a circle of students in business suits. And here at last was Hashimoto, my prize pupil, naked as a babe, his heels pinched and pulled at by yelling cops while those playful students, divinely laughing, raised him onto the float and cloaked his shame in somebody's pinstripe jacket.

14

FLIGHT PATHS OF THE EMPEROR

I: That autumn the Emperor's death seemed imminent, but he surprised the whole nation with a last-minute rally. By November the daily reports from Tōkyō were encouraging: Hirohito-sama was in stable condition, eating regularly, rising after meals to take light exercise and each day enjoying the televised *sumō* he had always loved. Still, Ōsaka's dirty air seemed to hum with an electric tension. The old man's time was coming, that much was clear, and his death might set in motion a series of complex and precarious changes. Even in a time of fabulous prosperity, the advent of a new era was cause for concern.

In mid-December, snow appeared in the last range of hills you cross travelling north towards Ōsaka. Sandra and Nick were returning to the city by train after spending the day on a mountain dotted with temples and old tombs.

'You're cold,' Sandra said to him, testing the silence, wrapping a warm, thickset arm round his shoulder. The train entered a tunnel and harsh lights snapped on above their heads. Nick looked away.

'I'll be fine,' he said. 'I'm not really cold.'

'You're shaking. I can feel it.'

'I'm not cold.'

'Anyway we're almost home. Are you hungry? You must be hungry by now.'

The train came out of the long tunnel and he turned back to her. Snow-covered hills framed her tired face.

'I said you must be hungry.'

'We should have left at two,' he said, turning from her and glaring into the aisle. A few rows ahead an old woman slumped sidelong out of her seat, half blocking the aisle, white head and tiny shoulders trembling to the rhythm of the train. She tried briefly to rouse and straighten herself, then yielded to the embrace of gravity. Her mouth lolled open as if frozen in mid-phrase. For a moment Nick hated the slack mouth, its snoring.

'I thought you wanted to see the place,' Sandra said.

'We saw it this morning in two hours. It was nice. We didn't need to stay all day.' He shivered. The mountain's chill had settled into his limbs and bones.

She pulled her arm away and looked out the window.

'You know we couldn't leave at two, Nick. We promised my boss ...'

'You promised,' he said. 'I'm the one who found the grave.'

'You mean the tomb.'

'You know what I mean.'

'Come on, Nick, we were going up anyway, it's custom-ary for friends ...'

'Not on their day off it isn't. Christ. You do more than enough for him as it is.' He shook his head and saw her pale knuckles tighten on the armrest.

Dusk was falling behind the mountains. To the north the glow of the city's lights crept upward, gathering strength.

'Nick, please, I've apologized. All right? I really didn't think it would take so long to find.'

'Like trying to find a friendly face,' he said softly, 'in an Ōsaka crowd.'

219

She stiffened. Her eyes were a soft, aquatic green, but in anger they would freeze up with a biting, brittle glint, like marbles or the glass eyes of a doll. 'Oh I'm sure you'd have no trouble doing that,' she whispered, 'if you liked. Maybe you've already found a friendly face or two. Maybe I have myself.'

'I don't believe you.'

Her head sagged. 'Don't, then. Why should you? You know by now what I'm like ... And I know you.'

Looking numbly into his lap he saw the dull, delicate ellipse of his wedding ring, the chilled hands open, palms upward, as if showing they had nothing to hide. 'I told you I was through with that when we left Canada.'

'But now we're going back.'

'You say it as if it's my fault.'

'You mean it's mine,' she said, and he saw that he had, he had meant that exactly, it was her fault, or at least her mother's – they were going back on her account.

'Look – not yours. I'm sorry. I'm glad we're going back.'

'I know you're not.'

'I am. I am, really. Sandra? Look, I'm glad we're going back.'

The news hadn't been so much of a surprise. Dorothy's illness had almost kept them from leaving home in the first place. Of course she had urged them to go, but under her bright brisk entreaties was a plaintive, despairing strain, another voice with its own sharp message: *Go, hurry up and go, why stay and watch a fat old lady fall apart when you can tour the Orient? You're still young, you have your health, I know you want to leave me ...*

Promises. A promise to sprinkle water on the tomb of the Takamuras. A promise to return if Dorothy's condition should worsen. A promise to love, honour and cherish, and so on.

His father-in-law's letter was curt and pointed. Dorothy might be gone by Christmas ...

Sandra's body was turned from him now. Her heavy

shoulders quivered. Softly she blew her nose. He checked the surrounding seats and made sure most of their neighbours were asleep; the middle-aged women across the aisle reading fashion magazines had kindly granted them the status of ghosts. In Japan it is rude to blow one's nose in public, and ruder still for a couple to fight.

'Sandra?'

She spun round. Her face was strange to him, twisted by opposing urges, her sudden hatred and the wish to be reconciled. Now she would collaborate, conniving at the cheapest, most slapdash dénouement, forced by the broadcast warning that Namba Station was just minutes away into more and more tawdry, outrageous devices; anything, anything. That was how it would be. The overhead lights came on again, adding years to her face and startling him with the knowledge he had the power to make her ugly.

II: The next day at the school is taken up with farewells. His students are disappointed to see him go, but not especially surprised, since foreign teachers seldom stay long and always leave unexpectedly. His principal is frankly suspicious about 'the illness of his wife's mother'; too many teachers, she probably feels, have killed off friends and relatives in order to escape their obligations in Japan.

'To judge from the teachers I have employed in the last ten years,' she says, 'you North Americans are a uniquely unhealthy race. Never have I seen so many friends and parents and uncles and cousins die suddenly. Oh, it is a terrible thing! So many of them struck down in the prime of life. And so often the day after I distribute pay cheques or generous advances.'

No doubt her suspicions are heightened by her never having met Sandra, whose existence she is too polite to call into question. She wants to know if he will return to the school when things are taken care of at home.

But Yamaguchi-san,' he petitions her, 'my contract expires on the first of March anyway. Surely it would be more reasonable –'

'It would be more reasonable for you to honour your contract.'

'Of course. I realize that. But I'm afraid under the circumstances ...'

'Yes, yes, I know. You foreigners are always pleading circumstances. As if a contract is conditional upon ideal unchanging circumstances. But life is not like that, Mr Asher. Perhaps the Japanese ability to face and endure adversity in lieu of shying away from it is the main factor behind our current economic success. And our social stability. Why, look at the divorce rate in America these days ...' And she removes her glasses to indicate the interview is at an end.

He bows slightly, then excuses himself and hurries into the classroom for his last lesson. As he enters the room he overhears his students discussing him in Japanese, and for a disconcerting instant learns that he is about to die. Then realizes his mistake: in Japanese *to go away* and *to pass away* sound almost the same.

At the end of the class he hands out goodwill gifts his stepmother made for him before his departure – seven felt pencil-cases embroidered with scarlet maple leaves – and the students instantly retaliate with baskets of persimmons, Japanese tea-cakes, a summer kimono, fountain pens, notebooks, and from Teruyo, his best student, a miniature brush painting of butterflies in a temple garden. She seems to find her young teacher's fondness for the old culture quaint and charming.

On his way out he trudges up the half-lit, flickering hallway to Yamaguchi-san's office. Her door is open. He stands in the doorway ready to announce his departure, but she is stiff in her chair, unaware of him, her enlarged eyes unfocused as she listens to a news report from a hidden radio. The Emperor, he thinks. Gone. He can make out only a few words ... Ah, the

Emperor is still alive. But fallen into a profound sleep. His doctors are extremely worried ...

Yamaguchi-san sees him and asks him what he wants. She adjusts her glasses and behind them her weak eyes blink repeatedly, as if finding it hard to bring his face into focus. She frowns. In her mind he already belongs to the past, not the future that is now bearing down on her, and his present apparition does not demand the usual courtesies.

'Well? You're on your way?'

'Yes. I'm sorry about what happened ...'

'These things cannot be helped. There are other teachers.'

There are other schools, he has a cruel urge to say – but does not. He knows her school is in trouble. And it is clear to him as he watches her how quickly she is aging. The dusty fluorescent lights guttering above her head give her figure a dim, flickering cast, like a dead actress in an early film; he reminds himself she is of the generation that local youths – students not much younger than he – refer to as 'already ancient'.

On the train from Kōbe to Ōsaka he savours for the last time the felicitous imprecision of Japanese English. Even now the earnest blunderings of subway billboarders coax a smile from his exhaustion. Across the aisle an ad for some kind of hair tonic leaps out over the slumped shoulders of two dozing salarymen: NOT ONLY DRESS UP LIKE FOP BUT TO PERFORM HIMSELF MAN MAKES UP OWN HAIR SYLE. THERE'S SOMETHING THAT MAKES MAN LOOK SHINY.

He covers his smile with a hand, in the Japanese way. But as the emptying train emerges from the underworld and crosses a high trestle he sees among the office towers and neon billboards a great red crab pulsing above a famous restaurant. His mind makes the necessary connections. *Cancer* is the word no one uses when talking of Dorothy and her treasonous bowels; a word that sounds today more and more like a knell, an irreversible sentence, as Black Death must have sounded to

223

medieval ears. And if Yamaguchi-san was right about the alarming rate at which Western marriages were dissolving she would have to admit also that cancer was now the scourge of the industrially poisoned home islands. In the last year several of his students had lost parents to the epidemic. Side-effects of the new era. Perhaps Yamaguchi-san was becoming ill herself ...

He gets out at Nagai and heads toward the apartment for the last time. From now on, everything he does will be transformed by this sense of finality. He wonders if there is an inkling here of how it feels having only weeks to live – when at last the fabulous is seen in the banal, in the faded sheen off antique faucets, late sunlight creeping over warped linoleum and the lovely, squalid muddle of shoes by the door ... He notices tonight that the Love Hotels he always passes are turning a brisk trade. The coffee-shops are closing up, and a drunk man reeling out of the American Dream smiles and asks him for a light. In the glow of the flame the man's round face is a rich amber, like an old moon on the rise, or a paper lantern at New Year's. There's something, he thinks, that makes man look shiny.

III: But illness wasn't just a reason for return; it was illness that caused your departure. Your parents divorced years ago and at home you watched your father and stepmother, who lived not far from your apartment, infect each other with their ennui and spite. It was open war. Your stepmother waged a more audacious campaign and you could not help foreseeing her eventual triumph – but on some points the two of them were still allied. For example, the two of them could not conceal (from you or themselves) their view that you might have done a bit better than Sandra. When you visited for Sunday dinner your stepmother would charge from the kitchen with a great basted bird, the raised legs tipped with crowns of frilled paper so it resembled a disgraced, murdered monarch – then present Sandra with a few eviscerate scraps that seemed to settle and wilt to nothing in the time it took father to mumble grace. She would never offer Sandra dessert, she would suggest a long walk after dinner, she would find other, more subtle ways to accuse her of obesity and ugliness. 'A teacher!' she'd cried on first meeting Sandra, and at the time you believed she had said it with pleasure.

Your career was devouring itself too. You were not cut out for office work. The idleness, the cramped spaces oppressed you. You thought marriage would admit you to a secure and roomy structure promising freedom and maturity and creature comforts along with its duties and responsibilities – but its unexpected confines brought out the ogre in you, the wayward, wilful child. On your desk for several years you kept a picture of your wife on your wedding day and insisted to yourself with pious regularity that this was the Sandra you'd married; and every evening when she came home (exactly twenty minutes after you) she looked less and less like the woman you spent your coffee breaks recreating. To fortify your image of the old, authentic Sandra and buttress her memory against the onslaught of this pudgy impostor, you erected along the edges of your desk a breastwork of wedding and pre-wedding pictures. And still the two of you could laugh together when recalling an incident from an office party: Gareth loudly presenting his girlfriend, a secretary from accounting who dressed plainly and used no cosmetics but had arrived made-up like an auditioning stripper – 'This,' he roared several times in the course of the evening, his pink face puffy with bourbon and pride, 'is the *real* Barbara.'

Your work suffered. Your boss dropped hints, then began to make warnings. *You'd better shape up, Asher. You call in sick too often.* And you felt his sceptical eyes upon you at the Christmas party.

You started an affair, as Gareth had long predicted you would.

'Listen, Nick, a guy can't hold out forever. Times are changing, join the club.' Gareth always sounded like the

Dictionary of Phrases you later used in classes in Japan. 'It's the way of the world. You're only young once – better make hay while the sun shines.' He leered and licked a silver fleck of beer-foam off the edge of his moustache. 'At least that's my personal opinion.'

Randi was a celluloid goddess, a high-profile big-city model with an anorexic mind. Years of indiscriminate praise and the scheming deference of suitors had atrophied her brain like a cancer. When you made love to her she behaved as if your eyes were the attentive lenses of two Hollywood cameras. It was not till two years later in Japan that you found in subway ads and t-shirt inscriptions an analogue of her crippled speech.

You could laugh at her, and you could laugh at Gareth. You could even laugh at yourself. But you could not stop what you were doing.

Sandra knew all about it. You returned one afternoon from a taxing rendezvous and her look told you everything. She was sitting on the sofa under the window, her face grey in the pale light seeping through those cheap gauze curtains she'd insisted on. During your affair she had steadily put on weight – as if billowing with pent-up shame, indignation. Dorothy sat beside her discussing laxatives. Jim, as usual, had appropriated your La-Z-Boy chair and was drinking your last Export, while visibly fending off sleep. In their tired faces you saw Sandra's face shadowed as if in a crude, distorting mirror, a mirror marred by hairline cracks that map out an appalling future in wrinkles.

Terrible thoughts you were having. You felt them crawling inside you, multiplying, probing icy tentacles into your outermost parts. Clearly you were now a monster. But monsters are not immune to fear; and so, night after night, while dawn's official duties spun towards you out of the dark, you lay awake in the arms of premonitions: you and Sandra at seventy, chastened and respectable, leaving the ballet for streets where angels in designer blue-jeans scamper by just out of grasp. You are ugly and weak, indistinguishable from your own shadow; Sandra is grey, matronly, the deep scores round her mouth puckered in a chronic reproach.

At night you thought of Dorothy's symptoms. They had become too grim for her to invent. And Randi, beautiful Randi, solace of rent-by-the-hour afternoons, whose aerobic physique agreed in every particular with the latest commercial norms – Randi was accusing you of letting things at home get in the way. And she was right.

So that when Gareth mentioned to the boys at the office that he was going to Japan where there were countless jobs and good money and nice Japanese girls and chances to travel (and no parents-in-law) you asked him for more information.

He was always happy to help out a friend.

Japan! The Land of the Rising Sun! A new start! An exotic eastern fief that still had an emperor, for Christ's sake! A country enjoying untold prosperity! Not to mention the longest life expectancy in the world.

iv: Tōkyō in mid-December. Amplified Christmas carols in gar-bled English, flashing ornaments and parcel-laden crowds swarming through the Ginza. You find a traditional inn tucked between two giant banks on a street behind Ueno Station. Make several trips to the headquarters of Japan Air Lines where you confirm reservations and where, if you are not very much mistaken, a bowing kimono-clad doorman exclaims in fervent English, 'We hope you have enjoyed our hostility.'

Silence in the East Garden. Over one of these granite walls, behind some ornate, immemorial door in the heart of the Imperial Palace, the Mikado is dying. This morning's *Japan Times* informs you that he is in critical but stable condition – a contradiction in terms you have never understood. You learn that Hirohito-sama's problems are not particular but generalized

227

and systemic. The old man is dying of his age. He ascended the throne, you recall, in 1925. Over sixty years as 'Heaven's Emperor'. The miracle is that he survived the crushing defeat his kingdom endured at the end of the Second World War. It was the death of an era, an empire, and a god. A middle-aged mortal, short and slight of build, stripped of power and god-hood, lived on.

Silence in the East Garden. You and Sandra walk together in the bitter air through a light, untimely fall of snow. Not even a breath of wind. The carefully tended maples, hedges and barren flower plots maintain a breathless repose. The crooked pines under the Palace walls are static, stiffly poised, like the moment itself – frozen. Things are about to be explained. Sandra takes your hand in hers and after a moment's hesitation you grip her stubby fingers. But your hand is cold and will not thaw and she soon withdraws her own hand for the relative warmth of a pocket.

Silence in the East Garden. You see an old man, shrunk and gnarled as an antique *bonsai*, hobbling away up a crossing path. It is Hirohito, the humbled Emperor, meditating perhaps on the nature of dreams and the vanity of human wishes.

'Don't be ridiculous, Nick. You know it's not him.'

When you tell her it would be easy to mistake him – the old folks of that generation are all small and stooped – she explains it's because of an excess of salt in the diet which eats away the bones from inside. Sandra had been obsessed with pathology since her mother became ill.

In a nearby museum you admire a painting called 'Moon Through a Spider's Web'.

That evening on television there are more reports on the Emperor, who once again has defied all expectations and ral-lied. Your shaggy translation of the commentary yields this rough gem: 'And so, once more, the epoch is preserved ...' There is weather, of course – snow expected to continue into tomorrow – and *sumō* highlights. It seems Chiyonofuji, the Emperor's favourite wrestler, will have to settle this year for second place; the winner is a 200 kilogram import from Hawaii.

Some time after midnight, grieving, choked with desire, you wake from a dream you cannot remember and reach out. With shivering fingers you touch her exposed nape but she sleeps on, her face to the wall, her broad shoulder shrugged above you like a stone slab or the cliffs of an island. For the briefest span the mark of your fingers remains in her flesh. How deep the snow must be now in the East Garden.

v: No beating around the bush. Japan was a healthy break in an otherwise run-down marriage. In Japan there were centripetal pressures that drove us together, threw us back on mutual resources, taught us to love, honour, cherish and revere. Or words to that effect. Now we were being called back, as I knew we would be, to a painfully familiar place, by the centrifugal powers of duty and disease.

In the dark flickering hull of the 747, hemmed in by strangers as in our narrow eight-*tatami* flat, issued a mediocre meal and with only stale soporific films for diversion, there was nothing left to do but turn and face each other and try to talk. This might be the last time we could give each other such attention.

'You don't want to see the film,' I predicted, waving toward the screen where a khaki-clad adventurer faced a doddering chieftain. My voice boomed in the silent fuselage.

'I've seen it,' she said. 'It's old. I saw it before I knew you.'

At least eight years. 'Who with?'

'I can't remember. No wait – it must have been Marco.'

Marco. 'You should have married him,' I said lightly, taking a gulp of Kirin. 'He would have treated you better. He wanted to marry you, didn't he?'

On the screen two grimacing tribesmen grabbed the adventurer and menaced him with spears. I finished my Kirin.

'His family wanted him to. They were crazy about me.'

Light from the screen flashed cinematically across her face. 'Like mine, eh?'

The adventurer shook himself free and yanked a huge handgun from his trousers. Cowardly tribesmen scattered into the jungle. The adventurer managed to shoot two or three. In the seats around us, earphoned spectators were laughing robustly – perhaps at some amusing remark on the sound-track.

'Let's not talk about it,' she whispered. 'They won't be at the airport, will they?'

'I doubt it.'

She gnawed at a stale bun. 'Tell your stepmother I lost ten pounds in Japan. Maybe now she'll be able to love me.'

'I don't know ... Maybe if you'd flunked Teacher's College the way she did ...'

'She'd hate me more.'

'She doesn't hate you.'

'God, Nick, it was forty years ago she failed! Why can't she forget?'

'She doesn't hate you. It's just that – I don't think she ever learned how to love. You or anyone else.'

'Sometimes I think the same about your father.'

I choked down a forkful of rice. In a close-up, the dashing, unshaven adventurer poked the barrel of his revolver into the chieftain's slack throat. The old man rolled his eyes like a minstrel in black face.

'You don't understand my father. Don't say things like that about him.'

Something we couldn't hear made the adventurer spin round. Cut to a close-up of a native armed with bow-and-arrow cowering at the edge of the jungle.

'You could have had other women. Your parents would have been happier. Hey, are you listening to me?'

The native, smirking like a sinister cupid, drew his bow and shot an arrow, then slumped back with a bullet hole between the eyes.

'You could have had other men,' I said.

Cut to the chieftain, crumpled now against a palm tree with his own man's arrow sticking out of his gut. Clearly the nimble adventurer had leapt aside in the nick of time. He stood now, proud, monumental, a smoking revolver in his sinewy fist. Leering smugly he made some remark the surrounding audience enjoyed. It struck me that at this very moment we might be plummeting out of control to the sea.

'You were it,' she said.

'For better or worse.'

The adventurer blew a fume of smoke from the tip of his revolver.

'I do love you,' I said.

VI: At Seattle airport we have a few hours to kill before boarding our connecting flight to Toronto. After reduced-scale Ōsaka we find ourselves dwarfed by hordes of *sumō*-sized specimens gobbling hamburgers and potato chips and foot-long dogs. Sandra is sitting by the windows, her manner unnaturally stiff, eyes furtive, as if waking just now to the presence of her body. She watches jetplanes with exotic insignia taxi in from the runway. I buy a copy of the *Seattle Post* and enclose myself in the aloof, comforting shell of far-off disaster.

A small story on the second page mentions that Hirohito is failing again and is not expected to see the New Year. But we know by now that the Emperor, like the old epoch, is more resilient than anyone would think.

In the back pages I find another, smaller story:

HIROHITO STIRS BRIEFLY FROM PROLONGED SLEEP

TOKYO (Reuter) – Japan's Emperor Hirohito, who collapsed in mid-September, awoke briefly from his long
sleep yesterday and looked around his bedroom, a palace
official said. 'I don't think His Majesty wanted anything
but he opened up his eyes and looked around the room,'
the official said. The 87-year-old emperor, whose condition is described as being close to a coma, lost a small
amount of blood overnight.

I close the paper. Sandra is still staring off towards the
runway.

Through terminal windows the huge white cone of Mt
Rainier looms like Fujiyama.

VII: Jim is waiting for you on the far side of customs. Without
Dorothy beside him he is insubstantial, an extra on a vast set
teeming with rangy, vivacious actors. He embraces his daughter as if you are a stranger, or a ghost he can exorcise only by
ignoring. His felt cap is too large for him, his beige eyes anonymous, glassy, and when he turns to give your hand a
perfunctory shake there is nothing to say. You smell beer, and
something stronger. On the way home those lonely bar-room
odours fill the car.

The burden of strength now squarely upon her, Sandra
swells with solicitude, kindness, her eyes lit up with a desperate
optimism. Like a new mother, all her fears have been transformed into a brisk, efficient energy. And after all the news is
not so bad.

On the way home Jim leaks the truth gently, gradually,
almost with reluctance, as if unwilling to forfeit the status of
victim. He seems confused by the turn of events. Perhaps he
doesn't know what to feel. Dorothy, it turns out, had made
great progress. The doctors are puzzled but impressed and judge

232

that if watched and encouraged this respite could last for years. *Remission*, that is the word they are using – an echo from made-for-TV movies about cancer victims and their unstinting families. An echo from the liturgy you recited in childhood – something about the remission of sins.

You embrace Dorothy. She looks the same as before the trip, a touch thinner perhaps, but shimmering with her recovery, the pride of it, an old woman who has made a brazen unforeseen leap from the crumbling lip of her grave onto solid ground. She has put on a light floral dress, as if for an August supper on the patio. Anecdotes seethe behind her eyes. She apologizes for not coming to the airport and assures you she feels fine and could have made it if the doctors hadn't been so fussy, insisting she stay in till after New Year's ...

She has been granted a reprieve. You suggest a drink to celebrate, and ask Jim for a double. He pours two. Well, cheers, he says, his voice an anaemic, squeaky whisper. Because of a simple diagnostic error you have been summoned back into the glittering web, and trapped. Your marriage, you understand, will be slowly exterminated. You can't be sure by whom. The old cling to life and link you with the dead. There will be no brave new era.

VIII: A few days into the New Year we visit my father's parents in Buckingham, Québec. My father tells me how excited they are about our coming; our visits have been an annual rite but this year they've expected us to be off in Japan, and perhaps have sensed (I've hinted at it enough in my letters) that we'll renew our contracts and stay another year, then another year after that ...

The night before driving up we have dinner at my father's house.

'They can't wait to see you,' my father says, nodding sharply so that his glasses slip down his nose and he can peer at me over the rims. This is meant to prepare me for a serious remark. 'It's a good thing you came back.'

'In some ways,' my stepmother corrects him. 'After all, they had to break their contracts. And don't forget the reason. Illness is hardly a good thing. Care for some more potatoes, dear?'

Before she can reply, my stepmother ladles a steaming cairn of mashed potatoes onto Sandra's plate; out of deference to Dorothy's reduced condition, it seems, she has relaxed her campaign to save Sandra's figure, or remind her of it, or both.

'We're so glad to hear how she's improved,' she says, reddening as she struggles with a piece of chicken. 'We've been calling every couple of days.'

'Unfortunately your grandfather has not improved,' says my father. 'Physically he's still fine, but I'm afraid his mind' – he taps a forefinger against his temple – 'well, he hardly knows who I am any more. He spends most of his time sleeping, or staring at the TV.'

'And think of the stations they get up there!' my stepmother cries, sitting back and fingering the scarab brooch on her cardigan. 'Almost all of them French! He must be miserable.'

'It comes to us all,' my father reflects.

'I don't think he knew me the last time we went up,' I say. 'He seemed to think Sandra was a French barmaid he'd known during the First World War.'

'*Ma chère Danielle, ma chère Danielle*,' chants Sandra – and with a brisk manual motion my father replaces his glasses, chuckling politely. The evil stepmother casts Sandra a baleful glance, perhaps feeling that mirth – especially in bilingual form – is unseemly in the awkward and the ugly, who should be more penitent in their misfortune. But tonight I ignore her. I feel generous, expansive, I accept second helpings and recklessly propose a bottle of wine. Naturally there is no wine in the house, but tonight my motion is not even condemned, and since it's allowed to stand – to breathe, as it were – it seems intoxicating of itself. Tomorrow, after all, we are going on a trip, and even if the destination is near and our hosts not exactly foreign it is a kind of adventure, a kind of escape.

With arthritic fingers my stepmother smooths the skin round her carefully designed lips. She is what fashion and film magazines dub 'well-preserved'. But now her opaque, ash-coloured eyes seem punctured, drained by our laughter, deflated; not an evil stepmother, I think, at all.

'You be careful tomorrow in the car,' she says. 'You don't know how your father worries about you when you're off on your travels. It gives him grey hair and lines above the eyes.'

'We'll be careful,' we promise.

'Especially once you cross over into Quebec,' she goes on, relentless in her concern, 'you know how they drive up there. And the roads! It's just terrible. When I was a student about your age I lived for a year in Montreal and' – she breaks off, having received some private signal from my father, who is peering again over the rim of his glasses. Tonight her mood is delicate, frangible as fine china; usually he cannot stop her so easily. He begins to speak. 'I read in the papers today that they expect Emperor Hirohito to die by tomorrow morning.' And gives his napkin an urbane twirl, as if to congratulate himself on this subtle gambit. No doubt he thinks he has changed the topic to something new.

IX: There had been a thaw in the night, and when Sandra took the wheel near Prescott he was free to sit back and study the passing landscape. A midwinter thaw is a kind of remission; this far north it never lasts for long. Nick looked out over a country of dark fields, deserted farms and trailer parks, gas stations, old churchyards under a marble sky.

Outside Hull the highway began to disintegrate, but the

murderous drivers his stepmother had promised them were nowhere to be seen. It was Sunday, midafternoon, a time for digesting sermons or heavy dinners and peering out through frosted window-panes, not for trying to get anywhere.

Sandra and Nick hardly spoke from Kingston to Buckingham. In a small car on a midwinter's day, he thought, the centripetal forces that fused them in Japan should be active, irresistible. And they said nothing. Sandra's free hand lay by the gearshift, twitching now and then. Her eyes glared straight ahead up the empty road. On New Year's Eve they had made love with a tentative, awakening ardour, like shy lovers giving themselves for the first time; and feeling the generous warmth of her breasts and large body around him he had been sure he could never love another woman. But the next morning she was silent, sullen, their ecstatic communion a victim of poor sleep, anxious dreams or some abrupt recognition. Now that Dorothy was flagrantly well, the energy Sandra had conjured to support her seemed to vanish. The sheen passed from her eyes, the bloom from her cheeks. She moved heavily within her skin, her body had a sad, abandoned look, as if she herself had left and caught a flight to a far-off country. Again Nick felt a nagging urge to escape her, a desire for the youthful, conspicuous good looks that asked so little effort and promised eternal life. There were times Nick thought he knew the future, and times he thought he understood the past. He always turned out to be wrong. On the train to Ōsaka, faced with the prospect of an early return, resurrecting old grievances and finding them undecayed, he'd foreseen with absolute clarity the death of his marriage. On the flight home and on New Year's Eve – and even the night before at dinner, teamed with Sandra against a flagging stepmother – he'd been equally sure they would survive. How many times he had flown between the two extremes, a trapped commuter who never seemed to touch down. And he knew, if he knew anything at all, that he never would touch down.

They reached Buckingham at three. The streets were deserted. Already lamps glowed in most of the windows.

Ed was sleeping when they entered the peeling clapboard house that he and Emily had owned since the war. Seeing their car in the driveway Emily had tried to rouse him but he'd barked at her to leave him alone, let him rest. 'I told him it was Danielle,' she beamed, her gentle face a shrivelled browless version of his father's. Her wandering left eye, he saw, was now completely free of her will. Her apron and house dress sported badly faded but plucky floral designs. 'Danielle from Paris, I told him, but he didn't understand. He thought I meant there was somebody French at the door.' She winked. 'You know how he feels about them.'

Nick knew. His grandparents were of Loyalist blood and solemnly stuck to principles of remote but hallowed origin. For forty years they had resisted the French language with such determined gallantry that Gran could now claim with good conscience she hadn't learned a single word. *Picked up* was the way she liked to put it; *I haven't picked up a thing*, she would say, as if talking of trash from a gutter or a contagious, possibly fatal disease. But times were changing – that much she would allow. She and Ed were the last of a dying breed. At one time they'd had a lot of English friends here.

Grandmother's devoted bigotry was an old joke in his family, so he was startled when she asked them over tea and buttered scones about their experiences in Japan – then listened closely to their answers. She wanted to know how the older Japanese felt about the Emperor's illness, which she had been following in the papers. Then she recalled reading about his coronation in 1925. At that time she had been just thirty. Thirty years old!

She shook her head, as if at the farfetched remark of a guest only she could see. The lamplight crossing her pale hairnet made it shimmer like a web.

237

'Nicholas, if you'd only come here before your tour instead of leaving in such a hurry I might have taught you some Japanese.'

Nick asked her, politely, what she was talking about. He reminded himself that Edward's Alzheimer's was not infectious.

'Not more than a few words, mind you. Just a phrase I learned as a girl.'

He put down his teacup.

'I was only ten. I'm not sure I can remember ...' She broke off and stared at the untouched plate of scones. 'You're not eating, Nicky.'

'I'll have one in a minute, Gran, I promise – but how —'

'I spent half the morning baking them. Please. You loved them as a boy. Now when *I* was ten ... when *I* was ten my parents worked as missionaries in Churchill. Churchill is a small town in northern Manitoba.'

He nodded. He knew. She had spoken of it many times before.

'One of their friends – another missionary – returned to Churchill from Japan. It was after a war, some war they'd just fought ... Sandra dear, please, you'll waste away —'

'The Russo-Japanese war,' he said. '1904–05.' Sandra and he exchanged looks and he could see she was feeling the same wonder, the miracle of dead figures and dry bones revived by an old woman's breath.

'Yes, that war. I forget the man's name. Now I remember – Sandberg, Reverend Sandberg. A big man, bald. He brought gifts for my sister and me. I can't remember what Vicky got but he gave me a doll. *Ningyo*, he said. That means doll.'

Nick leaned over the table. 'Yes. Yes it does.'

Her fingers, gnarled like the roots of a tiny, ancient tree, carved rectangular shapes from the air.

'It came in one of those wooden boxes – Sandra, dear, you

must know them – the crates they put mandarin oranges in – and it was in a bed of crumpled paper. A little boy, a little warrior in a kimono with a silk belt and a small wooden sword. And when he gave it to me Reverend Sandberg taught me to say what it was in Japanese. '*Honto*,' she said, squinting, focusing cloudy eyes on the scones. '*Honto no – ko – kotaishi.*'

'That means "a real prince".'

'Yes, yes,' she said, impatient with herself, seizing her teacup and glaring into it, a fortune-teller reading tea-leaves. 'But he taught me to say a full sentence.'

Her right eye fixed on his face while the other seemed to study another guest, invisible beside him. He saw her struggling to exhume the final honorific. As a teacher he'd learned never to intervene.

'*Honto no kotaishi*' – she paused, squinting – '*de gozaimasu*,' A real prince, it is.'

Nick beamed and nodded. 'Old Japanese,' he said, 'extremely polite. And you still remember this?'

She looked at him with playful disdain. 'My mind's not gone yet,' she said. 'You'd be surprised at the things I remember.' She turned her trembling head towards Sandra. 'I could tell you some things about your husband here, as a little boy ...'

'*Honto no kotaishi de gozaimasu*,' he interrupted, shaking his head. The words were simple and familiar enough but on the tongue of a woman he'd known since birth and who'd long since lost the power to surprise him they had a fabulous, exotic sound. She had heard them half a century before his birth, then harboured the echoes all those years like a family secret. They loomed up in his mind, immense as a continent; they took on trappings like a spell or a mantra. Nothing could ever pass away.

'Do you still have the doll?' Sandra asked.

'The doll?' she snapped. 'Oh, well, I've really no idea at all what became of it. When we left Winnipeg after the war it must have been lost in the move. Or else when I was married

239

and left home. But I still remember the doll's face: very proud, a noble little warrior, a samurai.'

Emily shuddered, as if trying to shake herself from a dream. She stood up and reached with fluttering fingers for the teapot. She was still a businesslike woman, hurried and brusque, lavishly energetic like someone half her age; she never let conversations linger on her own affairs.

Sandra and Nick rose together to offer their help but she brushed them away and had them know she wasn't ready for a nursing home yet.

There was a groan from the bedroom.

'It's him,' Emily said, glancing at the tiny wristwatch she had worn for as long as Nick could remember. 'He'll be needing me now. No, please, I told you, leave the tea things alone. Make yourselves comfortable for a few minutes while I go and see him. In a little while I'll bring him out for a visit. We won't be long.'

Nick poured Sandra some tea and then, in the Japanese manner, let her replenish his own cup. The sound of the trickling fluid filled the small kitchen. The windows were clouding over with steam so that patterns a dreaming finger had traced appeared and spread outward over the panes: transparent paths, cursive and meandering, illegible as a line of characters. A fit of coughing erupted from the bedroom and then, like a lullaby, soothing sounds. Over steaming cups Nick and Sandra watched each other with a new patience that was close to love.

ACKNOWLEDGEMENTS

The stories in *Flight paths of the Emperor* were previously published in *Canadian Fiction Magazine, Critical Quarterly, The Fiddlehead, Descant, Hawai'i Review, The Laurel Review, Matrix, The New Quarterly, PRISM International, Queen's Quarterly, Stand*, the Kingston *Whig-Standard, White Wall Review*, and *Writ*. 'On Strikes and Errors in Japanese Baseball' was reprinted in *Best Canadian Stories 89* (Oberon) and *Engaged Elsewhere* (Quarry Press). 'How Beautiful upon the Mountains' appeared also in *Best Canadian Stories 92* (Oberon) and in *The Journey Prize Anthology* (M&S, 1992); 'A Man Away from Home Has No Neighbours' also appeared in *The Journey Prize Anthology 1992*. 'Five Paintings of the New Japan' was reprinted in *Best Short Stories 1992*, eds. Giles Gordon and David Hughes (London, Heinemann), *The Minerva Book of Short Stories 5*, eds. Gordon and Hughes (London, Minerva, 1993), *The Best of Best Short Stories 1986–1995*, eds. Gordon and Hughes (London, Minerva, 1995), *The Literature of Work* (Phoenix, University of Phoenix Press, 1991) and *The New Story Writers* (Kingston Quarry Press, 1992); 'Sounds of the Water' was also reprinted in *The New Story Writers*, and appeared along with 'The Battle of Midway' and 'A Protruding Nail' in *Coming Attractions 90* (Oberon).

Thanks to Acuff-Rose Music Incorporated for permission to quote lines from 'The Tennessee Waltz', by Pee Wee King and Redd Stewart, copyright © 1948, renewed 1975.

Thanks to New Directions Publishing Corp. for permission to use Kenneth Rexroth's translation of a poem by Bunya no Asayasu in *One Hundred Poems from the Japanese*, copyright © 1974, 1976 by Kenneth Rexroth.

Thanks to Penguin Books for permission to quote from Lafcadio Hearn's *Writings from Japan*, edited with an introduction by Francis King, copyright © Francis King, 1984.